THE TIGER'S EGG

terest level : grades 4 -8

R points : 13.0

TOS book level : 6.5

THE WEDNESDAY TALES ~ NO. 2

THE TIGER'S EGG

JON BERKELEY

ILLUSTRATED BY BRANDON DORMAN

THE JULIE ANDREWS COLLECTION

HARPERCOLLINS*PUBLISHERS*

Library of Congress Cataloging-in-Publication Data
Berkeley, Jon.
   The tiger's egg / Jon Berkeley ; illustrated by Brandon
Dorman. — 1st ed.
      p.   cm. — (The Julie Andrews collection) (The
Wednesday tales ; no. 2)
   Summary: While working for the newly revamped circus,
orphaned eleven-year-old Miles gains information about his
past and sets off with his angel companion, Little, on a quest
to find a mystical tiger's egg before it falls into the hands of
their nemesis, the Great Cortado.
   ISBN 978-0-06-075510-2 (trade bdg.)
   ISBN 978-0-06-075511-9 (lib. bdg.)
   [1. Adventure and adventurers—Fiction. 2. Circus—
Fiction. 3. Angels—Fiction. 4. Orphans—Fiction. 5. Tigers—
Fiction.] I. Dorman, Brandon, ill. II. Title.
PZ7.B45255Tig 2007   2006039842
[Fic]—dc22   CIP
                                                      AC

Typography by Christopher Stengel
1 2 3 4 5 6 7 8 9 10

First Edition

For Mum and Dad—
A rare matching pair in the sock-basket of life

CONTENTS

THE TIGER'S EGG

CHAPTER ONE
A LOOSE CANNON

Along a hospital corridor marched a man on squeaking shoes, dressed in an outsized orderly's uniform. He had a small round head and pale gray eyes, and he called himself the Great Cortado. Stuck to his upper lip, where his magnificent mustache had been only minutes before, was a tiny square of tissue paper with a spot of blood at the center. He was walking quickly toward the hospital entrance, away from the room where he had spent the past three months under lock and key. The room was locked again now, and the key was in his pocket. The uniform he wore belonged to the real hospital orderly, who lay unconscious on the floor of the locked room, his wrists and ankles tied with strips of torn bedsheet. The orderly had been hit over the head with a heavy steel tray, and would not be waking up anytime soon.

The Great Cortado squeaked through the reception area, past the desk where the night doorman sat reading his paper. The doorman looked up and frowned. "Knocking off early?" he said, glancing at his watch. "Shift doesn't end till four."

"I'm going on strike," said Cortado, "for better conditions."

The doorman put down his paper and raised an eyebrow. "Strike?" he said. "Is it official?"

"Whatever," said the Great Cortado, and he pushed the revolving door and spun himself out into the frosty night air.

His foggy breath was lit by the lamps that lined the gravel driveway, and the cold bit his upper lip. A snigger escaped him, and he clamped his mouth shut. Better nip that in the bud. Once he started it could get the better of him. He marched out through the gates and along the tree-lined street beyond, his head filled with a tumult of sounds and pictures, of cackling and howling and falling and spinning. Night and day this freak show went on inside his mind, and he walked a tightrope through the chaos, sometimes slipping off and losing himself for days. Now was not the time, he told himself, and he fixed his eyes on a spot ten feet ahead of him as he walked. One step at a time. Left, right, left, right, up, down and sideways. No skipping. Another laugh bubbled up and he forced it back down. "Concentrate," he muttered. "You are the Great Cortado."

"You *were* the Great Cortado," said a voice at the back of his head. He spun around, but there was no one there. "Nobody here but us chickens," he said. "I *am* the Great Cortado. Just a minor setback. Once I get back on my feet, then we'll see who's laughing."

He marched on unsteadily into the night, the once Great Cortado, sudden giggles exploding from him like hiccups. As the cold air washed the hospital drugs from his system his old plans and schemes began to rise up through the madness, stranger than they had been before, darker and more crooked. An army of slaves. A city of bones. A military-industrial complex bristling with rockets and roaring with ire. He breathed deeply and allowed himself to laugh aloud. No matter what monstrosity he chose to build or how he trampled his way to power, there was one thing he knew for sure. At the gates of his empire there would be a tall straight pole, and on that pole would be the head of

Selim, the boy who had brought down the Palace of Laughter. "Item one on my shopping list," said the Great Cortado to the empty streets, "Selim's head on a pole. Then we'll see who's laughing!"

The Circus Bolsillo came to Larde on a crisp February morning. From the moment the first wagons appeared over the brow of the hill it was clear that this was a circus without equal. A pair of elephants led the parade, painted and tasseled and each with a waistcoated monkey perched between her ears. They were followed by a gap-toothed man with slicked hair, juggling a dozen flaming clubs. A troupe of tumblers cartwheeled along the frosty road, their breaths tracing spirals of vapor that vanished at once in the winter sun, and behind them came a procession of wagons and trucks, painted in bright colors and each one more exotic than the last. They rode in on a wave of drums, whistles and gongs that could wake the dead, and the strange hoots and rumbles of animals from far-off jungles and distant deserts. The lead wagon was painted with the words THE INCOMPARABLE CIRCUS BOLSILLO in reds, blues and yellows, and in the large round Os were painted the grinning faces of three little clowns with pointed teeth.

A small girl and a coffee-skinned boy sat on the

parapet of the stone bridge that led into Larde, oblivious to the cold and waiting eagerly for the circus to reach them. The boy's name was Miles, and the girl was known as Little. Sitting side by side on the cold stone they might seem unremarkable enough, if you did not know that Little was over four hundred years old and had the outline of a pair of lost wings etched into the skin of her back, or that Miles had befriended a talking tiger and carried in his pocket a small stuffed bear that could dance like a drunken sailor.

The lead wagon drew closer, and Miles and Little could see the Bolsillo brothers themselves, Fabio, Umor and Gila, balanced on the roof like a small totem pole. As they rumbled across the bridge the totem pole made a triple bow. "How are you, Master Miles?" shouted Fabio over the racket of the circus band. "And the little lady, Lady Little?" called Umor, and Gila showed his pointy teeth in a broad smile.

"Fine, I suppose," shouted Miles. "How's the new circus shaping up?"

"Can't complain," called Fabio.

"Yes we can," shouted Gila.

"But we won't," said Umor, his voice almost lost in the cacophony.

Miles and Little fell into step with the Bolsillo brothers' wagon, which was drawn by two enormous cart horses with legs like fringed pillars, but were soon caught up in the dense crowd that had spilled onto the streets, and stopped where they were to watch the rest of the parade go by.

The Circus Bolsillo could not have been more different from its predecessor, the Circus Oscuro, which had crept into town in the dead of night not six months before. That sinister outfit was disbanded now, and its ringmaster had been locked away in a secure hospital, but from its remains the Bolsillo brothers had built a brand-new circus, as colorful and chaotic as the Circus Oscuro had been eerie and dark. They had brought in new performers to replace those who were missing or jailed, and as their fabulous procession rolled by, Miles could see just what a remarkable show they had created.

There were many more wagons, brightly painted with the names of exotic acts and sideshows: the Toki sisters from the Far Orient, Countess Fontainbleau and her Savage Lions, K2 the Strongman, Doctor Tau-Tau Presents Your Future. Something about the name on that last wagon sounded familiar to Miles, but he was distracted by a cage fat with crocodiles that rolled by in its wake. The sleepy reptiles were draped across each other like saggy statues, their crooked grins hinting that they might just be quietly digesting a small child or two. Miles was secretly hoping to catch a glimpse of a tiger somewhere in the colorful parade. There were animals from every corner of the world, but he was not really surprised when the last wagon passed and the only stripes he had seen were on whinnying zebras and folded canvas.

Miles and Little followed the tail of the Circus Bolsillo, even as the first wagons were pulling into the long field at the bottom of the hill. Lady Partridge, who ran the orphanage that they called home, had told them that the circus was coming, although she could not say when, and that they would be quartering their animals in the old stables behind Partridge Manor for a few days before taking to the road for the spring season.

By the time Miles and Little arrived at the long field, the wagons and trucks had arranged themselves in a broad circle around its edge, and those first to arrive had already spilled from their traveling homes with their dogs and children and washing lines and folding chairs and basins and chickens and oil lanterns. Canvas canopies cracked in the wind as their corners were lashed to nearby trees. A generator on a small yellow truck roared into life, and Fabio Bolsillo appeared from behind it, wiping his hands on an oily rag. At the sight of Miles and Little his face broke into a grin, and he shoved the rag into the back pocket of his overalls and turned a quick cartwheel that brought him right up beside them. He bowed low, and gave Miles a sly wink.

"Thought you'd come sniffing around," he said.

"Like flies around horse dung," said Gila, who had appeared from nowhere.

"Where's Umor?" asked Little.

"Cooking," said Gila.

"We're expecting guests," said Fabio.

"Oh," said Miles. "Then we'll go. We just came to say hello."

"Go if you want," shrugged Gila.

"Then we'll have no guests," said Fabio.

"All the more for us." Gila reached out, quick as a flash, and tweaked Miles's nose. "*Ommadawn,*" he said.

As they walked toward the Bolsillo brothers' wagon, Fabio gave Miles a sidelong glance from under his bushy eyebrows. "I suppose you've heard the news from Flukehill?" he said.

A cold feeling stole over Miles. "What news?" he asked.

"The Great Cortado escaped from the secure hospital last week," said Fabio.

"Hit his warder over the head with a steel tray," said Gila.

"Shaved off his mustache with a sharpened butter knife."

"Dressed himself in the warder's clothes and marched straight out of the door."

"Told the guard he was going on strike."

Miles felt his stomach tighten, and for a moment the ground seemed to tilt away beneath his feet. He could see Little looking at him anxiously from the corner of his eye, and he made himself smile at her. "I don't think he'll get far before they catch him again," he said. He pictured Sergeant Bramley and his two trusty constables, filling in the crossword over mugs of steaming tea, and quickly pushed the thought from his mind.

"I wouldn't be so sure," said Fabio.

"He's a master of disguise," said Gila.

"And handy with a knife!" said Fabio.

"He's been sighted in Nape, and Iota, and as far away as Frappe," said Gila.

Fabio pulled Gila's cap down over his eyes. "Rumors and lies," he snorted, "unless he's sprouted a propeller since we saw him last."

Miles laughed, and the knots in his stomach eased slightly, but still he felt that a cloud had stolen over the day, and he reached into his pocket for the reassuring feel of his orange-gray stuffed bear, Tangerine, who had been sung to life by Little on a moonlit autumn night. Tangerine said nothing, but he gave Miles's fingers a squeeze that said more than a pocketful of words.

CHAPTER TWO
A TIGHT SHIP

Umor Bolsillo, sloe-eyed and quick-fingered, danced a complicated jig in a cloud of smoke that smelled of pork and sage and wild mushrooms. He sang in a strange language as he danced, and he poked the meat that sizzled on a spit over the open fire. The other two Bolsillo brothers and their guests sat on wooden stools that Gila had brought from the wagon in a teetering pile and set down in a half circle around the fire.

"Well, Master Miles," said Fabio, "tell us your news."

"There's not much to tell," said Miles. "The orphanage is nearly finished. Lady Partridge is busier than ever. Baltinglass of Araby comes by now and then, when he can hitch a ride from Cnoc."

"And The Null?" asked Fabio, watching Miles from under his bushy eyebrows.

"The Null is much the same," said Miles. He thought of the nameless beast that he had saved from execution, even after it had tried to crush him to death, and which now lived behind stout bars in the gazebo in Lady Partridge's garden. He was in the habit of visiting The Null each morning, but today he had been distracted on the way by the arrival of the circus, and he knew the beast would be hunched in a corner, gnawing on a bone and brooding darkly. "Sometimes it has quiet days, sometimes not," he said. "I read to it every morning from the paper, and that seems to calm it somehow."

Fabio nodded. "I doubt you'll ever get further than that," he said.

"Some tried to master the beast, while it still lived in the Circus Oscuro," said Umor.

"But they all failed."

"Even the ones that survived."

"I don't want to master The Null," said Miles. "I just think it needs a friend."

"A friend," echoed Fabio, and gave Miles a thoughtful look.

"You have so many new acts!" said Little, who had been looking around at the colorful wagons. "Where have you been since we saw you last?"

"Here and there, little Sky Beetle," said Gila.

"But mostly there."

"Small towns, largely."

"Little shows."

"Big people."

"Settling in the new acts," said Fabio.

"Training them up."

"Sawing them in half," laughed Umor.

Fabio leaned forward and dropped his voice. "Working on a new show," he said.

"Sort of Rutfal fo Salap," said Gila.

"Rufta what?" said Little.

"It's backwards," said Miles.

"Palace of Laughter," said Fabio.

"But in reverse," said Gila.

"Grub's up!" called Umor from the smoke.

They sat around the warm fire, eating roast pork from cracked plates. The Bolsillo brothers told, in their usual leapfrogging chatter, how they had put on a series of shows over the winter months in small towns and villages while they searched for new acts to bring the limping circus back to life. There were bills to pay and animals to feed, but they had also been working hard on a new and more spectacular show for the coming year. The clowning routines would be of particular importance, for the brothers were quietly trying to devise a performance that would reverse the effects of the Great Cortado's laughter hypnosis, with which he had sucked the laughter from the people, town by town and village by village, so that he could sell it back to them in small green-labeled bottles. Since Miles and Little had brought this odious racket to an end a creeping grayness had spread through parts of the country, and Fabio, Umor and Gila had set their minds to creating a show that could undo the damage.

"And that," said Fabio to Little, "is where you come in, little Sky Beetle."

Little wiped gravy from her chin with her shirt (a habit that Lady Partridge had tried to rid her of without success) and tucked her short blond hair behind one ear. "What do you mean?" she asked.

"You've got the song we need," said Fabio.

"There's bad music to be untwisted," said Gila.

"And bad laughter to be upended."

"We heard a little of your singing, back in the Palace of Laughter."

"You could sing the sourness off milk."

"And the fur off the trees," said Gila.

"Fur doesn't grow on trees," said Umor.

"You always told me there were fur trees."

"If I did, then there must be."

Little shook her head. "I can't use the One Song for that," she said. "I'm no longer a Song Angel. I can't use it at all, not now."

Fabio put his finger to his lips. "Shh-shh!" he said. "We don't want to know about that."

"None of our business," said Umor.

"Tell us anyway," said Gila.

Miles looked at the stubborn set of Little's mouth, but he knew her almost as well as she knew herself. She had bent the rules to follow Silverpoint to Earth, and when she had saved Miles from The Null by singing the creature's name she had broken them altogether. He knew she would not take much persuading to tiptoe around them again.

"Maybe you could work with the circus band in some way," he said.

"Just what we were thinking, Master Miles," said Fabio.

"We were?" said Gila.

"He was thinking it for you, save you the bother," said Umor, sucking the juices from his fingers.

"You could be the World's Youngest Bandmaster."

"We've already got the World's Tallest Midget."

"Not to mention the Tiniest Flea."

They sat on their wooden stools, the coffee-skinned boy, his adopted little sister and three tiny men with black curly hair and eyebrows like caterpillars. A chilly wind whipped gray ash around them as the embers began to cool, and Miles felt his heart sinking as he realized that there was no place in this plan for him.

"I wouldn't want to go without Miles," said Little.

"We'll be back before the year's end," said Fabio.

"From rains to rains is the season," said Umor.

"That's if Lady P. will release you from your schooling."

"Baltinglass of Araby says there's more education to be got from a day of adventure than a month reading books," said Miles. He had not forgotten his promise to make Little's new life as magical as the one she had left behind. A season with the Circus Bolsillo seemed like an excellent start, and he was torn between the excitement of the adventure that beckoned her and his disappointment at the prospect of being left behind.

"Don't worry," said Gila, looking at Miles with his little black eyes. "We'll look after her good."

"Like she was our own niece," said Umor.

"Or our little spindly grandmother, even."

Miles nodded, a lump in his throat. He looked at the colored wagons and the currents of people swirling around them, eating and working and tending their animals. The wistful sound of an accordion drifted from one of the small campfires, and from the window of a blue wagon came the sound of a girl shouting, and the crash of a plate. It was like a village that had appeared in the space of an hour, and would disappear just as quickly; a moving mirage that no one could hope to enter unless by invitation. When he turned back to the fire, Gila was playing with his gray mouse, Susan, and Umor was noisily stacking plates, which he balanced on his head as he trotted up the steps and disappeared into the wagon.

Miles cleared his throat. "Maybe I could . . . ," he began, but Fabio shook his head. "Circus is a tight ship," he said.

Gila looked up from his mouse. "No room for passengers," he said.

There was the sound of another piece of crockery smashing in the blue wagon, and the girl's voice shouted, "When I go, Hector go too. You don't feed him even!"

"But Miles works hard," said Little. "He could help with the tent, or look after animals."

"Can he walk a wire?" asked Fabio.

"Or show a lion?" asked Gila.

Miles shook his head.

"He could wash the dishes," came Umor's voice from inside the wagon.

"Everyone in circus must do two or three things, Master Miles," said Fabio. "It's the only way we can survive."

From the corner of his eye Miles saw a small muscular girl step out of the blue wagon, slamming the door behind her so that the windows rattled. Her glossy brown hair was tied back with a ribbon, and she wore an oversized coat. A small monkey sat hunched on her shoulder, and her eyes flashed with anger. She marched toward the Bolsillo brothers' campfire, staggering slightly on her platform shoes under the weight of a large suitcase and a worn carpetbag. A sparkling pink sleeve hung from the suitcase, its end dragging in the mud.

"I will not anymore work with that animal!" she said in a voice much larger than herself. She dropped her bags and folded her arms, glaring at Fabio.

Fabio looked at the monkey curiously. "He's a good little performer," he said.

"Tchah!" said the girl. "Not little Hector. The

monkey is beautiful human being." She jerked her head over her shoulder. "Stranski is the animal! He never wash, smell like a badger's bum. He never say please, never thank you, always so much rude."

"Stranski can't speak, Julia," said Gila.

"Not since his accident," shouted Umor from inside the trailer.

"Hasn't said a word in twenty years," said Fabio.

The girl sniffed. "I know that! It's not what he don't say. It's the way he don't say it. Always push me into the box, pull me out, pinch me with hard fingers. He never feed the monkey, always I give him from my own food. I finish with Stranski now, and I take the monkey with me. We finish with this circus for good!"

"You can't leave now," said Fabio.

"Stranski needs an assistant," said Gila.

"You have a contract," said Fabio.

Julia bent down and rummaged in her bag until she found a crumpled sheet of paper with spidery writing crawling over both sides. "This contract?" she said, and she rolled it into a ball and stuffed it in her mouth. She chewed for a minute, her head high and her hands on her hips, and swallowed the paper with an exaggerated gulp, then without another word she picked up her bags and staggered off in the direction of the road. The monkey turned back to face the circus, chattering loudly and pulling at the girl's ear, but she shook her head resolutely and kept walking. Just before she reached the road Hector leaped from her shoulder and ran, dodging between wagons and under clotheslines, straight back to the blue wagon from which they had come. Julia paused for a moment and stared back after the monkey with a wounded look, then she turned and was gone.

There was silence around the campfire. Umor appeared on the top step and looked sadly after the girl. "Pity," he said. "I liked her."

Fabio stared into the embers for a minute, a frown knitting his bushy eyebrows together, then he looked up at Miles and smiled.

"How would you like to be sawn in half?" he said.

CHAPTER THREE
THE CANNY RAT

Miles Wednesday, bone-tired and chest-inflated, wheeled a barrow of elephant droppings over the stone bridge into Larde, with a broad grin on his face and Little skipping by his side. After Julia's unexpected departure from the circus he had been hired on the spot as tent boy, junior beast man and assistant to Stranski the Magician, an expert knife thrower and trick swordsman who did indeed smell like a badger's bum.

"Some people are just in the right place at the right time," Umor had said, leading him over to the small elephant enclosure in the corner of the field.

"And you're not one of them," added Gila, handing

Miles a shovel. He pointed to the miniature mountain of dung that Tembo and Mamba had already managed to produce. "Load up the wheelbarrow there, Master Miles," he said.

"You have to ask their permission first," said Umor.

"And mind they don't step on you," said Gila.

After several hours of backbreaking work he had been sent with Little to the Parks and Gardens Department of the town hall. The barrow of elephant dung, to which had been added a cocktail of exotic droppings from four continents (and a couple of incontinents), made an excellent manure, and selling it would help to pay for the animal feed. Miles's hands were blistered by the shovel, and the handles of the barrow stung. He stopped in a narrow alley and put the barrow down gingerly.

"Is this it?" asked Little, squinting up at the sign that hung from the grim building beside them. Her progress in learning to read was slow, as she could not grasp how the music of speech could be tied down with such clumsy stitches. "T-heh . . . Can . . . ny . . . ," she began.

"The Canny Rat," said Miles. "No, this isn't it— I'm just giving my hands a rest." The sign showed a sleek white rat with pink eyes, rearing up against a striped shield as you would see a lion do on a coat of arms. The rat held a glass of stout in one paw, and a large key in the other. Above the sign a bare light-bulb burned weakly in the shadows of the alley, suspended from a tangle of black wires.

As Miles bent to pick up the heavy barrow, a large thatched head poked out from the gloom of the pub doorway. Miles straightened up in surprise. There was no mistaking that mean squint and the heavy lower lip that dangled like a moist pink slug over a stubbly chin. It was Fowler Pinchbucket, who together with his flinty-thin wife had run the county orphanage—where Miles had once lived— like a juvenile prison.

"You can't park that thing 'ere," said Fowler. Miles picked up the barrow hastily. He knew that Fowler Pinchbucket usually had to squint at something for a few seconds before he could identify it, and he wanted to use this narrow opportunity to make good his escape.

"'Ang about," said Fowler, stepping into the road and blocking the way. "I know you. You're Wednesday, ain't you?" He folded his arms and peered from Miles to Little with a puzzled frown.

"Never heard of him," said Miles, "and you're standing in the way of fresh manure on wheels. You might want to reconsider."

Fowler Pinchbucket didn't budge. "You can't fool me," he said, forgetting that Miles had done so on many occasions. "I never forget a face."

"Fow-ler!" barked a hard voice from the gloom inside. "What are you doing out there—discussing the weather? There are barrels that need changing."

Little glanced at Miles. "We have to go now," she said to Fowler Pinchbucket, but having failed to identify her he found it easier to ignore her.

"Found two of ours," Fowler called over his shoulder. His voice was thick, as though he had swallowed a sock. "The Wednesday lad, and a girl I can't remember."

"We're not yours!" said Miles, and he pushed the wheelbarrow into Fowler's shins. Fowler's mouth opened in a grimace, waiting for a word to arrive from his brain. The sound of Mrs. Pinchbucket's voice had made knots in Miles's stomach, but while Fowler blocked the narrow alley there was no way around him.

"*Which* Wednesday lad?" shouted the voice from inside. "We had a dozen of them."

"Ow!" said Fowler. "It's the one that got away. The dark one."

Mrs. Pinchbucket appeared at the doorway in an

instant. In contrast to her husband, who appeared to have been pieced together from a number of blubbery and mismatched bodies, Mrs. Pinchbucket was dried and wrinkled like a single stick of vanilla. Only her face was smooth, so stretched by her tightly tied hair that it looked as though it had been lacquered. "Miles Wednesday!" she said, her eyebrows climbing her forehead. "What a nice surprise. You've grown so *big*! And you've found a little friend, I see."

Miles stared at Mrs. Pinchbucket as though she had sprouted feathers. In the eight years he had suffered the gray tedium of Pinchbucket House, he could not remember ever hearing a pleasant word from Mrs. Pinchbucket or her husband.

"She's . . . she's my sister," he said.

"Your . . . sister!" echoed Mrs. Pinchbucket. A sickly smile bisected her face. "Well come in, the two of you, and we'll get you a drink of . . . pop, or whatever. I hear rumors that you've been saving the town in our absence. You must tell us all about it."

"Thank you, but we have to go," said Miles, with as much politeness as he could muster. "We're already late," added Little.

"Nonsense!" said Mrs. Pinchbucket. "Fowler, park that wheelbarrow while I show these children our new establishment. We just opened on Friday," she said to Miles.

Fowler Pinchbucket grunted, and grabbed the rough handles of the barrow. He was just as puzzled as Miles, but had long since learned to avoid any delay in carrying out his wife's instructions. With reluctant curiosity Miles, followed by Little, stepped over the threshold of the Canny Rat.

If you have ever seen a place decorated by two people with absolutely no taste or talent, who like parting with money about as much as having their legs chewed off by a cannibal, you will have a pretty good picture of the interior of the Canny Rat. The Pinchbuckets had tried to scrub years of greasy dirt from the bile-green walls, on the basis that soap and water is cheaper than paint, but Fowler's homemade ladder had buckled under his weight before they were finished, leaving a tidemark just below the ceiling. Three bare lightbulbs gave off such a feeble light that it was hard to be sure they were switched on. Mrs. Pinchbucket had splashed out on one tub of paint, a gallon of special-offer pink emulsion, which she had applied to the bar and part of the floor around it until the paint had run out. It made the bar look like a half-melted block of ice cream.

"Make yourselves comfortable," said Mrs.

Pinchbucket, pointing at a straggle of hard stools along the bar, "and I'll get you both a drink. What would you like?"

"Orange juice will be fine," said Miles.

"Don't hold your breath," said Mrs. Pinchbucket in a chirpy voice.

"Water?" ventured Little.

"Tap's broken," said Mrs. Pinchbucket. "Two bitter lemons." This last remark was aimed at the far end of the bar, beyond the reach of the feeble lightbulbs. Miles could just make out the figure of a girl polishing glasses in the gloom.

"Two bitter what?" asked the girl.

"Bitter lemons. Bitter lemons," snapped Mrs. Pinchbucket. "Behind you on the right, in the glass cabinet."

The girl slid into the light and placed two bottles on the bar, and Miles recognized her immediately as Julia from the circus. She had evidently found a new job as quickly as Miles himself had. "Two bitter lemons," she said in a bored voice.

"Well," said Mrs. Pinchbucket, settling herself stiffly behind the bar. "How do you like our little pub?"

"It's . . . different," said Miles, looking around. There did not seem to be another customer in the place. In the corner was a stack of boxes with the words EXPORT ONLY stenciled on them.

"I'm glad you think so," said Mrs. Pinchbucket. "We get very busy in the evenings, of course. But you must tell me about yourself, and your little . . . sister. Are you still living in a moldy old tub?"

"My barrel got flattened," said Miles.

Little took the straw out of her mouth. "We live with—" she began, but Miles shot his elbow out and sent the two sour drinks flooding across the bar before she could say another word.

"Oops!" he said loudly.

Mrs. Pinchbucket glared at him, then stretched her mouth into a smile. "Accidents will happen," she said. "Julia?"

"The cloth is where?" said Julia from the gloom.

"Hanging from the tap, girl," said Mrs. Pinchbucket, "and bring two more drinks, chop chop!" She moved to a dry spot on the bar. "Now," she said to Little, "I don't believe I got your name, child."

Miles stepped down from the stool. "We really have to go now," he said. "We have some important manure to deliver."

"Then you must come again," said Mrs. Pinchbucket, the sweetness in her voice stretching thin. "Where will you be if we need you? There are always odd jobs in places Fowler is too big to crawl into."

"I already have a job," said Miles, but he was interrupted by a squeal of delight from Little. Following her gaze he saw two sleek white rats, like the one on the signboard outside, running along the bar top toward the spilled drink. Before Julia could start to mop it up they had dipped their pink snouts into the sticky puddle and were lapping it up greedily.

"Fow-ler!" shouted Mrs. Pinchbucket, her voice once again hard as industrial diamond. "Get in here and box those rats of yours."

"Where are they?" said Fowler, shambling in with a plywood box under his arm, the wire-netting door swinging open. He spotted the two rats on the bar. "How the blazes did you get in here?" he said, and slammed the box down heavily on the bar. The rats flinched, but they carried on drinking. "Titus. Larry. Get back in yer box," said Fowler thickly. The rats ignored him. "Back in yer box," he wheedled. "Come on, don't be pigheaded."

Miles and Little forgot their hasty departure for a moment, watching the unequal struggle between man and rodent. Little, who could understand all animal speech, gave a giggle. "You should hear what the rats are saying," she whispered to Miles.

Fowler grabbed one of the rats, but it struggled from his grip and managed to bite him in the process. He swore, and sucked his thumb.

"This way you will not succeed," said Julia. "You must *talk* to them. Find out what they want." Miles and Little exchanged glances.

"What do you know about rats?" said Fowler. "I've been breedin' 'em for years, me."

Julia said nothing, but she reached under the bar and produced a packet of nuts. She opened it and held a couple of peanuts out on her open hand. The rats paused in their drinking and sniffed, their whiskers twitching.

"I bet you like some of these, don't you, boys?" said Julia. She did not speak to them in rat language, as Miles had half expected, but her voice was soft and he could see they were listening to her. He wondered why the monkey had chosen to stay with Stranski. "It's time to return back in your box. Come on, Titus; come, Larry," said Julia quietly, and she put a handful of nuts in the box. The rats hesitated for just a moment, then trotted inside. Fowler slammed the door and glared at her, as though she had just done him a disservice.

"Let's go," whispered Little, and as they stepped out into the alleyway they heard Mrs. Pinchbucket say, "Those nuts will come out of your wages, girl."

CHAPTER FOUR

SPECIAL DEVILRY

Stranski the Magician, mute and malodorous, plucked the last of his twelve knives from where it quivered in the scarred and painted board by Miles's left ear. Like most circus performers he was short and compact and looked as though he could be packed away neatly in a large suitcase. His head was shaved bald, and a bushy beard fringed his chin, which had made Little comment the first time she saw him that his head was on upside down.

An intricate pattern of waxy scars covered Stranski's arms and throat, a legacy of the trailer fire that had almost killed him many years before. His terrible injuries had ended his career as an acrobat, and Gila said that this had robbed him of his good humor as well as his voice, although Miles was sure he must have been short of patience all his life. He poked Miles none too gently in the chest, and wagged his head from side to side like a metronome. Miles had become used to Stranski's sign language, and he understood this as a reprimand for moving his head. He was sure he hadn't moved at all, but he was wise enough to heed the warnings of a man who threw razor-sharp knives at him every evening, when he wasn't sawing him in half.

Stranski was no less gruff with Hector the monkey. It was the monkey's job to sneak under the banked seats, pick the pocket of someone in the audience and slip the stolen wallet into Stranski's own pocket without being noticed. Stranski would keep an eye out for the monkey's little hand as it reached up from under the seats, and at the end of the act he would single out the unwitting victim and astonish him by producing the wallet from inside a colored handkerchief, before it had even been missed.

There was a lot to be learned in the days before the circus took to the road. During the day Miles tended the circus zoo under Umor's and Gila's instruction. They taught him how to feed and care for the animals, how to keep them healthy and calm and how to end the day with the same number of limbs with which he started it. With every animal bite and aching muscle he felt himself grow in confidence and strength.

Sometimes, when no one was around, he would try to talk with the lions, but they would gaze at him disinterestedly for a moment and return to their grooming, or to pacing the length of their wheeled cages. Then Miles would talk instead to Tangerine, who would poke his head out of Miles's inside pocket and smile his lopsided smile at the lions. The life that Little had sung into the stuffed bear while she was still a Song Angel allowed him to climb like a koala and walk like a gin-soaked sailor, but his mouth was a row of clumsy stitches, and he was no more capable of uttering a word than he had ever been.

Little worked with the circus band for most of the day, coaxing from them an unearthly music that grew sweeter as the days went by. The other performers, too, were tightening up their acts and perfecting their routines, and though Miles spent most of his time with the animals he was soon on nodding terms with everyone in the circus. Everyone, that is, except Doctor Tau-Tau. The fortune-teller's wagon stood at the end of the field, shaded by a tamarind tree and with its curtains drawn day and night, and never a sign of its mysterious occupant. Miles passed the wagon every evening on his way home to Partridge Manor. Sometimes he would be startled by a jet of steam from the narrow stovepipe on the roof, or a burst of tuneless singing that would break off abruptly as he approached, and he felt his curiosity grow with every passing day.

"Have you ever seen him?" Miles asked Little as he locked up the elephants' pen for the night.

"No," said Little. "There's a small bird in his wagon—I've heard her talk, but from Doctor Tau-Tau I have only heard snores, and snores speak of nothing."

"I wonder what he's hiding from?" said Miles.

"Maybe he has two heads," suggested Little.

"One called Tau," laughed Miles, "and the other called Tau."

Little put her finger to her lips.

"Nobody's listening," said Miles, looking around.

"I am," said Little. "Listen. The bees are singing the flowers. That's just the sound I needed."

"Bees don't sing," said Miles. "That humming is made by their wings beating."

Little laughed. "Of course they sing, Miles. They hum that part of the One Song that makes the flowers grow, and the flowers feed them in return."

"I thought it was you Song Angels that sang the One Song," said Miles.

"The Song Angels look after the One Song," said Little. "They tie it all together, but everything has its part. The bees sing the flowers. The crows sing the thorn bushes and the seagulls sing the wind. Everything is connected, Miles."

They were approaching Doctor Tau-Tau's wagon now, and as they drew closer Miles was sure there were voices coming from inside. Little looked at him, wide-eyed, and they crept forward and stopped behind the trunk of the tamarind tree.

"You can't blame that on me," a voice was saying.

"Oh, but I do," said another, with an unpleasant titter. "Who else should I blame?"

"I didn't have enough time," said the first man, and Miles thought he could hear a slight quaver in his voice. "No one should have to work under those conditions."

"You lost me my associate," said the other. "I gave you the job of bringing him back from the cliff, and instead you pushed him right over the edge. You're an idiot masquerading as a fool, Tau-Tau, and you've chosen the wrong time to come out of hiding. It's not even you I was looking for, but you'll do for starters!" The man dissolved into a giggling fit, although there was nothing very funny in what he was saying.

"Wait . . . wait!" said the other voice, sounding genuinely frightened. "I know what you're looking for, and I think I know where to find it. I'm getting close. We can work together . . . can't we?"

The other man tittered again. Something about the sound made Miles's skin crawl. He felt Little grip his hand tightly. "Tell me," said the voice, "and you had better not waste my time."

The other man lowered his voice. He began to speak rapidly without taking a breath, but Miles could no longer make out the words. He looked at Little, crouched beside him in the grass. "We should leave," she whispered. Miles nodded, and they crept out onto the road that led to Partridge Manor.

"Do you think we should tell Lady Partridge?" said Little.

Miles shook his head. "There's not much to tell really, and she'd only worry about us leaving with the circus. If we tell anyone it should be the

Bolsillo brothers, but I'm not sure it's any of our business anyway."

They walked on in silence toward the big square mansion with its glowing windows, and when Miles glanced over his shoulder he thought he saw a small figure slip out of Doctor Tau-Tau's wagon and steal away into the night.

Lady Partridge, gowned, groomed and freshly scented, sat at the head of the table on the night before the circus took to the road. She had invited the Bolsillo brothers to dinner, and they sat in the new dining room, which was smaller and more friendly than the original one had been. In place of the marquises, duchesses and theater directors who once would have been her guests, Lady Partridge felt unaccountably pleased to find herself hosting a dinner for three small acrobat clowns, a boy who befriended tigers and a girl who had fallen from the sky.

The conversation at the meal was lively. The excitement of their imminent departure had chased the weariness from the circus performers. They had spent the morning unpacking the big top and laying it out in the long field for a final inspection. Every rope and pole and eyebolt had been counted, and the smaller children had walked the spread-out canvas in their bare feet, looking for tears and burst seams. Every hole had been patched and every frayed rope replaced; blocks had been greased and checked for rust, and the whole structure had been packed away again and loaded onto the three long trucks that would carry it from town to town.

The animals were restless too. They had lived their lives on the road, and knew as they were led into their hosed-down wagons that before dawn they would be starting on their own strange migration through the smells and sounds of the thawing countryside.

"Red sky at night," said Gila, gesturing toward the window with a pork rib.

"Gives my dog a fright," said Umor.

"That means good weather, doesn't it?" said Miles.

"My dog affects the weather?" said Umor.

"A red sky," said Miles.

"That depends," said Little. "A red sky means the Council of Light is meeting. The weather that follows depends on how the meeting goes. Usually many things are resolved, so of course there will be calm skies, but if the meeting ends in anger there will still be a storm afterward."

"Well," said Lady Partridge, "let's hope this meeting goes smoothly." She tapped a knife on her glass, waking a couple of cats who were dozing on the sideboard. "A toast to the Circus Bolsillo," she said. "May the new season surpass all expectations."

Drinks were raised and glasses clinked.

"I'll drink to that," said Fabio.

"I'll drink to anything," said Umor.

"Among the reasons I invited you here," said Lady Partridge to Fabio, "was to ask if you would do me the favor of keeping an eye on Miles and Little for me."

"We can look after ourselves, Lady Partridge," protested Miles.

"Indeed you can," said Lady Partridge, "and better than many of your elders, as you have already demonstrated. But it worries me that that dangerous little Cortado man is on the loose again. You may have outwitted him once, but that only gives him more reason to bear a grudge. Only yesterday there was a report in the *Weekly Herald* that he had been sighted in Shallowford, and while I don't place much reliance on that bundle of fish wrapping, I can't say I feel comfortable about you being out on the road while he is still at large."

"Well if he was seen around these parts, maybe it's better that we're leaving for a while," suggested Miles.

"Perhaps," said Lady Partridge, though she did not sound convinced.

"Don't you worry, Lady P.," said Umor.

"We'll watch them like our own cash box," said Gila.

"Besides, we're more than a match for that little half-pint."

"Even if we're just quarter-pints."

"There are three of us."

"Which makes us a liter."

"Thank you, boys," said Lady Partridge with a smile. "That makes me feel a lot better."

There was a soft knock at the door of the dining room, and a small boy in pajamas poked his head around the door. "There's a man at the door. He says he has a special devilry," said the boy, who looked half asleep.

"Thank you, Marcus," said Lady Partridge. "I rather hope you mean delivery."

The boy nodded. He turned to leave, but the door swung open and Fowler Pinchbucket pushed past him, carrying a heavy box and almost knocking Marcus off his feet. "Pardon the interruption," he grunted, and tried to remove his cap, forgetting for a moment that he had his hands full with his special devilry. He caught the box before it slipped from his grasp, and plonked it down on the sideboard, scattering the cats. "Imported," he said, as though that explained everything.

"What on earth . . . ?" said Lady Partridge, inflating dangerously.

"A present for Lady Pinchpartridge from the Rat Bucket," said Fowler, clearly flustered by Lady Partridge's daunting glare. He began again: "A present for Lady Partridge, from the proprietors of the Canny Rat."

"I'm not expecting any deliveries, and certainly not at this hour," said Lady Partridge frostily.

"Yes, well," said Fowler, "apologies for that. We keep odd hours, being in the licensed trade, and as soon as we heard that you had taken in the Wednesday boy as well as the rest of our old work . . . our orphans, Mrs. Pinchbucket insisted that I deliver this token of our appreciation. If you see what I mean."

Lady Partridge eyed the sweating man suspiciously as he opened the box and lifted out a large mantel clock. It had a black lacquered case, arched at the top and otherwise completely plain. The face was painted with roman numerals, and the hands stood at a minute to midnight.

"Very nice," said Fabio, breaking the silence.

"Your house'll never blow away with that in it," said Umor.

"Well, thank you, I'm sure," said Lady Partridge, rather taken aback. "Can I offer you a drink before you leave, Mr. Pinchbucket?"

"No thanks," said Fowler, touching the brim of his cap. "I'm needed at the taps."

As he made to leave, a whirring sound came from the clock, and everyone turned to look. It began to chime, and what a chime it was! The sound was as light and pure as the clock was plain and heavy. It swirled around the candlelit room, carrying with it a flavor of foreign lands that was so strong you could almost smell it. No one moved or breathed until the last echoes faded into silence. Even Fowler Pinchbucket stood transfixed, his hand on the door handle, and a smile invading his sulky face.

"Why, that's absolutely beautiful," breathed Lady Partridge.

"Like a lark in a cinder block," said Gila. "What would you say, Sky Beetle?"

"I like it," said Little. "Whoever made that lives beside water, and has listened very well to the songbirds."

"Is anyone eating that?" said Fowler Pinchbucket, pointing to the last pork rib on the platter.

CHAPTER FIVE

A DEEPER SECRET

Miles Wednesday, scarf-wrapped and half-awake, sat on the box seat beside Fabio, who drove the Bolsillo brothers' wagon at an easy pace along the road that led from Larde to the distant mountains. The birds were beginning to awaken in the trees, and the sky ahead of them lightened toward dawn. Fabio spoke softly to the massive horses that plodded slowly ahead of them, and Miles listened in comfortable silence, not yet awake enough for conversation. He tried to make out what Fabio was saying, but the words were unfamiliar, and punctutated with little chucks and whistles that did not seem to have any meaning.

The three long trucks that carried the big top had gone well ahead of them, and were long since swallowed up by the orange blob of the rising sun. With them had gone the tent boys, K2 the Strongman and the Bolsillo brothers' hardworking elephants, Tembo and Mamba. They would reach Shallowford well before the rest of the circus, and there they would make ready the tent to be raised, once more hands had arrived.

Miles had been allocated the spare bunk in the Bolsillo brothers' wagon. He had cleared it of polka dot socks and luminous wigs, and found a space among the ropes, the hoops, the cymbals and horns and greasepaint for the small trunk that Lady Partridge had packed for him. Little was to ride with the Toki sisters, a troupe of contortionists who had arrived just weeks before from the Far East. Miles had seen the Toki sisters at practice, tying themselves into a fantastic beast with four heads and many limbs, and he had heard that they could fold themselves up like deck chairs, or make themselves into hoops and roll effortlessly around the ring.

He leaned out and looked back along the road to see if he could spot Little. Directly behind them came the blue and silver wagon of the mysterious

Doctor Tau-Tau, and behind that was the lion cage, driven by the haughty Countess Fontainbleau, and the battered van belonging to Stranski the Magician, followed by the Zipplethorpe family's horse trailer, but the Toki sisters' wagon was still lost in the morning mist.

"When did Doctor Tau-Tau join the circus?" asked Miles.

"Just after Christmas," said Fabio.

"He was abroad for many years," said Gila.

"But he was with Barty Fumble's before that," said Umor.

"Why does he never leave his wagon?" asked Miles.

Fabio shrugged. "Who knows?" he said.

"None of our business," said Gila.

"People join the circus for many reasons," said Fabio.

"And it's not always a good idea to ask."

"A man's wagon is his castle."

Miles pulled his overcoat tighter to keep out the biting cold. There seemed little point in trying to tell them about the conversation he had overheard from Doctor Tau-Tau's wagon, and in any case the fragment he had heard would mean little on its own. He wondered how many secrets the circus carried with it as it wound through the countryside.

Perhaps a clue to his father's disappearance still lurked in one of the painted wagons. He always pictured his parents in a wagon with a magnificent tiger's head painted on it, but he was not sure why, and he knew of no such wagon in the circus.

"Which wagon belonged to my parents?" he asked. "Is it still with the circus?"

Fabio cleared his throat. "Yes," he said.

"And no," said Gila.

"What they mean," said Umor's voice from inside the wagon, "is that all the wagons change hands."

"They get repainted."

"And refitted."

"They get married and separated."

"Sometimes we make a new one from two old ones."

"I once tried to turn one inside out," said Gila, "but I couldn't get the wagon through the door."

Miles waited for them to finish. "Which one is it?" he repeated.

"Tau-Tau's wagon," said Fabio, staring straight ahead.

Miles leaned out to the side and looked back along the road. Tau-Tau's wagon was directly behind them, and for once he could see Doctor Tau-Tau himself, perched on the box seat in his battered fez.

His face was round and red, with a little tuft of beard dangling from it so that he looked like a goat in a coat. Miles tried to picture Barty Fumble himself sitting on that very seat with Miles's mother beside him, but while he could clearly see his barrel-chested father in his mind's eye, his mother was as indistinct as a noonday ghost.

He turned back to Fabio. "What was my mother's name?" he asked. For years he had known nothing about his parents, but in the months since he had learned of his mother's death in childbirth and the subsequent disappearance of his father from his own circus, he had begun to think that it was time to start filling in the new and hollow feeling that had grown within him.

"There's a village up ahead," said Gila.

"That'll be Hay," called Umor from inside.

"Nice little inn there," said Gila.

"Very reasonable too," said Umor.

Fabio kept silent, watching the horses' broad backs.

"You told me you knew my parents well," said Miles, carefully keeping the impatience from his voice. He had long since learned that getting information from the Bolsillo brothers was like catching fish with your bare hands. A lot of patience was required, and there was no guarantee of success.

"As well as anybody, Master Miles," said Fabio.

"I don't know anything about my mother," said Miles.

Fabio sighed. "Your mother's name was Celeste," he said, "and she came from down south, across the water."

"She had hair like midnight," said Gila.

"And eyes to match," said Fabio.

"Always smelled of warm coconut," said Umor, his head poking out from between the curtains at the front of the wagon.

"And when Barty laughed, she would just smile," said Gila.

"Like she knew a deeper secret," said Umor.

"Celeste knew all the secrets, Master Miles," said Fabio.

"Do you have any pictures of them?" asked Miles. "Of my parents?"

"Of your father, yes," said Fabio.

"Your mother didn't like cameras," said Gila.

"Or they didn't like her," said Fabio.

"She didn't like to be trapped in a picture, did Celeste," said Umor, poking his head out from the wagon once more.

He held out a small photograph in a dark wooden

frame. Miles took it with trepidation. He was almost afraid to look, in case what he saw did not match his expectations. The frame contained an old black-and-white photograph, faded by age to a brownish color. A number of bleached yellow blobs floated like giant amoebas in the center of the photograph. Beside them a large man stared out from the picture, his head tilted back and a smile creasing his face, though little of it could be seen behind a bushy black beard. The man wore a double-breasted ringmaster's coat with two rows of shiny buttons and elaborate epaulets. Behind him could be seen a wagon painted with a rearing tiger, almost exactly as Miles had imagined it.

The man in the photograph, who of course was Barty Fumble himself, stood with his arm around a slender woman in a dark dress, but the largest of the yellow blobs floated just where the woman's face should be. A tangle of beads could just be seen hanging below the blob, but not a trace remained of her features. Miles stared at the picture as though he could will his mother's face to appear. He felt cheated.

"It's a good one of Barty," said Gila.

"But not a great likeness of your mother," said Umor.

"What happened to the photo?" asked Miles.

Fabio shrugged, making a clicking noise to the horses as he did so.

"Who knows?" he said.

"She didn't want it taken in the first place," said Umor.

"But Barty insisted."

"The photo came back all right."

"But before the week was out, her face had disappeared."

"When Barty saw it, he just laughed, and threw the picture away."

"But we kept it."

"And now it's yours," said Gila. "If you want it."

"Thank you," said Miles. He took another long look at his father, who smiled out at him as though he knew that Miles were there, then he slipped the picture into his inside pocket, feeling Tangerine wriggle around to make room for it.

"Have you ever looked for my father," he asked Fabio, "since he disappeared?"

Fabio said nothing. Gila jumped up from the box seat and ducked into the wagon to help Umor with some unspecified task.

"Has anyone ever searched for him?" asked Miles, looking at Fabio. "He can't have just vanished off the face of the earth."

Fabio stared ahead in silence. They rumbled over the bridge into the small town of Hay, where Miles and Little had stopped to find something to eat on their long journey to the Palace of Laughter the previous autumn. As they approached the Surly Hen Inn, Fabio turned to Miles, a fathomless expression in his little black eyes.

"Your father is dead," he said. For once there was no echo from the two brothers in the wagon.

"But how do you know?" said Miles. He could feel tears welling up in his eyes, and he fought them back. "You said he had disappeared."

"Just believe me, I know," said Fabio. "Barty Fumble is dead and gone."

He called softly to the horses, and they pulled in to the yard beside the Surly Hen and drew to a halt before the dark, silent forest.

CHAPTER SIX
A STOLEN NAME

Tangerine the bear, birdbrained and half-stuffed, felt his master's hand reach into the warm pocket where he lived. He gave Miles's fingers a soft squeeze, and the fingers squeezed back. Miles was in the habit of checking on Tangerine regularly, both to make sure he was still there and to keep him from showing himself in company. A bear that could walk and dance generally attracted the wrong sort of attention from strangers. As he sat at a heavy wooden table in the corner of the Surly Hen, Miles checked on Tangerine more frequently than usual. This was, after all, the place where he had lost the bear once before, and it was not an experience he wanted to repeat.

The inn, which was normally quiet this early in the morning, was crowded now with circus folk. The landlady and her daughter were bustling between the contortionists, lion tamers and sword swallowers, balancing above their heads plates of fried breakfast and steaming mugs of coffee. At the bar sat a scattering of farmers, making sure they had a good feed under their belts before embarking on the hard labor that separated them from lunchtime, and staring at the circus folk with open curiosity.

"I'm starving," said Little, sliding onto the bench beside Miles with a knife and fork at the ready. "The Toki sisters talked about food the whole way here. It was mostly stuff I never heard of, but it made me hungry all the same."

Miles felt empty too, but he could not tell how much of this was hunger and how much was the yawning hole left by Fabio's insistence that his father was dead. He was sure that Fabio would never tell him an outright lie, but he couldn't shake the idea that he was not being told the whole truth either. He tried to put thoughts of Barty Fumble out of his mind as two enormous breakfasts arrived on the table. They were followed a moment later by

Doctor Tau-Tau, whose own breakfast was piled so high on the plate that it was in danger of keeling over. He sat down gingerly to avoid shaking the table. His face was weathered to a brick red, and his bulging eyes took in Miles and Little as he speared a large sausage with gusto.

"Doctor Tau-Tau, clairvoyant and master of nature's remedies," he said through a mouthful of sausage. He held out his hand. "You must be Stranski's new boy and the little bandmaster." A gold tooth glinted through his half-chewed breakfast, and his faded red fez perched on grizzled brown hair. It looked as though both he and the hat had spent many years in the sun.

"That's right," said Miles. "I'm Miles, and this is Little."

Miles was rather surprised to be addressed so heartily by Doctor Tau-Tau, who had never even shown his face since they had joined the circus. Perhaps, he thought, it was the open road that had lightened Tau-Tau's mood.

Doctor Tau-Tau pointed at them with his fork, and chewed vigorously to make room for speech. "I can see many things in your past," he said eventually in a sausage-muffled voice. "And your futures are an open book to me."

Miles was not sure if this odd statement, spoken in a thick foreign accent, required an answer, so he concentrated on taking the edge off his own hunger. Little ate too, her clear blue eyes fixed on Doctor Tau-Tau's face.

Doctor Tau-Tau took a noisy slurp from his tea and leaned across the table. "Reality is a veil," he said, "and the truth swims behind it like a golden fish with ruby eyes and fins of . . . some silvery stuff. Few are the people who can pull that veil aside, but I have that gift. That gift, young travelers, is one that I have."

"Is the veil in the water?" asked Little, mopping her plate with a piece of bread. "Or is the fish flying?"

Doctor Tau-Tau sat back in his chair and laughed. "You are sharp, little girl," he said. "There are many kinds of veils in the water. There's . . . er . . . a water veil, for a start." He paused for a moment, and a frown creased his forehead. "And the fish of truth can of course fly. . . ." His voice tailed off as though he had just thought of something else, then suddenly he sat bolt upright and turned back to Miles. He put his fingertips to his temples. "Ask me a question," he said, fixing Miles with his goggly eyes and looking not unlike the fish of truth himself. "Anything at all."

Miles thought for a moment. "Okay," he said, suddenly remembering where he had seen the fortune-teller's name before. "Did you invent Dr. Tau-Tau's Restorative Tonic?"

A shocked look came over Doctor Tau-Tau's face. "Infamy!" he spluttered. "I never had anything to do with the stuff. I hope no drop of that insidious juice ever passed your lips, young man."

He straightened his fez with a hand that shook slightly. "My name was stolen, if you must know, by a villain named the Great Cortado. He hounded me from the circus and stole my possessions! My books, my herbs and remedies, even my name he took for his vile concoctions, and I was left to start again in foreign parts with nothing but the clothes I stood up in." He took a gulp of tea, and it seemed to restore some of his composure. "And, of course, my uncommon talent," he added.

"You used to be with Barty Fumble's circus, didn't you?" said Miles.

Doctor Tau-Tau nodded. "Many years ago," he said, "I was apprenticed to a fortune-teller named Celeste. My unparalleled knowledge of the divining arts was built on the foundation of her teaching. She also taught me much about the ancient healing properties of plants, and with my innate talent I was able to develop a number of excellent potions and cures from her simple remedies, although unlike that infamous tonic, few of them have received the recognition they deserved."

"What kind of potions did you invent?" asked Little.

"Well, there was my powerful sleeping draught, which could calm the most nervous of people and send them into a deep and dreamless sleep for an entire day. I also perfected a cure for gastric distress, and of course my patented Bearded Lady lotion remains an untried marvel to this day."

"A Bearded Lady lotion?" said Little.

"Absolutely," said Tau-Tau, chewing the last of his sausage. "Two drops of this liquid applied to the chin of the daintiest lady would be enough to produce a beard of magnificent quality in minutes. Think of the money an enterprising girl could make as a sideshow. I can't imagine why no one has ever consented to try it."

"Very odd," said Miles, who was far more interested by the mention of his mother than by Doctor Tau-Tau's back catalogue of untried marvels. He tried to keep his tone casual, but he was burning to know more. "What was she like?" he asked.

"I told you I never found anyone brave . . . I mean,

enterprising enough," said the fortune-teller sadly.

"I mean Celeste," said Miles. "What was she like?"

"Ah!" said Tau-Tau, and he paused for the first time since sitting down at the table. He seemed to be lost for a moment in another time. "Great clairvoyants don't come along every five minutes, young man," he said at length. "I, of course, am the greatest fortune-teller and healer alive, though I don't like to blow my own trumpet, but Celeste was certainly something special in her day. She made you feel like you were made of glass, and your beating heart was suspended there for her to see."

"But what did she look like?" asked Miles.

"What did she look like?" repeated Doctor Tau-Tau. He was silent again for a while, except for a loud belch that started deep in his stomach and rumbled its way out without disturbing his train of thought. "Funny you should ask that," he said eventually. "I remember her well, but I just can't see her face for the life of me. For the life of me," he repeated, "I just can't see her face."

"You must have known Barty Fumble too," said Miles. He wondered to himself what kind of fortune-teller would be unaware that he was talking to the son of his own mentor, but he thought it best not to mention this for the time being.

"Of course," said Doctor Tau-Tau, coming out of his reverie. "Big overweight chap. He would have been nothing without his tiger."

Miles was almost too surprised to be annoyed. He had never heard anyone speak of his father with anything less than affection and respect. "It wasn't his tiger," he said shortly. "No tiger can be owned by a man."

"Ah!" said Doctor Tau-Tau, tapping the side of his nose and looking pleased with himself. "I think you will find that you are wrong. I know many of the secrets of the striped cat. You won't find the important details in picture books, my boy."

"I think your fish has slipped behind your veil," said Miles indignantly. "I happen to be good friends with a tiger, and he told me so himself."

Little clattered her cutlery loudly on her empty plate. "People are leaving," she said. "We'd better get back to the wagons, Miles."

For a moment Miles and Doctor Tau-Tau held each other's stare, then the fortune-teller straightened up and showed his gold tooth in a broad smile. "Forgive me!" he said. "Sometimes a man with my talents can be blinded by overconfidence. You do indeed bear the mark of a tiger friend—I see it now." He reached across the table and grasped

Miles's hand warmly. "Perhaps you will ride with me for the rest of our journey. Such a gift is rare, and I would be honored to hear more about your friendship."

"I'd rather not talk about it," said Miles. He was uncomfortably aware that Little was trying to steer him away from the fortune-teller, but at the same time he could not help being flattered by the interest Doctor Tau-Tau showed in him. Sometimes he almost forgot how unusual a thing it was to have been befriended by a talking tiger.

"Of course, of course," said Doctor Tau-Tau. "As you wish, my boy. But please ride with me anyway, both of you. We will be many months on the road together, and we should not be strangers."

"Thank you, but I promised the Toki sisters I would help them with their costumes," said Little. She shot Miles a meaningful glance. "They need a lot of help," she said.

Miles shrugged. "I'm not much good with a needle," he said. He had just remembered that the wagon in which Tau-Tau was traveling had once belonged to his parents, and he was curious to take a look inside. "I'll see you when we get to Shallowford." He leaned close to Little as they made their way out into the cold morning. "Don't worry," he said. "I think he's harmless."

"The man who was in his wagon the other night didn't sound so harmless," said Little. "Just be careful what you tell him." She turned and jumped onto the back of the Toki sisters' wagon just as it began to roll toward the open road.

Miles sat up beside Doctor Tau-Tau on the box seat of the small wagon, swaying with the rhythm of the wooden wheels, his belly comfortably full with a warm breakfast.

"A real tiger," sighed Doctor Tau-Tau, almost to himself. "And you say he spoke to you? It is a sign of great fortune. But of course, if you don't want to talk about it, you certainly shouldn't. Not so much as a word, my friend."

CHAPTER SEVEN
HALF A BOY

Miles Wednesday, belly-full and fire-warmed, closed his eyes and let the soft echoes of applause and sweet music wash through him. The first show of the season was over, the townspeople had all gone, and the animals were fed and settled in their cages for the night. Now the two-legged performers sat around a large campfire in the center of their wandering village, eating their supper and laughing over the small mishaps and major triumphs of the night's performance.

The show had been a resounding success. It seemed that every man, woman and child in Shallowford had squeezed themselves into the big top until the canvas bulged. In truth, many of them had come because they had seen Doctor Tau-Tau's name painted on his circus wagon, and the rumor had spread like wildfire that the circus would be dispensing Dr. Tau-Tau's Restorative Tonic. The townspeople had dropped their tools and forgotten their appointments and flocked to the circus, elbowing each other in their anxiety to buy tickets for the show.

Once inside the tent they had filled every seat, and settled themselves in the aisles between, anxiously looking for signs of the small green bottles of the tonic, which was the only relief they knew from the the grayness that had enveloped their lives since they had fallen under the Great Cortado's sinister hypnosis at the Palace of Laughter.

There was, of course, no tonic on offer at the Circus Bolsillo, but it was not long before the townspeople forgot all about the temporary relief of the little green bottles. Instead they found themselves watching a magical show of such warmth and gaiety that it seemed to shine a light on their troubled souls. The animals were beautifully groomed, powerful and well-trained, the acrobats flew like birds, and the clowns put all their heart into their craft, gently sending up everything that was sad and funny and flawed and good in human nature, and bringing out laughter that was born where it should be, in the heart.

But the best thing of all was the music. Such music had never been heard in the town of Shallowford in living memory! It was funny and strange, and it flowed through the night air like a gurgling stream of happiness, smoothing frowns and lifting hearts until the people began to laugh with pure delight, in a way they could not remember laughing for what seemed like a lifetime. Its echo could still be heard among the firelit circus folk now, as from time to time one of the musicians would pick up his trumpet or his flute to make it sing that phrase just one more time, and others would be unable to resist joining in.

Little smiled to herself, sitting beside Miles in her sparkling acrobat's costume, with his old overcoat wrapped around her. She had joined Henna and Etoile, the dark-haired trapeze artists, to form a treble act in which Little walked a high wire while the girls somersaulted through the air, and Miles had watched her through a gap in the backstage curtain. He had found himself holding his breath at the sight of her, glowing in the spotlight and perched high above the audience, as she had been the very first time he'd seen her, at the Circus Oscuro.

"You were very good," he said to her. "Weren't you afraid up there, without your wings?"

Little shook her head. "It felt good to be up high again," she said, "and we have practiced a lot. Were you afraid?"

Miles shrugged. "Not really," he lied. "Stranski's never skewered anyone yet. At least not as far as I know."

He could still feel the glow from the applause that had greeted his act with Stranski the Magician. It was a new experience for him, and he allowed his tired eyes to close so that he could relive his moment of triumph.

There he was, padlocked in a star-painted box with his knees tucked up and only his head showing, while Stranski stood in the center of the ring and held a long saw in the air for all the people of Shallowford to see. The saw's teeth glinted as the magician turned it under the spotlights, then he turned suddenly on his heel and began to saw vigorously through the center of the box. The crowd gasped, and Miles only just prevented himself from flinching as the saw's teeth bit through the wood.

Stranski wheeled the two halves of the box apart to show beyond doubt that the boy had been halved. From the other half, Miles knew, a pair of shoes would be wiggling frantically, but Stranski had not revealed even to him whose feet they might be, or how they came to be alive. When the box was rejoined and Miles released, Stranski gave him a curt nod, which was the closest thing to praise that he ever bestowed on his helper. Miles smiled as he stretched his arms wide and did a complete turn under the spotlights, and applause swept through the ring.

Miles was jolted from his reverie by the sound of shouting from somewhere beyond the firelight. There was a thud and a gasp, and a woman's scream, then a man's voice bellowed, "Bet you didn't predict *that*, Mr. Presents Your Future."

The fireside conversation stopped for a moment, and Fabio and Umor slipped away toward the sound of the scuffle. Fabio tapped K2, the enormous strongman, on his shiny bald head as he went. K2 lumbered to his feet and followed them into the night. They were back a few moments later. K2 sat down heavily on the end of the log he had vacated, causing Gila, who sat at the other end, to bounce several inches into the air.

"What happened?" asked Little as Fabio sat down beside her.

"Telling fortunes is a dangerous game," said Fabio.

"Especially when your customer is a pretty girl," chuckled Umor.

"Tau-Tau predicted she'd find new love in the spring," said Fabio.

"What's wrong with that?" asked Little.

"Her husband was listening outside," said Umor.

"And he didn't think it was funny."

Gila produced his harmonica and began to play a comical tune. Other band members joined in, and Tariq the juggler snatched a couple of burning sticks from the fire and began to toss them in the air, the ragged flames sputtering as they wove arcs of light against the night sky. Miles watched for a while, the warmth of the fire on his face, and sighed contentedly. He was in a strange place, surrounded by stranger people, and he had never felt so at home.

"You're feeling homesick," said a voice by his ear, "but it will pass in time." It was Doctor Tau-Tau, his words whistling slightly through a broken tooth.

"No I'm not," said Miles.

"You don't have to be shy with me," said Tau-Tau. "You know your mind is an open book to someone with skills such as mine." His bulging eyes glistened in the firelight, and he sipped gingerly from a small china cup with no handle, which he refilled from a silver pot that he placed between his feet. A large bruise was spreading across his swollen jaw.

"That must hurt," said Miles.

"Ah," said Tau-Tau, "it's just one of the hazards that attend greatness."

Miles thought about the irate husband's words. "Couldn't you have avoided it?" he asked.

"You mean by looking into my own future?" Tau-Tau shook his head. "Absolutely not. It's the first thing Celeste taught me about clairvoyance. A fortune-teller can see the paths of others' lives like veins in a leaf, but his own future remains in darkness, and with good reason."

"But why?" asked Miles.

"Because it would lead to madness. To madness, my friend, is where it would lead. Imagine you could see all the pitfalls in your life, right up to your own death. You would be forever dodging and turning like a hunted fox, but fate cannot be tricked, and it would master you anyway. To see into your own future would rob you of the ability to live in the present."

He took another sip from his china cup, and sighed deeply. "Masala tea," he said, smacking his lips and grimacing with the pain. "The best way that man has yet devised to usher in the night."

"It smells nice," said Little.

"And it tastes even better," said Tau-Tau. "I would pour some for you, but I'm afraid I have a head cold that I wouldn't like to pass on, and my other cups are in my wagon."

"I'll get them," said Miles quickly. He had been looking for an excuse to see the inside of Tau-Tau's wagon, but the chance had not arisen on the ride to Shallowford.

"Perhaps another time," said Doctor Tau-Tau.

"I won't disturb anything," said Miles, "if you just tell me where to find them."

"Very well," said Tau-Tau. He fished a key from his pocket. It was tied by a ribbon to a small wooden figure with matted hair and tiny cowrie-shell eyes. "In the purple cupboard to the right of the door when you enter."

Miles got up and faced into the darkness. As he headed in the direction where he judged the wagon to be, Doctor Tau-Tau called after him, "And touch nothing else, my friend."

Away from the fire Miles could see the stars clearly, twinkling like frost in the moonless sky. His breath made clouds before him, and the grass crunched underfoot. Here and there a lantern glowed softly under the eaves of a wagon, but he was guided as much by his nose as by the little he could see. He left the musty odor of the lions' cage to his right, and passed by the oily smell that surrounded the llamas' enclosure. As far as he could remember, Tau-Tau's wagon was the third one after the swampy reek of the crocodiles' tank.

When he reached the wagon he thought for a moment that he had found the wrong one. He could hear drawers opening, and what sounded like soft muttering, from inside. He stopped for a moment on the steps, the key raised halfway to the lock. He leaned backward, and read the words that were faintly visible on the side of the wagon. DOCTOR TAU-TAU PRESENTS YOUR FUTURE, they said. He waited for a moment more, but the sounds had stopped, and he could hear only the faint laughter and music carried from the campfire on the cold night air. He shrugged. "Must have been from another wagon," he said quietly to Tangerine, wishing he had brought a lantern with him. Tangerine, it seemed, was also listening closely. Miles took a deep breath and opened the door.

There was a flurry of movement in the darkened wagon, and the sound of a bottle smashing. He thought he glimpsed someone disappearing through the open window opposite him, and a moment later another figure leaped up onto the sill and turned for an instant to stare at him. He could see its hairy outline, no bigger than that of a six-year-old child, silhouetted against the rectangle of starry sky. Its movements were quick and sudden, like a bird, and two black eyes glittered faintly with reflected firelight. Miles had the odd feeling that if he entered the wagon he would be stepping into a dream, and he froze where he was on the top step. He heard the creature's feet scrape on the wooden sill, then it dropped from the window and was gone.

Miles stood frozen on the top step of Doctor Tau-Tau's wagon. The darkness inside seemed to yawn with silence, and he wondered if there might be more of the creatures lurking in it, just waiting for him to make a move. He fumbled inside the door, feeling for a light switch behind the heavy clothing that hung there. The impulse to shut the door and run had almost overtaken him when his fingers found the switch, and he flicked it on.

The inside of the wagon was filled with a dim red light, and it was a moment before Miles could make sense of what he was seeing. It looked as though a violent storm had passed through the little room. A round table lay on its side in a sea of scattered envelopes. Every cupboard had been ransacked, the drawers pulled out and emptied onto the carpet. A fleet of small bottles had sailed across the slightly tilted floor and come to rest in an untidy pile in the corner. Pictures hung askew, and at one end of the wagon a mattress sagged from the bed to the floor, as though it had tried to escape and been brought down by the sheets that were twined around it. Over all this chaos the faint aroma of the masala tea that Doctor Tau-Tau had brewed earlier still hung in the air.

A sudden movement in the corner made Miles jump, but it was only a tiny bird flying up from the floor to perch on the curtain rail. The bird was gray, with a black head and tail, and it looked at him with curiosity. In the corner from which it had appeared, Miles saw a small wooden cage lying on its side with its door wide open. Miles picked his way across the floor to shut the window. A small pile of books lay in the shadow of the capsized table, and they toppled over as he passed. There were assorted books on numerology and geomancy, and two leatherbound notebooks. The notebooks were old and well worn, blotched with overlapping stains and frayed at the edges. A loose page had fallen from one of them, and Miles picked it up with his thumb and forefinger, as though it might fall apart at his touch.

The paper was thin and crisp like an onion skin, and densely covered with tiny writing and strange diagrams. He looked at it curiously, but the symbols that covered the page seemed to swim and wriggle in the dim light, and he could make no sense out of them. He opened one of the notebooks and carefully inserted the loose page.

It was an uncomfortable feeling to be shut in the ransacked wagon, ankle-deep in Doctor Tau-Tau's personal possessions. He felt as though he had walked in and surprised him in his underwear. The thought made him laugh despite himself, and it was at precisely that moment that the door swung open, and Doctor Tau Tau stepped inside.

The fortune-teller opened his mouth to speak, a look of mild irritation on his florid face, but as he did so he noticed the sea of wreckage spread across the floor. His bruised jaw dropped farther, and he winced with the pain. Without a word he strode across the floor and snatched the notebook that Miles held in his hand. For a moment Miles expected to be struck, but Doctor Tau-Tau merely fixed him with a wounded stare as he tucked the notebook into his waistcoat pocket.

"*Why*, boy?" he croaked.

Miles folded his arms and looked at him indignantly. "It wasn't me!" he said. "It was . . ." He struggled to think of a way to describe the intruders that would not sound like a tall story. He could hardly expect Doctor Tau-Tau to believe that they were small hairy creatures that had escaped through the window like monkeys.

Doctor Tau-Tau's eyebrows disappeared into his fez. He was waiting for an answer.

"They were small hairy creatures who escaped through the window like monkeys," said Miles. "I only caught a glimpse of them in the dark. I think there were two of them."

"Monkeys, you say?" repeated Doctor Tau-Tau. He was staring at Miles with an odd expression, as though something rang a bell that he did not want to hear.

"They weren't monkeys," said Miles. "The monkeys are all locked in their cage. I have the key in my pocket."

"Are you sure . . . ," whispered Doctor Tau-Tau, leaning close to Miles and enveloping him in his oriental breath, "that it wasn't your *tiger* friend?"

Miles was lost for an answer to such a strange suggestion. He was about to ask why on earth a tiger would want to ransack Doctor Tau-Tau's wagon, when he spotted the little gray bird that had startled him earlier. "Look!" he said, glad of the distraction. "Your bird is loose."

Doctor Tau-Tau turned to look. "Satu!" he said. "What are you doing out, you little feathered rascal?"

The bird hopped among the small red and gold envelopes that lay scattered across the carpet. She stopped suddenly and tugged one of the envelopes free with her fat red beak, then she hopped forward until she came to rest by Doctor Tau-Tau's embroidered slipper.

Doctor Tau-Tau bent down and held out his hand, palm upward. The bird jumped on board. The fortune-teller took the envelope and opened it, as though he had forgotten about Miles altogether. He removed a small yellowing card and read it with with a frown of concentration. "Impossible," he murmured to himself. He glanced at Miles from under his bushy eyebrows, then he looked at the card once more, before slipping it back into its envelope.

"What does the card say?" asked Miles.

"Oh, nothing, nothing," said Doctor Tau-Tau vaguely. "The cards were scattered, and Satu has had a fright. In such circumstances a mistake is understandable." He delved into his trouser pocket and brought out a few seeds, which he fed to the little bird, then he crunched his way across his scattered belongings, righted the cage and placed her gently inside.

"What kind of mistake?" persisted Miles. He was curious to know what the card could have said to make Tau-Tau's anger dissolve so quickly into puzzlement.

"Let's just forget about it, eh?" said Tau-Tau, forcing a smile. "It's the wrong card. It couldn't apply to you. Why don't you just come back first thing in the morning and help me straighten the place out, eh?" He tucked the little envelope into his waistcoat pocket, beside the notebook, and Miles noticed that his hands were shaking.

CHAPTER EIGHT

A PAIR OF WINGS

Tariq Ali Mohammad III, bare-chested and oil-slicked, opened his mouth and blew a mighty ball of flame that would have put a dragon to shame. The audience gasped—indeed some of them ducked, and he blew another, just to keep them on their toes. Miles loved to watch Tariq make fire, but he had no time to watch now. He was behind the curtain, helping the tent boys to line up the big round platforms on which Tembo and Mamba would perform for the people of Nape.

A roar of applause told him that Tariq was taking his bow, and as the fire-eater marched through the curtain, spitting the last of the paraffin to one side, Miles slipped past him and ran into the ring with a large rake. He quickly smoothed the sawdust as the tent boys came out behind him, rolling the heavy platforms on their sides like hula hoops. Miles ran back through the curtain, ducking under Tembo's trunk as she ambled in from the darkening field outside, led by Gila in a green suit with gold braiding.

"Steady, Master Miles," said Gila.

"Don't knock over the elephants," added Umor, who was following close behind with Mamba.

"I'll try not to," said Miles.

"Can you help me with these wings, Miles?" said Little.

She was dressed in her sparkling suit and white ballet slippers, and a small pair of wings sat lopsidedly on her shoulders. They had been carefully stitched together from goose feathers by Delia Zipplethorpe, the horse mistress. She had done a fine job, but no amount of clever needlework could match the luminous beauty of the real wings that had once graced Little's shoulders. A tracery of graceful lines in the skin of her back was all that remained of them now; a faint reminder of what she had lost when she sang her real name to release Miles from The Null's monstrous grip, and in doing so tied herself forever to Earth.

Miles tugged at the elastic straps that held the wings to her shoulders. They made him feel slightly sad, and he wondered how much worse it must be for Little herself. "Are you sure you want to wear these?" he asked.

"Of course," said Little. "Haven't you seen the playbill? I'm Little, the winged acrobat." She smiled at him over her shoulder.

"I know," said Miles. "But you don't have to be. I could ask Fabio to change it." He took a step back to check that the wings were straight.

Little turned and hugged Miles around his waist. She smiled up at him. "Thank you, Miles. I do miss my wings, but wearing these makes no difference to that. This is a circus, and people want to see something magical. That's why we're here, isn't it?"

Another wave of applause followed Tembo and Mamba as they loped out of the ring and pushed through the curtain. They knew they had performed well and they were in a hurry to find out what treat might await them with their evening meal. As they trotted out under the stars, the slim figure of Etoile, the dark-haired acrobat, strode in past them, patting both their trunks in turn as she made for the curtain. Her sister, Henna, stumbled along after her in spike-heeled shoes.

Although they looked alike, Henna and Etoile could not have been more different. Etoile was immaculately dressed and perfectly made up at any hour of the day. She was always polite, never late, and despite the circus's harsh work ethic, no one seemed to mind—or to notice—that she never troubled to get her hands dirty.

Henna, by contrast, was usually to be found in overalls, a cigarette dangling from her lips and her hair looking as though the macaws had been nesting in it. She mucked out the animals, shaved and shod the Zipplethorpe family's fine Arab horses and scrubbed down the wagon, inside and out, that she shared with her sister. She never even thought of getting ready for a performance until ten minutes before it began. She would still be touching up her mascara right up to the moment she walked into the ring, but as she stepped through the star-strewn curtain a transformation came over her. It was as though she could throw on like a costume the elegance and poise that her sister wore all the time, and once under the spotlights it was hard to tell the two apart.

"*Vite, chérie!*" called Etoile to Little.

"No time for the gossip," added Henna, making

last-minute adjustments to the straps of her costume.

"See you later," said Little. She fell into line between Etoile and Henna, and the band struck up a whirling tune as the three acrobats, heads up and backs straight, strode into the center of the ring, and the dark-haired sisters stepped out of their high-heeled shoes, ready to begin.

Miles busied himself helping the tent boys to stack the rectangular sections of the lions' cage, ready to be quickly assembled during the intermission. Countess Fontainbleau and her Savage Lions always opened the second half of the show, and the cage had to be built in the time it took the audience to buy a bag of popcorn and drop half of it down between the seats. The work helped to take his mind off the knot in his stomach, which began to form as the time approached for his own act with Stranski the Magician. The rise and fall of applause washed through the curtain like waves breaking on a beach, and when he glanced upward he could see the shadows of the acrobats curling gracefully across the canvas roof.

On a final wave of applause Henna and Etoile came hurrying through the curtain, followed by Little, whose face glowed in the dim backstage light. Henna produced a cigarette from the sleeve of her costume and clamped it between her lips, and Papaya the clown lit it for her as he passed by on flapping shoes.

"How was it?" Miles asked Little.

"Good," said Little. "I slipped a bit on the rope, but I think the audience finds it more exciting when that happens."

"There you are, Little," said Countess Fontain-bleau, the lion tamer, bringing the chill air with her as she strode in from the darkness. "Did you speak to my Perseus for me?"

"Yes," said Little, who had never lost her ear for the music of animal speech, "and you were right. He has a toothache."

The countess, dressed in an immaculate red coat with gold braiding, gold tights and pink fluffy bed-room slippers, sighed theatrically. "Then I will have to go on with just Nestor and Eunice," she said, "and Nestor is so *lazy* when Perseus is not there to bite his backside."

"It's okay," said Little. "Perseus says he'll perform tonight, as long as you get the dentist to look at him after the show."

Countess Fontainbleau's face brightened up, and her haughty expression melted into a smile. "Thank you, Little, you're a princess!" she said, and she blew her a kiss before turning and stalking out of the marquee.

"Oh, Countess!" called Little.

The countess stopped and turned, the lamplight picking out her long neck and high cheekbones. "Well?" she said.

"Perseus said not to put your head in his mouth tonight, unless you want to finish the show without it."

The countess gave a whinnying laugh, and disappeared into the gloom.

"Master Miles!" barked Fabio. "Where are you supposed to be?"

Miles thought for a second. "Elephants," he said. "Helping Umor and Gila."

"Then get moving, before you take root," called Fabio, and he disappeared through the curtain.

"I'll come with you," said Little. "I want a word with Mamba before she goes to sleep."

They walked quickly between the trailers, through the bustle of animals, performers and their props. Everyone was busy preparing for the second half of the show, or packing away their acts from the first. Miles and Little ducked the flailing tail of a crocodile as his trainer, Gina, wrestled him into a carved wooden box on wheels. The elephants were munching the last of their apples in the small enclosure that surrounded their wagon.

"Here he is," said Umor.

"I thought there was something missing from this shovel," said Gila.

He held the handle of the shovel out to Miles. Miles attempted to tweak his nose, but the little man was far too quick for him, and skipped out of his reach.

"No good, Master Miles," he chuckled.

"A snail could do better," said Umor.

"And they have no fingers."

Miles took the shovel with a sigh, and began to scoop up the elephant dung and tip it into the waiting wheelbarrow.

"Did Doctor Tau-Tau find out who broke into his wagon?" asked Little. Miles opened his mouth to answer, but he was interrupted by Umor.

"'Course he didn't," called the little man.

"Nothing to tell," said Gila.

"Just the local kids," said Umor.

Miles shook his head. "They weren't kids. I saw them. They were covered in hair."

Gila dunked a brush in a bucket of soapy water and began to scrub at Mamba's wrinkly hide. "Kids are very hairy these days," he said.

"I blame the parents," said Umor.

"Me too," said Gila. He paused for a moment in his scrubbing. "Why?"

"Man with a beard. Woman with long hair," said Umor, emptying his bucket in the corner. "Recipe for disaster."

"Either that," said Gila, "or too many vitamins."

"Vitamin H," called Umor. "That's the culprit."

Miles pictured the strange little figure with the birdlike movements, perched for a second on the darkened sill. He shook his head. "They weren't kids," he repeated, "and they weren't monkeys."

"There's nothing between," said Umor.

"Kids or monkeys," said Gila. "That's all there is."

"Your barrow is full," said Umor, "and there's a man waiting to saw you in half."

Miles shrugged and picked up the heavy barrow. He pushed it with difficulty through the soft mud, heading for the manure truck. Little walked beside him, leaving no footprints.

"They didn't like that question, did they?" she said when they were out of earshot of the two little clowns.

"It's hard to tell with them," said Miles. "Doctor Tau-Tau wouldn't answer me either. He just kept changing the subject and asking me about the tiger." He took a run at the wooden ramp that leaned against the manure truck, and heaved the contents of the barrow into the back.

"You should be careful," said Little.

"I feel a bit sorry for Tau-Tau," said Miles. "Lots of the other performers won't talk to him."

"Maybe there's a reason for that," said Little, jumping over the rope by which K2 was dragging a brightly painted cannon toward the big top. Hector the monkey was perched on top of the cannon, and he jumped onto Miles's shoulder as they passed, chattering softly in his ear.

"What's he saying?" asked Miles.

Little laughed. "He says you should watch more carefully when he's picking pockets tonight. Stranski relies on you to spot the ones he misses."

"Ask him why he always seems to pick people who smell of cheap cologne," said Miles, scratching the monkey behind his ears. Hector and Little chattered back and forth for a minute, then the monkey dropped to the ground as they passed Stranski's wagon and scampered up the steps.

"He said that if you lived with someone who smells like Stranski," said Little, "you'd seek out people who smell a bit nicer. He used to think Stranski might take the hint, but he never did. Now Hector just likes the smell of cologne from the wallets he borrows."

Miles rummaged for his keys as they approached the Bolsillo brothers' wagon, where his costume was kept. "I don't really think Tau-Tau means any harm," he said.

"Maybe not," said Little. "His song is not a bad one; he just doesn't seem able to hear anyone else's. I can just hear Silverpoint saying, 'Don't trust that Doctor Tau-Tau. He has a nose for the wrong path.'"

"By the seven hills of Hades!" came a voice from the darkness. "Have I made such a bad impression?" Doctor Tau-Tau appeared around the corner of the wagon, his faded red fez perched on his head and a smile stretched tightly across his face. He looked as though he were mastering his annoyance with difficulty. "And who might this *Silverpoint* be, who would think so ill of me?"

Little turned her clear blue gaze on his brick-red face, and smiled. "Silverpoint's a friend of ours. He's not from around here, and he never trusted anyone," she said. "And it's just that you're so . . . mysterious."

Doctor Tau-Tau straightened up and tugged the creases from his jacket. "Well, yes," he said. "I suppose I am." The smile was gone, but he looked rather pleased with himself. "I am," he repeated, "indeed very mysterious."

CHAPTER NINE

PAJAMAS

Miles Wednesday, sleep-wrapped and goose-pimpled, sat up suddenly in his foldaway bed, the remains of a dream clinging to him like a cobweb. The night was as black as a crow's eye, and a bullying wind rocked the trailer on its springs. Stranski had been in his dream, his mouth opening and closing mutely as he tried to tell him something of great urgency. Miles was sure that the tiger had also passed silently through his sleep, just out of sight as always. He could hear horses whinnying, and the loud banging of their hooves on the doors of their mobile stable, and he realized that this was not a part of his receding dream. He pulled aside the curtain and looked out into the night, where he could just make out the tops of the trees lashing back and forth against the blue-black sky.

The Zipplethorpes' horses had taken fright, and it seemed to Miles as though they would soon kick their trailer to matchwood. He saw Darius Zipplethorpe and his son, Dulac, tumbling from their stately wagon in dressing gowns and slippers. Dulac was around the same age as Miles and a miniature copy of his father, short and stocky with a thatch of straw-colored hair and pale eyebrows that made his face hard to read. He could do a handstand on the back of a cantering horse, but Miles had never seen him smile.

Dulac and his father ran to the trailer to calm the frightened horses. The lamp that usually glowed under its eaves had been blown out, and the brass wind chimes rang a crazy alarm. Miles strained his eyes to see. His breath was fogging the window, and as he wiped a clear arc with his sleeve he saw Delia Zipplethorpe emerging from the trailer too, holding a lantern, which she tried to shade with her shawl from the gusting wind.

As the Zipplethorpes unbolted the half doors of the trailer in the fluttering light, Miles was distracted by a movement behind them. A piece of the wagon's shadow broke away, then another, and a third. The hairy shapes of three tiny figures scurried off, stooping to run beneath the trailers that stood between them and the woods bordering the field, until moments later they had joined the shadows beneath the tossing trees and disappeared from sight.

Miles stared after the tiny figures, holding his breath as if that might somehow draw them back into the open where he could see them. He recognized the quick little movements from the raiders of Doctor Tau-Tau's wagon, and he had no doubt that these were the same creatures, or their close cousins at least. He wondered if he was still dreaming.

A shout brought his attention back to the Zipplethorpes and their horses. One of the stable doors had flown open, and the piebald mare leaped out as though from the starting gate of a steeplechase. She was bucking like a rodeo horse, and as Dulac fought to calm her she reared and kicked out, sending him sprawling in the grass. His mother gave a cry and ran toward him, the lantern falling from her hand. The light flickered once and died. Miles leaped from his bed and pulled on his old overcoat, stumbling across the darkened wagon.

The door whipped open before he reached it and a gust of wind barged in as Fabio Bolsillo slipped out into the night.

Together they ran toward the place where Dulac Zipplethorpe lay motionless on the ground, his mother bending over him in the darkness. Her shawl stood out sideways, cracking like a whip in the breeze.

"Is he all right?" shouted Miles. The wind whipped the words from his throat and left him gasping for breath.

Delia Zipplethorpe turned. There were tears streaking her cheek. "Help him," she said to Fabio. The little man bent to examine the gash on the forehead of the unconscious boy. A dark patch of blood matted his straw-colored hair. Darius joined them, having returned the frightened mare to her stall. "I'll go for a doctor," he bellowed, and he disappeared into the night.

"Your coat, Master Miles!" shouted Fabio. "I'll get some brandy."

Miles slipped Tangerine from his pocket and tucked him away inside his pajamas, then he struggled out of the heavy coat and laid it over Dulac, pulling the collar up to his chin. The boy's face was deathly pale. Delia Zipplethorpe began to moan softly, grasping her son's limp hand and rocking back and forth as though the wind had taken her over, and for the first time Miles realized that the boy might die. A panicky feeling spread from his stomach, and he wondered if he should run to get Little. He doubted there was anything she could do.

"Wipe the blood from his eye, boy," said a voice from behind him. He turned in surprise and saw Doctor Tau-Tau, wrapped in a dressing gown and staring at Miles with his bulging eyes as though he, and not Dulac, were the center of attention. "The blood!" repeated Tau-Tau. "Wipe it away."

Miles turned, puzzled, to Delia Zipplethorpe, but she seemed aware of nothing but her son's fading spirit. He saw the trickle of blood that had made its way down Dulac's pale forehead and into the corner of his eye, and reached out to wipe it away. The wind that had been gusting in his face dropped suddenly and the night became strangely still. Miles took a deep breath. He felt dizzy and light, as though he would blow away when the wind returned. His lungs seemed to have expanded to fill his entire body, and the cold clear air went right down into his fingertips. Dulac's forehead felt surprisingly hot, and as Miles wiped the sticky blood away he thought he might faint. He closed his eyes and sat back suddenly in the cold grass, waiting for the weight to pour slowly back into his body.

When he opened his eyes he was surprised to see that Dulac was sitting up, supported by his mother. Some of the color had come back to his face, and Fabio was kneeling in front of him, tipping a small glass to the boy's lips. His eyes were open and he pulled a face as the brandy burned his throat.

Dulac Zipplethorpe got shakily to his feet, helped by his mother and leaning on Fabio's shoulder. As they turned toward the Zipplethorpes' wagon, Fabio looked back at Miles. "Well done, Master Miles," he said. He glanced over Miles's head, and said, "Take him to the wagon, Tau-Tau. Umor will make him something hot to drink."

"No need, no need," said Doctor Tau-Tau. "I have a pot already brewing. On your feet, lad." He reached out a hand and beamed proudly at Miles, as though he had just knitted him from a ball of leftover wool.

Miles Wednesday, breeze-blown and pajama-striped, sank gratefully into a beanbag in Doctor Tau-Tau's warm wagon. His legs felt weak, and the short walk was as much as he could manage. Now the wind was shut outside and his shivering began to subside. A cup of hot masala tea was pressed into his hand by the still-beaming Tau-Tau, who stared and smiled, and smiled and stared as he bustled around amidst his clutter until Miles felt distinctly uncomfortable.

"You feel disorientated, but it will pass," said the fortune-teller, lighting a fistful of incense and placing it in a brass burner by the sink. "You have had a bit of a shock."

Miles nodded. "I thought he was going to die," he said.

"Nonsense," said Doctor Tau-Tau. "It wasn't his time. I would have seen it in the cards." He picked up the stack of red and gold envelopes and shuffled them absentmindedly. Miles felt irritated by his certainty. He thought about the card that the bird had picked out after Tau-Tau's wagon had been ransacked, and how the fortune-teller had refused to tell him what it said. A smile began to spread across his face, and he hid it with a yawn. "It's all just for show though, isn't it?" he said.

Tau-Tau paused in his shuffling and frowned down at Miles. "What is?" he said.

"All that stuff with the cards and the bird," said Miles casually. "You just make it up as you go along, don't you?"

"Make it up?" spluttered Tau-Tau, his face darkening.

"Certainly not! Clairvoyance is a rare gift, and it's brought to a fine focus only by years of study and practice."

"Then the cards must have shown you that Barty Fumble was my father," said Miles.

Doctor Tau-Tau looked at him blankly for a moment. "You? Barty Fumble's son?" His eyes bulged and he cleared his throat hastily. "Of course, boy. I spotted that right away. The cards can hide nothing from me. Nothing except my own future, of course." He lifted the birdcage down from a high shelf in the corner. "Try me," he said. "Just ask me anything at all."

"What happened to Barty Fumble?" Miles asked.

"What happened to . . ." A nervous look passed over Tau-Tau's face for a moment. He busied himself spreading the cards in front of the birdcage. "We will have the answer for you in no time," he said. "In no time at all, we will have an answer for you. Is that not so, my little feathered prognosticator?" Tau-Tau was mumbling to himself now, glancing at Miles from time to time as if he might disappear at any moment. "Now we shall see," he muttered, "what our little oracle can tell us." He opened the door of the birdcage. The little red-beaked bird hopped out onto the row of envelopes laid out in front of her, bent down and tugged one of them free. Tau-Tau took the envelope from the bird and slid the card out from inside it. His bushy eyebrows crept upward, and he glanced at Miles, and back at the card. "Then it's true," he muttered. He stroked his goatee in silence, while Miles watched him with growing curiosity.

"Can I see the card?" he asked finally.

Doctor Tau-Tau looked as though he was weighing this request carefully, then he held the creased card out between his thumb and forefinger for Miles to see. It was covered with a close pattern of little squiggles that looked like they had been painted with a brush. Miles was not sure what he had expected to see, but he felt slightly disappointed. "I can't make anything out of that," he said.

"Of course not, my boy, and for two reasons," said Tau-Tau. He slipped the card back into its envelope. "There are two reasons," he repeated, "for that. First, the cards are written in Chinese, an ancient language with which you are unlikely to be familiar. And second, only someone with extraordinary skills such as mine can hope to divine their true meaning."

"What does it say?" asked Miles. "Is it the same card she drew the other night?"

"It is, my boy," said Tau-Tau, pulling a small stool over to the beanbag where Miles sat, and settling down on it with a sigh. "And it does indeed concern your father, Barty Fumble."

Miles felt his heart miss a beat. The hope that someday he might find his father alive was never far from his thoughts, and he feared that the little bird might drown that hope forever. He forced himself to meet Doctor Tau-Tau's eyes. "What does it say?" he asked.

The fortune-teller poured another cup of masala tea for himself, and one for Miles. "I was a fool not to trust the card the first time it was drawn," he said, lowering his voice as though there were conspirators listening from behind every drape. "It seems that the old fraud has been alive all along!"

Miles looked at him in astonishment. "Are you sure?" he whispered.

"The oracle is sure, my boy," said Doctor Tau-Tau. "And that is good enough for me. What's more, I think I know where we could start to look for him."

Miles struggled out of the beanbag and leaped to his feet. The dizziness had left him completely, and in his excitement he barely noticed the less-than-flattering way in which Tau-Tau spoke of his father. "Where?" he asked. "Can we go now?"

To his surprise, Doctor Tau-Tau also sprang to his feet. "Indeed we had better!" he beamed, "but we shall have to find you something more fitting than pajamas to wear if we are going to be mixing with royalty. To mix with royalty," he said, looking around his cluttered wagon in a distracted fashion, "you will need something more fitting, my boy, than pajamas."

CHAPTER TEN
HELL'S TEETH

Doctor Tau-Tau, fez-topped and sparrow-led, huffed through the night at a considerable pace, and Miles had to trot to keep up. He was still in his pajamas despite his appointment with royalty, but wrapped around with an embroidered dressing gown that the fortune-teller had lent him to give the boy, as he put it, some semblance of dignity. Tau-Tau had insisted that they leave at once, without a word to anyone. He would not let Miles return to his wagon for clothes, nor would he hear of him retrieving his overcoat from the Zipplethorpes' trailer.

"I still don't see why we couldn't bring Little,"

Miles panted. "She wouldn't say a word to anyone, and she's very useful in a tricky situation."

"Out of the question," called Tau-Tau over his shoulder. "The people we are going to see don't make a habit of welcoming visitors. My great negotiating skills will be stretched to their fullest to get the information we need, and one more hanger-on would make it ten times harder."

"Who are they, the people we're going to see?" asked Miles.

Doctor Tau-Tau stopped to unsnag his own dressing gown from a bramble. "Don't bother me now with questions, boy," he said tetchily. "It's a good few years since I've been this way, and if you continue to pester me we may end up going in circles."

They marched on in silence for a while. The wind still gusted strongly, and at times it was as much as Miles could do to keep moving forward at all. It was a moonless night, and the faint light of the stars was all they had to guide them. Miles could make out the dark bulk of the mountains to their right, but most of his attention was focused on the ground before his feet. The countryside was hilly and dotted with small trees whose knobbled roots were well suited for tripping the unwary, and now and then they would stumble as they stepped suddenly into a hidden rabbit hole. Despite the cold wind Miles began to sweat in the heavy dressing gown, and his throat was as dry as sand. The fat doctor's labored breathing came back to him on the breeze.

"Is it much farther?" called Miles when they seemed to have been walking forever.

Doctor Tau-Tau said nothing, but a minute later he stopped in the shelter of a tall pinnacle of rock that rose from the side of a hill. "This will do," he said in a hoarse whisper, when Miles had caught up with him. "We'll take a short rest here."

Miles flopped gratefully down in the long grass, checking for Tangerine in the dressing-gown pocket where he had put him when Tau-Tau wasn't looking. The bear seemed to be shivering slightly, and Miles kept his hand in the pocket to warm him. "Are we nearly there?" he asked.

Doctor Tau-Tau put a long finger to his lips. "Shhhh," he said. "You don't want to be hollering around here like a schoolboy on an outing."

"But we're in the middle of nowhere," said Miles, whispering nonetheless. "There's no one for miles around."

"Don't be so sure," said Tau-Tau. His bulging eyes shone faintly in the darkness. He produced a thermos flask from inside his dressing gown, and poured himself an inevitable cup of spiced tea. When he had emptied it he poured another and handed it to Miles. The cold had begun to bite again now that they had stopped, and Miles gulped it down gratefully.

"You said we were going to see royalty," he whispered.

"Well, in a manner of speaking," said Tau-Tau, pouring himself another cup. He slurped noisily, presumably forgetting about the need for stealth. "The people who live in these parts have been here for countless years, since before your ancestors or mine ever set foot here. Your ancestors, that is, not mine," he corrected himself. "I come from a distant country that you will never have heard of."

"That depends," said Miles, "on what letter of the alphabet it starts with."

The fortune-teller snorted, and promptly began to choke noisily on the tea that had shot up the back of his nose.

"It's true," said Miles. "I've got all my education from Lady Partridge's encyclopedia. I'm up to the letter 'Q.'"

"My hometown begins with 'Z,'" coughed Doctor Tau-Tau.

"Maybe I'll know the country," said Miles, who

had always been fascinated by the pictures of far-off places in Lady Partridge's richly illustrated encyclopedia.

"Also 'Z,'" said Tau-Tau sharply. "Now if we don't press on, the sun will come up and the path may no longer be available to us."

Miles scrambled to his feet. The night was still dark, but away on the eastern horizon he could see the sky beginning to lighten. They were entering a strange landscape of small hollows and steep hills, out of which there grew more and more of the tall jagged rocks like the one that had sheltered them while they rested. In the darkness they looked like giant stone teeth, some tilted at a crazy angle, and the faint path wound among them and dipped into the empty sockets in between. The wind whipped around them, shredded by the stone teeth into gusts and eddies that ambushed them from every direction and dropped just as suddenly. Doctor Tau-Tau moved more slowly now, and every now and then he stopped and squinted at a battered notebook that he produced from the pocket of his dressing gown. Miles kept close behind him.

"What is this place?" asked Miles, as loudly as he dared.

"The locals call it Hell's Teeth," whispered Tau-

Tau. "It's been mined for thousands of years, which accounts for the holes, to an extent, but the wind and the rain have made most of it."

"It's not the kind of place where I'd expect to find royalty," said Miles.

Doctor Tau-Tau stopped so abruptly that Miles almost ran into him. He turned slowly and bent down until his face was inches away from Miles's nose. "We are only here for your benefit, my boy," he whispered hoarsely, "and we are getting very close, so you will oblige me by keeping your ceaseless chatter to yourself." He straightened up and began to creep forward with all the stealth of a buffalo.

If you have ever stood at the sink cleaning your teeth and become convinced that someone is staring at you from behind, you will be familiar with the feeling that came over Miles as he began once again to follow Doctor Tau-Tau through the forest of giant teeth. Perhaps it was the pajamas and dressing gown that did it, but he slowly became convinced that if he were to look around he would see a pair of eyes staring at him from somewhere in the shadows. The more the feeling grew, the more determined he was not to give in to it and look around. He was beginning to wonder if this midnight trip had been such a good idea, and he had to remind himself that it was his determination to find his father, or at least to discover his fate, that had brought him to this eerie place.

They came to a hollow that seemed to dip steeply into blackness on its far side. They descended carefully, their feet slipping on the damp grass. At the bottom of the hollow Doctor Tau-Tau paused and put his finger to his lips. He produced his notebook and peered at it for a minute, then he took out a small flashlight. It gave off a feeble yellow light, which flickered and died within seconds. Tau-Tau muttered something ugly, and tried to shake the flashlight back to life.

Strangely enough it was this attempt to pierce the darkness that made Miles finally lose his nerve and look behind him. Before his eyes had time to make sense of the shadows they had begun to move and break up, and a swarm of little figures was slithering down the steep sides of the hollow toward them, like the hairy outcasts of a hundred forgotten dreams.

"Doctor Tau-Tau!" said Miles in an urgent whisper, tugging at his sleeve.

"Not now, boy," said Tau-Tau, still squinting at his notebook, but as he fumbled once again with the switch on his flashlight, one of the hairy little men appeared at his elbow, reached up in an instant and snatched it from his hand. Doctor Tau-Tau's jaw dropped in astonishment, and at that moment a second little man jumped up nimbly and wedged a large clod of grass into his open mouth before the fortune-teller could utter a word.

CHAPTER ELEVEN
TWO HUNDRED KINGS
AND TWELVE

Miles Wednesday, dressing-gowned and hollow-trapped, stood in the center of a heaving circle of small, shaggy figures, none of whom rose above the level of his chin. The sky was still dark and they carried no lights, but at close range he could see them a bit better. Their hair was long and matted, and their faces almost completely covered with thick beards. In their noses they wore brass rings. They were dressed in a sort of patchwork of animal furs, but so hairy were the little men themselves that it was impossible to tell where their clothes ended and their own pelts began. They jockeyed and elbowed each other to get a better look at him, and some of them poked him with sharpened sticks, or reached out and pinched him with bony little fingers to see what he was made of.

He glanced at Doctor Tau-Tau, who was struggling to free his arms from the grip of their captors so that he could remove the clump of grass from his mouth, but although the hairy men were small they were wiry and strong, and there were far too many of them to be overpowered. Miles himself had been neither tied nor gagged, and he decided that it was better not to resist, and to wait and see what would happen next. He had no doubt that these little men were the ones who had been raiding the circus at night, and if anything this encounter increased his curiosity about them.

Their captors began to poke and prod them toward the deeper darkness at the far side of the hollow. Miles could just see Doctor Tau-Tau stumbling ahead of him, surrrounded by the jostling men, and soon he found himself pushing through thick bushes. He suddenly lost sight of Tau-Tau altogether, and before he had time to wonder where he had gone the ground disappeared beneath his feet and he tumbled into blackness. The hole into which he had fallen was not very deep, and moments later he found himself rolling down a rocky slope in absolute darkness. He could hear Doctor Tau-Tau ahead of him grunting and swearing as he bounced along. The grass gag had been jolted from his mouth, and he cursed and spat by turns as he tried to rid his tongue of the gritty soil.

As he tumbled down the underground slope Miles could hear a faint jingle of metal and the whisper of many leathery feet. He pictured (quite rightly, as it happened) the small army of hairy men running and leaping down the rocky slope on either side, without so much as a flashlight or even a flaming match to light their way. Just when he felt he had collected a bruise on every part of his body, he fetched up against the bulk of Doctor Tau-Tau, who was lying winded at the bottom of the slope.

"Get off me!" spluttered Tau-Tau. His hand found Miles in the darkness and groped its way around his face. "Oh, it's you," he said irritably, as though it were Miles who had led him to this place and not the other way around. Miles picked himself up carefully and checked in his pocket for Tangerine. The little bear gripped his finger shakily, but he knew better than to make a sound.

Miles felt little bony fingers take his elbows on both sides, but their grip this time was not hard, and it was obvious that their captors knew he could see nothing in the pitch darkness that surrounded them. He wondered why they did not make a light, but it seemed they needed none.

"Get your hands off me!" he heard Tau-Tau say. "I wish to parlay with the king. Which one of you hairy little devils is the king?"

A ripple of chuckles swept around them, and Miles could hear the sound of muttering and argument in a language he did not recognize. He wished, not for the first time, that Little were with him. He had never heard a language she was unable to translate.

The men gripping his elbows began to push him forward, and they stumbled for a while over uneven rock, Doctor Tau-Tau grousing loudly all the way. "Can't see a thing," he grumbled. "Surely even these gibbering pygmies have learned to make fire."

"Aren't these the people you were planning to meet?" asked Miles.

"Of course," huffed Tau-Tau, who must have been bent double to avoid cracking his skull on the rocky ceiling. "But I wasn't expecting their emissaries to be such an uncouth rabble."

"You said they didn't welcome visitors," said Miles. "Who exactly are they, anyway?"

"I told you," said the fortune-teller, "these are the people who lived here before your ancestors came from the lands to the east. They are known as the Fir

Bolg by the few people who believe in their existence. They don't get out much, as you may have noticed."

"But why should they know anything about my father?" asked Miles.

"That's a long story." Tau-Tau's voice echoed back along the tunnel. "I believe there was some connection between them and Celeste before she died, but it's too complicated to go into now. I intend to speak to their king, assuming he too hasn't descended to running around in rabbit skin and speaking gibberish."

A faint glow appeared ahead of them. It began to grow in size, though not in brightness, but it was relief to eyes that had spent so long straining in the inky dark. Miles began to make out the outlines of their Fir Bolg captors, swarming through the tunnel and out into a wider space from which the glow came.

They emerged into a large cavern filled with stalagmites and stalactites and lit with a feeble orange light. There were hundreds of the little hairy figures in the cave, arguing and laughing in their strange tongue, eating and fighting and crouched in groups playing games with small pieces of bone. There were women and children here too, even smaller than the men and distinguishable only by the fact that they had no beards.

The dim glow came from a sort of fireplace built in the center of the cavern. The fire was almost completely enclosed by a huge stone funnel, and in the stonework was a network of little gaps. These let out warmth and plenty of smoke, but very little light.

As Miles and Tau-Tau stood blinking in the smoky glow a silence fell over the crowd, and hundreds of faces turned to stare at them with glittering black eyes.

The silence did not last long. For a few moments there was nothing to be heard but the faint crackling of the enclosed fire, and somewhere in the distance a trickle of water, then all at once the Fir Bolg began to swarm around them—men, women and children, shaking their sticks and their fists, and all shouting at once. Miles and Tau-Tau were propelled into the cavern and half pushed, half carried toward the other side, which sloped steeply upward into the gloom. Doctor Tau-Tau's fez was knocked from his head in the scuffle, and what little patience he possessed deserted him altogether. His face turned a dangerous purple, and he threatened his hairy captors with the police, the plague and a hundred forgotten curses. The Fir Bolg did not understand a word.

Miles knew better than to put up a struggle, and

allowed himself to be swept along. The far side of the cavern was a stone slope dotted with smaller caves. Some were as large as a baron's bedroom, and others so small that they were just big enough for one of the little men to lie down in. Up ahead of him Miles could make out a knot of Fir Bolg manhandling Doctor Tau-Tau over the lip of one of these caves. The sight reminded him of a swarm of ants heaving a grub into their larder, and for the first time he wondered what the little men ate.

A moment later he was shoved into the cave after the grub, and collapsed beside him onto a carpet of dried grass. Tau-Tau was gasping for breath after his exertions, and no doubt the shouting had not helped. "Barbarians . . . ," he panted. "Troglodyte hooligans! . . . Clearly have no idea who they're dealing with." He produced his battered notebook from inside his dressing gown and rifled through it for a time in the faint orange light. He closed the notebook with a snap and poked his head out of the cave. "I wish to speak to the king," he said slowly to the knot of guards posted outside. The little men looked at each other and shrugged. "*On Ree,*" said Tau-Tau. "Get me *on Ree.*"

The guards broke into laughter, then began to argue and gesticulate among themselves. Eventually one of them received a poke from the blunt end of a spear, and set off back down the slope.

"That's more like it," said Tau-Tau. "There's nothing like an in-depth knowledge of the local lingo." Miles joined him at the cave mouth and looked out into the cavern. "Are you going to ask the king about my father?" he said.

"Yes, yes, all in good time," said Doctor Tau-Tau. "There are formalities to be observed first."

They waited for a long time, until it seemed that they had been altogether forgotten. Tau-Tau rummaged absently in his pocket and produced a fluff-covered chicken drumstick, but before he could get it to his lips one of their tiny captors ran forward and speared it deftly on his pointed stick. The fortune-teller was left with his mouth dangling open and his two hands grasping empty space, and the look of shock in his bulging eyes made the guards stop squabbling over their prize and hoot with laughter.

Eventually Miles spotted someone clambering up the slope toward them. As the figure got closer he could see that it was a woman, and that her wrinkled face was tattooed all over with a blue-black pattern of spirals and swirls. She wore three rings through her nose, each one larger than the last. Some of her matted hair was plaited into twisted tails and finished with brass beads, and she carried a switch that she cracked from side to side to clear a path for herself. Perched on top of her head was Doctor Tau-Tau's faded red fez.

Tau-Tau pasted a strained grin on his face as the tiny woman approached, and extended his hand, which she ignored. "I have business with the king," he said, with as much politeness as he could muster.

The woman spoke, and to his surprise Miles could make out some of her words.

"King," she said, and a grin split her face. "*Gaw cade dahreig!* Two hundred kings and twelve." Her bony arm swept out in an arc behind her.

"Two hundred and twelve? But there aren't much more than two hundred people here," said Doctor Tau-Tau.

"I think that's what she means," said Miles. "Maybe they don't have a ruler."

The little woman turned her black eyes on Miles. She reached out and grabbed his jaw, turning his head from side to side. "*Fasogue?*" she chuckled. "Where's your beard?"

"I don't have one," said Miles. "I'm only eleven."

The woman cocked her head to one side like a bird, and the rings in her nostrils clinked. She turned to Doctor Tau-Tau again and poked him in the belly with her switch.

Tau-Tau's smile began to crack. "Your leader," he said loudly. "Who is your leader?"

"Two hundred kings," repeated the little woman. "Speak to me. I am Fuat, daughter of Anust, daughter of Etar. I know your tongue. Who are you, and who was your mother and your mother's mother? What are you wanting here?"

Doctor Tau-Tau gave Miles a sidelong glance. "We need to speak in private," he said to Fuat, "and you are wearing my hat."

The woman poked him again with her switch. "Speak now," she said. "Fuat's ears are open. The hat is mine."

Tau-Tau shifted his feet uncomfortably. He leaned forward and muttered something in the little woman's ear. Miles could not hear what he said, but whatever it was did not remain a secret for long. The woman's eyes sprang wide and she went rigid, as though an electric shock had run through her. She turned slowly around, and in a surprisingly strong voice she boomed out her message to the entire cavern. *"Tawn t-Uv Reevoch egge!"* she said. A roar went up, and the Fir Bolg began to swarm up the slope toward them. Fuat shouted something else, and they stopped where they were. She snapped her fingers and pointed to the little group of guards, who piled into the cave and at once began a thorough search of the startled Doctor Tau-Tau's person. They poked in his pockets and rummaged in his hair. They took out his notebook and his eyeglasses, two squares of fudge and a number of used tissues, and examined them all minutely. Two of them yanked off his slippers and shook them out.

"Not me, the *boy*, you hairy little nincompoops!" spluttered Tau-Tau. "The egg is in the *boy!*"

Miles felt his stomach tighten. He had no idea what Doctor Tau-Tau was talking about, but he knew that it would be his turn to be searched next. He put his hand into his pocket, and grasped Tangerine firmly. If they found the little bear there was no knowing what they would do to him. Miles glanced around him quickly. The cave wall behind him was pocked with smaller holes, like a giant cheese. He spotted a Tangerine-sized hole just above him, and making sure that the Fir Bolg were still occupied in their search of Tau-Tau, he reached up and quickly tucked the bear into the hole, pushing him to the back and hoping against hope that for once Tangerine would stay where he was put.

CHAPTER TWELVE
THE SHRIVELED FELLA

Miles Wednesday, arm-raised and egg-baffled, squirmed as a hundred bony little fingers searched him from head to toe. It was like being tickled by a pack of miniature uncles, and despite the anger rising up inside him he could barely keep himself from laughing. A hairy face appeared inches from his nose, and he felt his jaws prized open while the face's owner peered down his throat. He wondered how they could hope to see anything in a dark mouth in a gloomy cave, but the lack of light didn't seem to hinder the little men in the least. They made a thorough search of his pockets, where Tangerine had snuggled moments before, but there was nothing to be found.

"What about my father?" Miles called to Doctor Tau-Tau, as soon as the fingers were removed from his mouth.

"Yes, yes, we'll get to that," said Tau-Tau distractedly. "This is hardly the time." He seemed to be watching the search closely.

It dawned on Miles that whatever his real reason for coming here, the fortune-teller had no intention of asking for information about Barty Fumble. Angrily he tried to shake off the remaining Fir Bolg, and received a none-too-gentle jab in his ribs from the blunt end of a spear.

"Excuse me, missus Fuat," he called to the tiny woman, who perched on her hunkers at the mouth of the cave. She cocked her head again in that birdlike way.

"Speak, *a stor*," she said.

"Do you know a man called Barty Fumble?" asked Miles. "A big . . . giant with a beard. We came here to look for him."

The woman shook her head.

"Barty Fumble," repeated Miles. "He was the husband of Celeste. Did you know Celeste?"

The mention of Celeste's name had a dramatic effect on the Fir Bolg, though none of them seemed to have understood another word of the conversation. The hard little fingers instantly stopped rummaging in his clothes, and the hairy heads of his searchers turned as one to look at Fuat. She remained where she was, but her eyes were fixed on Miles.

"Celeste of the *droch-fiach*?" she said. "You are from the line of Celeste?"

"I don't know what a *droch-fiach* is," said Miles. He pronounced the unfamiliar words with care.

"That which is borrowed and not returned," said Fuat. "Celeste took from us the *Uv Reevoch*—the Tiger's Egg. If you are of her house, the debt is now yours and you must return it. *Taw an t-awm cautcha.* The time is passed and gone."

Miles opened his mouth to tell the tiny woman that he did not understand what she was talking about, but Doctor Tau-Tau got in first.

"The boy is Celeste's son," he said. "He knows nothing of the Egg. It's inside him, as I keep telling you. He must have swallowed it as an infant."

"What egg?" said Miles. "I haven't swallowed any egg. Is this why you brought me here? You told me we were looking for my father!"

"And so we are, my friend," said Tau-Tau, "but we must find the Egg first. With the Egg we will be able to find your father. We can find you a dozen fathers!" His voice rose as he spoke, to be heard over the swelling chatter of the Fir Bolg.

"Wait!" shouted Miles nervously over the little shaggy heads. "What *is* a Tiger's Egg? Tigers don't lay eggs!"

"It's a tool of advanced augury," said Tau-Tau. "You wouldn't understand these things, and you don't need to concern yourself with it." In the dim light he looked a little nervous.

"I think I do," said Miles, "if you say this thing is inside me."

"We will open the boy," interrupted Fuat. She motioned with her switch for a little man with a particularly shaggy beard and a long butcher knife to come forward.

"Just a moment," squeaked Tau-Tau hastily. He opened the notebook that he kept in his pocket, which had been returned to him once the Fir Bolg had satisfied themselves that it contained nothing egglike. A number of pages fell from the notebook as he opened it, and fluttered to the floor like leaves. Beads of sweat glistened on the fortune-teller's forehead as he leafed quickly through the remaining pages. The Fir Bolg watched him curiously. And Miles? Miles held his breath and prayed that Doctor Tau-Tau had something more effective up his sleeve than a balled-up handker-chief.

"Ah yes," said Tau-Tau, looking up from the note-book. "Just as I thought. You can't use metal to get a Tiger's Egg. It will lose its power at once."

The Fir Bolg looked expectantly at Fuat. She translated Tau-Tau's words. There was a moment's silence, then the whole cave erupted in laughter. The man with the butcher knife advanced toward Miles, feeling the blade with his thumb. Miles felt his mind race. He wished more than anything that the tiger would appear now and save him, but in the smoky dimness he saw nothing but a mob of shaggy little men, waiting to see him unzipped like a purse.

"Wait," he shouted desperately. "What if there's no egg inside me?"

"*Fon, fon nomaid*," Fuat barked. The butcher stopped. Another loud argument followed, with everyone joining in, even small children who appeared to be shouting purely for the fun of it. "You have a notion there," said Fuat at last, when the hubbub had died down. "If the Egg is in you, the debt will be paid and that's an end. But if we open you and find nothing, then your life has been spent foolishly, and our debt will be to your kin. First we must find out the truth."

Miles felt the knots loosen a little in his stomach. He had no idea what would happen next, but at least the immediate danger of being "opened" seemed to have receded.

Doctor Tau-Tau cleared his throat. "Well, I'm glad that's cleared up," he said.

"Come," said Fuat, ignoring him. "We will visit the Shriveled Fella. There are few breaths left to him, but he might use one of them to tell us what we need to know. *Ar aigue liv.*"

They prodded Doctor Tau-Tau and Miles toward the cave mouth and marched at a brisk pace along the sloping side of the cavern, their guards banging the butts of their spears rhythmically on the ground to keep up the pace. Doctor Tau-Tau was soon panting with the exertion, and muttering darkly with what little wind he could muster. Ahead of them ran Fuat, shoeless and tattooed and swift as a ferret, and as she ran she sang a song of the darkness, the bones of Earth and her many, many children.

Fuat, daughter of Anust, daughter of Etar, nose-ringed and spiral-skinned, stopped suddenly at the mouth of a long, low cave, and ducked inside without a word. Miles and Tau-Tau stood waiting for their breath to ease and wondering what would happen next. It was not long before Fuat appeared and beckoned Miles inside. Doctor Tau-Tau made to follow, but a quick swish of Fuat's switch was warning enough, and he sank gratefully to the ground outside the cave's entrance. Miles held his breath as he entered the cave. There was a smell of dried things, crackling leaves or rustling grasses. What little light there was in the main cavern barely entered the cave, and he felt Fuat's strong grip on his wrist as she led him forward. They reached the far corner and there they stopped. Fuat began to speak to the wall in a soft voice, and gradually Miles's eyes began to make out the shape of the Shriveled Fella, lying on a stone ledge in the warm darkness.

The Shriveled Fella was by far the oldest person that Miles had ever seen—aside from Little, of course. His face was a tiny skull, wrapped in papery skin crisscrossed with a thousand fine wrinkles, one for every joy and sorrow the ancient man had collected in his long life. He lay on a bed of dried grasses, and the thin gray wisps of what once had been a fine mane of hair seemed to float in the air around his head. He lifted a bony hand and motioned to Miles to come closer, then he raised himself so slowly and stiffly that Miles was sure he would snap like a twig. The Shriveled Fella placed his papery ear to Miles's stomach and listened. Miles held his breath, afraid to move. Eventually the tiny man sank back down onto the bed with a crackling sound that may have come from his brittle bones or the grass upon which they lay.

"*Neel aon Uv air bi, inyeen,*" he said to Fuat in a dry whisper. "*Ach taw ruddee a raw lom.*"

Fuat turned to Miles. "There is no Egg," she said, "and he has words for you."

Miles leaned closer to the Shriveled Fella. The old man's voice was barely audible, a wheezing breath shaped into words. "The bright hands are on you, *buhall*," he said, "and the far eyes, but it's shut you have them." His breathing settled into a steady rasp, and Miles waited to see if there was more. After a while the old man whispered, "You have forgotten to leave, *a vic.*"

The smoky glow in the cavern seemed almost bright after the darkness of the Shriveled Fella's cave. Doctor Tau-Tau was slumped on the floor in his rumpled dressing gown, still without his fez. When he saw Miles he scrambled to his feet. "Well?" he said.

"Well, what?" said Miles.

"The Egg!" hissed Tau-Tau. "Is it in there or not?"

"Not," said Miles.

Doctor Tau-Tau's bulging eyes widened in surprise. "You're sure that's what they said?" he asked. Miles nodded.

"Well, that's a relief, eh?" said Tau-Tau, looking disappointed. He leaned closer to Miles and whispered, "Just as well I made up that stuff about the Egg losing its power under metal, eh?"

Miles looked at the brick-red face of the fortune-teller, who had almost had him killed but was grinning at him as though he had saved his life, his empty promise to help find Barty Fumble entirely forgotten. He felt his hand ball into a fist, and he turned away before he could plant it right on Doctor Tau-Tau's bulbous nose. A sound came from behind him, like a steam kettle beginning to whistle, and built up steadily into an eerie wail. The Fir Bolg turned as one toward the narrow cave, and one by one they took up the wail until the cavern rang with the sound. Miles felt the hair stand up on his scalp as the long cry of sorrow echoed around him, and he knew at once what it was. The Shriveled Fella, dried and brittle as a fallen feather, had surrendered his last breath, and the wailing of two hundred voices was his lament.

Miles turned to look, and beyond the puzzled face of Doctor Tau-Tau he saw Fuat standing at the cave entrance. Her tattooed face glinted with tears in the dim firelight. She raised her hands in the air, and the wailing subsided a little. She shouted something at the knot of guards, and they surged forward and grabbed Doctor Tau-Tau by both arms.

"What's going on?" shouted Tau-Tau over the deafening noise. "Get your hands off me! I am Doctor Tau-Tau, the great clairvoyant, you little bearded misfits!"

The banging of spear butts began again, and Doctor Tau-Tau was spun around and set in motion, down along the slope of the cavern toward a dark tunnel mouth at the far end from the one by which they had entered. No one this time grabbed hold of Miles, and he ran with them only so that he would not be left behind. "Where are we going?" he shouted to Fuat.

"To the mouth of hell," said Fuat.

"What's the mouth of hell?" asked Miles, though he was not sure he wanted to hear the answer.

"Truth comes out of it, if truth there is," said Fuat.

They emerged into a wide-open space and there

they halted. The rocky walls themselves gave off a faint luminous light, and by this they could make out what kind of place they were in. They stood on a narrow ledge in an enormous cavern, and below them yawned a vast hole that sank down out of sight and made Miles feel instantly dizzy.

"Beelzebub's aunt!" panted Doctor Tau-Tau. "They should have a guard rail here. Someone could plummet to their death!" Miles stepped forward cautiously and peered into the enormous hole. He could make out the rocky walls on the far side, extending downward into utter darkness. Sometimes they seemed to shimmer slightly in the heat rising up from the earth's heart.

"*Anish,*" said Fuat, breaking the silence. "The boy has no Egg, nor is it known to him. You brought him here, man with the red face, and if there is a nut of truth to be had between the pair of you, it's you that must give it up now."

"I'm afraid," said Doctor Tau-Tau, and his voice cracked. He began again. "I'm afraid there's been a terrible mistake." The guards began to prod him toward the edge of the ledge. The fortune-teller's voice raised an octave. "I thought they'd made him swallow the Egg as a baby," he squeaked. "It's just the kind of stunt his father would have come up with. The boy sees tigers, I'm telling you! How could I know that he was just dreaming?"

"Where is the *Uv Reevoch* now? Where is the Tiger's Egg?" shouted Fuat.

"I don't know," sobbed Doctor Tau-Tau.

"He doesn't know," said Miles. His throat was dry as chalk, and he was not sure they could even hear him. "Leave him alone. I don't think he knows anything."

Fuat, daughter of Anust, merely cracked her switch in reply. The sound echoed around the cavern, and before Miles could do a thing to stop them, the little men hoisted Doctor Tau-Tau bodily in the air and tossed him, shrieking, off the ledge and into the mouth of hell.

CHAPTER THIRTEEN

THE TIGER'S EGG

Miles Wednesday, ledge-bound and terror-tied, stared in disbelief at the flailing, wailing form of the fortune-teller. He could not understand what his eyes were telling him. It seemed as if time had frozen, and Doctor Tau-Tau was suspended in midair while the entire cave from the ledge downward had shattered into a million moving spirals, like the pattern on Fuat's face. A dozen heartbeats passed before he realized what had really happened. There was no deep hole before them, nor had there ever been. The mouth of hell was nothing more than the vast cave above them reflected in a wide, shallow pool that almost completely covered the floor of the cave. With no breath of wind to disturb it the pool lay deep underground like a perfect mirror, and the ledge they stood on was nothing more than a slice of the cave floor that rose above the level of the water.

Doctor Tau-Tau sat in the center of a web of ripples like a spider's breakfast. He had ceased to struggle as it dawned on him, too, that he had been deposited in a few inches of icy water instead of plummeting to his death far below. He was sobbing quietly now with a mixture of terror and relief, but even if you had been there you would not have heard him, for the moment he had landed with a splash on his backside the Fir Bolg had begun to laugh.

They hooted and cackled with laughter. They slapped their knees and bent double and dropped their spears with a clatter. Their laughter echoed around the cavern walls and Fuat, daughter of Anust, daughter of Etar, laughed the loudest of all. "The Shriveled Fella would have loved that one, may the gods put the juice back into him," gasped the little old woman. The tears streamed down her cheeks, and she slapped one of her hairy companions so hard on the back that he fell to his hands and knees.

Miles felt as though he would be sick. He stepped cautiously out into the pool, grateful that the image of the bottomless hole was still fractured into expanding ripples. The water was as cold as ice. He waded slowly forward until he reached the spot where Doctor Tau-Tau sat, and helped him to his feet. Tau-Tau shuffled through the water beside him, dazed and sniveling, until they reached the ledge. If he noticed the Fir Bolg's amusement at all he showed no reaction, but allowed himself to be led back along the tunnel, this time by Miles, who followed their giggling captors by ear through the inky darkness.

They were returned to their cave, where Doctor Tau-Tau collapsed quivering in a corner. Fuat spoke briefly to the guards, and turned to leave. "Wait," said Miles. "Why are you keeping us now? You know we don't have what you're looking for."

The little woman grinned at him. Her teeth were small and pointed. "You will be let go in the morning," she said, "but not the *far rua*."

"You mean Doctor Tau-Tau? You don't need him," said Miles. His earlier anger at Tau-Tau had drained away, and now he felt only pity. "He's been through enough."

Fuat cocked her head and raised her eyebrows.

"He had no right to come here, nor yet to leave."

"But you're letting me go. Why not him?" asked Miles.

"You have a debt to pay. You must return the Tiger's Egg to the Fir Bolg."

"I don't even know what it is!" protested Miles. He thought for a moment. "I'll need Doctor Tau-Tau to help me find it."

The woman cackled. "That one couldn't find his nose with his hand," she said, "but he will find his way into the pot. There will be feasting tomorrow for the last journey of the Shriveled Fella. The winter has been hard, and we are sore tired of running on empty bellies."

"You can't eat him," whispered Miles, thinking desperately. "What about his life? You'll be in debt to his family."

"That we will, *cyart go lore*," said Fuat. "A couple of rabbits should pay that, when the spring comes." She turned and cracked her switch at the guards, who hastily prodded Miles backward into the cave.

"We've had no food or water," Miles called after Fuat.

"*Amoroch*," she said. "Food there will be, tomorrow." She disappeared, laughing, into the gloom.

Miles looked over at Doctor Tau-Tau, who sat

slumped in the corner staring at the floor. He glanced out of the cave to make sure the guards were not watching either, then he reached up and groped anxiously in the small hole where he had left Tangerine. To his relief he found him at once. The little bear climbed into his hand and Miles lifted him carefully down and returned him to the pocket of his dressing gown with a sigh. "Now all we have to do," he whispered under his breath, "is to find a way out of here." Tangerine, always a better listener than he was a finder, grasped his master's finger happily and said not a word.

Miles sat himself down beside Doctor Tau-Tau. The fortune-teller was shivering in his damp dressing gown. He seemed to have physically shrunk since he had been hurled into the water, and in the dim light of the cave it looked as though his hair had begun to turn white. Miles searched for a way to distract him from his ordeal.

"Are the Fir Bolg related to The Null in some way?" he asked.

Doctor Tau-Tau sat up straight. "Why on earth would you think that?" he asked.

"Because they're so hairy," suggested Miles.

The fortune-teller snorted. "Both ants and antelopes have legs," he said. "That doesn't make them first cousins. Anyway," he added hastily, "I've never heard of The Null. Don't know what you're talking about."

Miles sighed. He wondered why it was so difficult to get a straight answer from anyone older than himself. He tried again. "It was the Fir Bolg who raided your wagon, wasn't it?"

"Possibly," said Tau-Tau cagily.

"What were they looking for?" asked Miles.

"For the Tiger's Egg, of course," said the fortune-teller.

"I need to know more about this Tiger's Egg," said Miles, "if I'm to get us out of here."

Doctor Tau-Tau thought about this for a moment. "It's a very rare thing, a precious stone that contains the captured soul of a tiger. It's believed there's only one still in existence, and that one was in the possession of Celeste, at least for a time. I've searched for it for many years, but it still eludes me."

"How can a stone contain the soul of a tiger?" asked Miles.

"It can be created only by a powerful shaman," said Tau-Tau. "The shaman takes the soul of a real tiger and traps it in the stone. The tiger can never die as long as his soul remains in the Egg. He becomes a sort of living ghost in thrall to the master of the Tiger's Egg, like a striped genie." He thought about this for a minute. "Like a genie," he said, "with stripes."

"But why would anyone want to trap a tiger's soul?" asked Miles.

"There's great power in a Tiger's Egg," said Tau-Tau, straightening himself up a little. "It contains the wisdom, courage and strength of the tiger who endowed it, but its owner must already be wise and strong to be able to control it. Some say that the Egg can also give immortality to its master."

"The Egg my mother had," said Miles, "did it belong to the Fir Bolg?"

"Celeste borrowed the Egg from the Fir Bolg for twenty-one years, in exchange for some service she was to render them; I never found out what it was. That time has now expired."

"And you brought me here to give it back?" asked Miles.

"Certainly not!" said Tau-Tau in a loud whisper. The background noise in the cavern beyond had fallen to a murmur. It seemed that whatever the Fir Bolg recognized as night had fallen, and they had settled in their caves and hollows to sleep. Miles felt a wave of tiredness wash over him at the thought. His stomach was hollow and his eyelids drooped.

"I don't understand," he whispered with an effort. "Then why are we here?"

Doctor Tau-Tau's shoulders slumped. "It's all been a misunderstanding," he said. "At first I was unsure if you were telling the truth about your encounters with a tiger. I didn't believe it was possible that you could possess a Tiger's Egg without knowing about it, but the Egg showed up clearly in your cards. Along with the fact that you were the son of Barty and Celeste," he added hastily. "I felt sure that you had swallowed the Egg as an infant, and that the Fir Bolg would know a harmless way to get it out of you. I was confident I could get us out of here easily, once I had it in my hands."

"But it wouldn't be yours, even if we had it. It belongs to the Fir Bolg, doesn't it?"

Doctor Tau-Tau shook his head. "It wouldn't be safe with the hairy little primitives. Cortado would find out where it was before long."

"The Great Cortado?" said Miles in astonishment. "How does he know about the Tiger's Egg?"

The fortune-teller shrugged. "No idea," he said. "But if it got into his hands we'd all be a tiger's breakfast. I'll only ever be safe if I get to the Egg first. And that goes for you too."

"*I'll* be safe?" said Miles angrily. "You nearly had

me killed just trying to find it!"

"Not at all," said Tau-Tau, smiling weakly. "They would never have cut you open. I had the situation completely under control."

"It didn't look like that when you were flying into the mouth of hell," said Miles sharply. He regretted the words as soon as they had left his mouth, but they could not be unsaid.

Doctor Tau-Tau cringed at the memory. "That's harsh," he said, then after a moment's thought he added, "but fair. Even a farsighted man such as myself can occasionally make an error of judgment. And now we'll probably rot in this damp hole, because there's little prospect of anyone finding us."

"They've told me I can go tomorrow," said Miles.

Doctor Tau-Tau sat bolt upright. "But you're just a tent boy!" he said. "What about me?"

Miles sighed. "I won't be going anywhere," he said. "I'm not leaving until I can get us both out of here."

"But you must!" exclaimed Tau-Tau. "You can go for help. How else will anyone know where I am?"

The fortune-teller's wheedling tone made Miles think of the conversation he and Little had over-heard under the tamarind tree in Larde, and suddenly the other voice they had heard from Tau-Tau's wagon clicked into place. "*You* told Cortado about the Tiger's Egg!" said Miles.

"What are you talking about?" said Doctor Tau-Tau shiftily. "I would have nothing to do with that little villain."

"He was in your wagon at Larde," said Miles. "I overheard you as I walked by."

"I-I . . . b-but . . . ," stammered Tau-Tau. He stopped and buried his head in his hands. "I had no choice," he said in a muffled voice. "I woke up with a knife at my throat and that lunatic sitting on my chest. I had to tell him something that would make him spare my life, and the Tiger's Egg was the first thing that came to mind."

"Why would the Great Cortado want to kill you?" asked Miles suspiciously.

"That goes back to Celeste's death," said Doctor Tau-Tau. "Cortado had always suspected Celeste held some power over the tiger, but he didn't know what it was. When she died he demanded that I reveal the secret to him. I told him I had learned nothing about the tiger from Celeste but he did not believe me. He flew into a rage and said that if I did not reveal the secret to him he would kill me. I had to flee for my life there and then. I traveled over-seas for many years, and I only came back when news reached me that he had been locked away in an asylum." He gave a bitter laugh. "I should have known that no hospital could hold him for long. As soon as he escaped he came to Larde to find the boy who had brought down the Palace of Laughter, and instead he found me in my wagon, with my name painted on the side like a signpost."

"What exactly did you tell him about the Tiger's Egg?"

"As little as possible. I just wanted to be rid of him until I could formulate a plan. I told him that the Egg was probably somewhere in Larde, where Barty and Celeste's son had supposedly died in the orphanage, or else it was still hidden in the circus. He told me to stay with the circus and continue searching for it, while he looked in Larde, just as I hoped he would."

"I didn't die in the orphanage!" said Miles.

"I can see that," said Doctor Tau-Tau, "but that was the story that was put about at the time, and I had no reason to disbelieve it until you . . . until the cards revealed who you were."

Miles sat back against the cold stone of the cave wall. "Then all we have to do is tell the police that the Great Cortado is hiding out in Larde," he said.

Doctor Tau-Tau sat bolt upright, and the whites

of his eyes shone faintly in the darkness. "Are you mad?" he hissed. "Those fools will just send him back to the hospital, and how long do you think it will be before he's back out and lying in wait with a butcher knife? Besides, it's not that simple. He has . . . something I need."

Miles looked at him in surprise. "What do you mean?"

"He has the notebook," sniffed Tau-Tau. "The one that tells how to master the Tiger's Egg."

"You mean it has an *instruction* manual?"

"In a manner of speaking," said Doctor Tau-Tau. "It's one of Celeste's old diaries, in which she was gathering everything she could learn about the Tiger's Egg. Cortado found it when he broke into my wagon, and he took it with him when he left, to ensure that I would come to him if I found the Egg."

"My mother's diaries?" said Miles. "How did *you* come to have my mother's diaries in your wagon?"

"Diary, my boy. I had only one. The other two were lost when I fled the Great Cortado in the first place. I took over Celeste's old wagon on my return, and I came across this one diary hidden behind one of the seats. It was only because I was repainting the wagon inside and out that I found it at all."

"Then if Cortado finds the Tiger's Egg in Larde,"

said Miles, "he won't need you, will he?"

Doctor Tau-Tau laughed quietly. "Don't be absurd," he said. "Only someone who has studied such things for years would be able to make head or tail of Celeste's notebooks, and Cortado knows it. They are written in a jumble of languages and symbols, some of which I'm sure she made up herself. I was only beginning to decipher the notebook when Cortado stole it from me, but he would not even know where to start. My . . . our only hope is to find the Tiger's Egg and somehow trick Cortado out of the notebook." Doctor Tau-Tau did not sound too sure of this part of the plan, but he leaned forward and his eyes bulged in the semidarkness. "With the power of the Egg," he whispered, "I would be safe from the little villain once and for all. The tiger is the only thing he's afraid of." He settled back into his dressing gown and closed his eyes.

Miles sat for a while, his eyes straining into the darkness until it seemed to crawl with a million tiny dots. It was obvious that Doctor Tau-Tau would be of little use in working out a way to escape. He would have to make a plan himself to get the two of them out of there, but before he knew it the weariness of the day had overtaken him, and he fell into an uneasy sleep.

CHAPTER FOURTEEN
A FLASH OF LIGHT

Miles Wednesday, bone-chilled and hollow-bellied, woke with a start with the now-familiar feel of a sharp stick being poked in his ribs. He had been dreaming of the tiger, who had peeled back the lid of the dark hole in which he sat, and was looking down at him with amusement, framed in the brilliant blue of a cloudless sky. His heart fell as he realized that he was still trapped in a cave, and the only person grinning down at him in the semi-darkness was one of the hairy little guards. Even worse, he had fallen asleep before he could even begin to think of a plan for their escape. Morning, he supposed, had come upon them, and he was being woken for his release. The guard was not one he remembered seeing before.

"*Arrye liu,*" said the guard, jabbing him again with the pointed stick.

Doctor Tau-Tau received a similar poke, and was on his feet before his eyes were fully open. "What?" he mumbled. "Are we there yet?" He peered around blearily in the darkness.

"Where's Fuat?" asked Miles. "I need to talk to her."

The guard showed no sign of understanding him, and hustled them outside to where the rest of the little men waited. Most of them, too, seemed to have just awoken. They jabbered among themselves, and two of them wrestled over a small flask, spilling most of the contents on the rocky slope before a drop could pass their lips. The new guard spoke sharply to them, and an argument broke out, with much gesticulating and everyone speaking at once.

Eventually agreement was reached. The guards got reluctantly to their feet and prodded their captives into the usual run, down toward the tunnel from which they had entered the cavern the day before, dodging sleeping knots of Fir Bolg who huddled here and there on the sloping floor. The dim light was soon left behind as they entered the tunnels, and they moved quickly through the darkness for some time. Miles's mind raced as they ran, but he quickly realized the futility of trying to overpower the guards. He could neither see where they were nor avoid their spears, and he could not hope to find a way out with no hint of light. Besides, Doctor Tau-Tau's breathing was becoming more labored by the moment, and it did not seem likely that he would be of much help in a struggle. He could only cling to the hope that wherever they were going, their course would bring them closer to the tunnel entrance, and the light beyond it.

"Must . . . stop a mo . . . a moment," panted Tau-Tau, as if to confirm what Miles was thinking. "Have to rest. . . ."

"Okay," said the new guard. He spoke to the others and they stopped abruptly. Miles himself was grateful for the rest, but something didn't seem right, and in a moment he realized what it was.

"You can understand us?" he said, facing the sound of the guard's voice. "Where are you taking us?"

"Cover your eyes," came the reply. Something about the guard's voice made Miles do as he was told, and not a moment too soon. There was a crack followed by a loud spluttering hiss. The cave was

filled with a pink light that was so bright it forced
its way between Miles's fingers and soaked through
his closed eyelids. He gasped with surprise, and
heard Tau-Tau give out a startled shout, but that was
nothing compared to the reaction of the other
guards. The unfortunate little men shrieked as
though they had been dropped into boiling soup,
and all around came the sound of their spears
falling to the ground. When Miles dared to open
his eyelids a fraction he saw that the new guard
seemed to hold in his hand a miniature sun that
flooded the cave with intense light, while his howling companions had curled up tightly in a ball, or
thrown themselves flat on their faces and were
squirming as quickly as they could away from the
light. Doctor Tau-Tau just sat on the floor, a floodlit,
dressing-gowned heap with his face in his hands
and his newly whitened hair standing out from his
head like cotton candy.

"*Gomo leshcule,*" said the Fir Bolg with the super-
nova. There was something about the guard's voice
that did not fit with the hairy little troglodyte it
came from. "Follow me," he said to Miles. "We
haven't got much time."

He turned and disappeared into a tunnel that led
from the cave. The intense light was beginning to

fade, and Miles quickly helped the dazed Tau-Tau to his feet before the pink glow could be swallowed up again by the darkness. They hurried along the narrow tunnel until once again it broadened out and they found themselves climbing a steep rocky slope. The Fir Bolg's light fizzled out, but they were not plunged into darkness as Miles had expected. From up ahead came a faint glow that he immediately recognized as daylight. The light was blue and fresh after the dull smoky orange that had lit their time underground, and he felt as though he were breathing for the first time in days.

At the top of the slope their hairy little guide disappeared into the light, and Miles and Doctor Tau-Tau clambered out after him, pushing through the bushes that hid the entrance to the subterranean world and emerging into the early evening of a cloudless day. They stood blinking in the bottom of the grassy bowl where they had first been captured, and Miles was rooted to the spot by the luminous beauty of the sky above them, which faded from a rich blue through salmon pink to the palest of yellows, where the sun neared the western horizon. He sucked in a deep breath of cold, outdoor air.

"Come on, Miles," called the hairy figure from

halfway up the grassy slope, "we've only got until nightfall to get a head start."

Miles blinked in disbelief. He could hardly believe his ears. "Little?" he said. "Is that *you* in there?"

"Of course it's me," said the Fir Bolg. "Who did you think it was?"

Miles turned to Doctor Tau-Tau, who was staring blankly from one to the other. "Come on," he said. "We'd better get moving." He started up the slope, trying to catch up with the tiny bearded figure of his four-hundred-year-old friend. He was weak with hunger, but a burning curiosity drove him and he soon left the panting fortune-teller behind.

"Wait," he called to Little, "wait for me!"

She stopped in the shadow of one of the tall rocky teeth. Behind the thick beard he could tell she was smiling.

"What . . . ?" gasped Miles as he caught up with her. "I mean, how . . . ?"

The hairy Little put her finger to her lips. "Shh," she said, "I'll explain later. First we have to get rid of Doctor Tau-Tau."

"How?" asked Miles. He could not take his eyes off Little now that he could see her better. Thick hair of a dirty grayish color grew from low on her forehead, sweeping back over her head like a disheveled waterfall that reached almost to her knees. She wore a magnificent beard that had been rather hastily plaited in a few places, and the rest of her body seemed to be covered in a matted tangle of filthy hair and animal furs, bound here and there with thongs of hide. Only her sky-blue eyes were recognizable, smiling from under an old man's bushy eyebrows.

"Leave it to me," she whispered, as Doctor Tau-Tau approached.

"What's going on?" huffed the fortune-teller, his bulging eyes almost popping from his head with the exertion. "Who is this filthy little fellow, and what's he up to, eh?"

"It's me, Doctor Tau-Tau," said Little. "It's Little."

Tau-Tau gaped at the hairy figure looking up at him. "By the twelve pillars of reason!" he said. "Where on earth did you get the outfit?"

"It's not an outfit," said Little. "It's an Untried Marvel. At least it was until I tried it."

"I'm not with you," said Doctor Tau-Tau.

It suddenly dawned on Miles what Little was talking about. "Your Bearded Lady lotion!" he said.

Doctor Tau-Tau stared at Little in disbelief. "Is this true?" he demanded. Little nodded. "You mean to tell me you entered my wagon and stole one of my valuable mixtures?"

"She did it to help us escape!" said Miles indignantly. His sympathy for Doctor Tau-Tau's underground trauma was rapidly wearing thin. "Would you prefer to be in a cooking pot right now?"

Doctor Tau-Tau cleared his throat and turned to Little. "Well, under the circumstances, I suppose we can overlook the trespass," he said.

"Thank you," said Little. "I just hope this will wear off soon."

"Wear off?" said Tau-Tau. "Yes, yes, of course. It will wear off in no time. In no time at all," he repeated, "you'll be bald in all the right places."

"Your lotion really is a work of genius," said Little, "and that's why you should get away as fast as you possibly can, while me and Miles create a diversion for the Fir Bolg."

"Really?" said Doctor Tau-Tau doubtfully. "But that would be very dangerous. I can't let you take such a risk."

"It's all right," said Little, "we won't get caught. And it's far more important that you get to safety.

Imagine if one of the world's greatest clairvoyants and healers ended up as supper for a pack of hungry cavemen."

"I see what you mean," said Tau-Tau with a look of ill-disguised relief. "Well, I'll be off then. Be careful, won't you?" He tightened the belt of his embroidered dressing gown and hurried away in the direction of the distant circus. "And if it does come to a tussle," he called over his shoulder, "see if you can get my hat back, would you?"

As soon as he was lost to sight, Little took Miles by the hand, her hairy fingers tickling his, and led him around to the other side of the rock that loomed over them. Somehow he knew what he would see before they even turned the corner. There in the grass, as large as life and twice as magnificent, sat the Bengal tiger, his deep amber eyes regarding Miles with faint amusement.

"Well, tub boy," said the tiger. "Here we are again, it seems."

Miles nodded, lost for words in his surprise and delight.

"I'm disappointed in your choice of traveling companion," said the tiger. "The fellow does not strike me as much of a guide. If he were of any value at all on a long trip, it would have to be as an item on the menu."

"That's exactly what he was," said Miles, a surge of happiness welling up inside him at the sound of the tiger's voice, "until a short while ago."

CHAPTER FIFTEEN

A BAG OF WIND

Miles Wednesday, spear-poked and light-rescued, sat down suddenly on a smooth rock that jutted from the grass. He felt dizzy after his run through the darkness, and he could not remember the last time he had eaten. "How did you know where to find us?" he asked.

"I didn't find you," said the tiger, "because I wasn't looking for you. I was taking a well-earned nap in a quiet spot when your little friend almost stepped on my tail. Not that I would have noticed, given that she weighs no more than a paper bag. If you want to know how you were saved from this particular scrape you will have to ask Little. Now climb aboard if you're coming. The tiger is leaving."

Miles climbed up behind Little onto the tiger's muscular back. It seemed an age since he had sat astride the tiger, but it was only a moment before he felt like he was right where he belonged, and every stripe of the mighty animal's pelt looked like a familiar friend. A chill wind was rising, and in Doctor Tau-Tau's silky dressing gown Miles found it harder than usual to grip the tiger's flanks. For a while he concentrated on keeping his balance, but he had too many questions to remain silent for long. "How *did* you find us?" he asked Little.

"I went to look for you the morning after Dulac's accident." Her words were whipped over her shoulder by the wind, and Miles had to strain his ears to catch them as they flew by. "No one knew where you were, and by the evening I was getting worried. I asked around the animals, but only Eunice the lioness had seen you leave. She could still catch your scent on the breeze for a long time, so she was able to tell me which way you had gone. I guessed you wanted your trip to be a secret, because you hadn't told me you were leaving, so I followed you on my own."

Miles felt a pang of guilt, though he could not tell from her windblown words whether she was hurt at being excluded. "I'm sorry," he shouted through chattering teeth. "I should have brought you with us. Doctor Tau-Tau said it would be a bad idea."

"Maybe it would," said Little. "If I'd been captured too, who would have come to get us? Anyway, I met a fox who had followed you most of the way. He said he could smell a chicken drumstick in the man's pocket, and he was hoping to catch him napping. Suddenly the fox disappeared, and a few moments later I almost ran into five of the Fir Bolg. They had been out hunting for rabbits, and luckily they were arguing over their catch and I managed to hide myself before they saw me. They disappeared into the hollow and they didn't come out, so after waiting awhile I moved to a closer hiding place to see where they had gone. That's when I bumped into the tiger.

"I was going to follow them down the hole, but the tiger said that they didn't look very friendly, and I wouldn't last five minutes. He offered to catch one of them for me and . . . well . . ." She sounded as though she was struggling to be diplomatic. "I didn't really like what he suggested," she finished.

"It was a perfectly logical suggestion," said the tiger. "And if it hadn't been for your squeamishness you would have had an authentic Fir Bolg skin and I would have had a light snack."

"Anyway," continued Little, "that's when I thought of Doctor Tau-Tau's lotion, and the tiger very kindly offered to take me back to the circus to get it."

"I don't recall offering, as it happens," interrupted the tiger. "In fact, whenever you appear on the scene you seem to end up clinging to my back, and I'm chewed if I can remember how it comes about."

"I was very grateful for your swiftness," said Little. "Without you I would never have got to the circus and back to Hell's Teeth before sunrise, and I wouldn't like to have been caught on the road with hair coming from everywhere so fast you could watch it grow."

Darkness was falling swiftly now, and the tiger hissed them to silence as they passed a lone figure trudging along the twilit road. It was Doctor Tau-Tau, his shoulders hunched and his eyes fixed on the ground, and as the tiger passed stealthily by through the woods Miles thought he could hear the fortune-teller muttering loudly to himself, his white cotton-candy hair flipped this way and that by the chilly breeze. The tiger picked up speed again, and the figure of Doctor Tau-Tau was swallowed by the gloom.

"I hope he makes it back all right," said Miles.

"Are you sure he deserves to?" asked the tiger.

"No one deserves to be eaten," said Miles.

"I think we shall have to differ on that point," said the tiger.

Miles was silent for a moment. He was hungrier than he could ever remember being, and his stomach felt as empty as a cave. He thought longingly of the campfire that burned in the center of the circus village each night, and wondered what delicious food Umor would have crackling on the spit when they arrived. He found himself thinking then of the strange, tiny men who lived their lives in darkness underground, and how they had fought over a cold greasy chicken leg garnished with pocket fluff.

"What did you say to the guards to get us out of the cave?" he asked Little.

"I told them that the soul of the Shriveled Fella had sent me, and that we had to bring you to the entrance to breathe sky air, or you would die."

"How did you know about the Shriveled Fella?" asked Miles in surprise.

"I spent that whole day among the Fir Bolg, finding out about them and where they were keeping you. I was there when he died."

"How did you make the light?" asked Miles.

"It was one of the flares that Big Dan uses in his act. You know when they fire him from the cannon? I brought it from the circus when I went back for the lotion. I had seen that the Fir Bolg came out on a moonless night to hunt, so I had a feeling that the light must be painful to their eyes."

The tiger slowed to a walk. The breeze had fallen to a whisper, and up ahead Miles could see the strings of colored bulbs swaying gently between the trailers, and the warm glow of the fire around which the circus performers would now be gathering to share their supper and swap stories of the day. The faint sound of an accordion reached his frozen ears. For a moment he wished that the tiger could just stroll into the circus with him and stay there as his friend, but as soon as it appeared the thought seemed absurd. It was impossible to imagine this lord of the distant jungle boxed in a wagon and trundling from town to town.

"This is as far as I go, tub boy," said the tiger. Miles slid to the ground and rested his hand on the tiger's flank.

"I have a question," he said.

The tiger turned to look at him. "I would be

surprised if you didn't," he said, "although you should not take that as the promise of an answer."

Miles took a deep breath. "Do you know anything about a Tiger's Egg?" he ventured.

"About as much as I know about a goat's wings," replied the tiger. "Or an elephant's gills. I see we are back to the riddles."

"It's just . . . ," said Miles, looking over the tiger's shoulder at the circus lights, "Doctor Tau-Tau says a Tiger's Egg is a sort of stone that contains the soul of a tiger. Or . . . something." He was sorry he had brought up the subject. The tiger stepped closer to him, his amber eyes drawing his gaze and making him feel like a small frightened herbivore.

"The only thing that could contain the soul of a tiger," said the magnificent beast, "is a tiger."

"I'm sorry if I offended you," said Miles. "I just wanted to know if you'd heard of such a thing."

"Ignorance does not offend the wise," said the tiger, "but I would expect more from you than to be taken in by the patter of a sideshow huckster. Be wary of that man. He looks to me like a bag of wind, and my impressions are seldom wrong. At least if they are," he said as he turned to leave, "I have yet to meet anyone who will tell me so."

"You will be back, won't you?" said Miles.

The tiger paused and looked over his shoulder. "More than likely," he said. "I'm beginning to enjoy the experience of talking to small animals without having to pick them from my teeth afterward." As he disappeared into the night Miles thought he heard the tiger mutter, "Though I can't imagine why."

CHAPTER SIXTEEN

THE BEARDED BABY

Gila Bolsillo, full-fed and brandy-warmed, turned the corner of his brightly painted wagon and came face to face with Miles and his hairy companion. The little man froze on the spot. He had left the campfire to collect his knitted Himalayan hat from the wagon before his frozen ears dropped off the sides of his head, and the last thing he expected to see was the missing boy and a figure about his own size covered from head to toe in matted hair. His black eyes narrowed and he squinted nervously at Little. "Who's your friend?" he hissed to Miles, from the corner of his mouth.

Miles laughed. "Have a guess," he said.

"I'd rather not," said Gila. He looked so rattled by the appearance of the hairy stranger that Miles felt sorry for him.

"It's Little," said Miles. "She used one of Doctor Tau-Tau's Untried Marvels. He says it will wear off soon."

Gila's eyes widened, and he peered closely at Little's bearded face. "Well, coat me in custard!" he said. "It's you, all right. What are you doing in there, Sky Beetle?"

"It's a long story," said Little, "and Miles is very hungry."

"Of course," said Gila. "Feed first, talk later."

The sound of laughter and the *parp-parrump* of a tuba drifted over from the campfire, carried on the smell of roasting meat and chestnuts and making Miles feel faint with hunger. Gila put his arms around their shoulders and steered them toward the fire, but Little pulled back. "I'm not hungry," she said. "I'll be in my wagon."

"'Course you're hungry!" said Gila, taking her elbow with a firm grip. "And don't worry about the hair. Even a walking hearth rug doesn't stand out among this lot. No one will even notice."

As they drew close to the campfire, Gila snapped

into ringmaster mode. He threw his head back, stuck out his chest and boomed, "Ladies and Gentlemen, you've heard of the Bearded Lady, but tonight we present, all the way from your darkest hour, the one and only Beeearded . . . Baaaabyyy!"

Little cringed. The tuba ceased its *parrump*ing, and twenty faces turned toward them in the firelight. Fabio rose slowly to his feet, staring at Little as though he had seen his long-dead grandmother wobbling past on a unicycle. Umor also stood transfixed, until the sausage he was toasting caught fire and he had to blow it out.

"It's all right," said Gila, "It's just Sky Beetle."

"Little?" said Fabio.

"She's been reupholstered," said Gila.

"I don't understand it," said Fabio.

"But I like it," said Umor.

"She can't go on the wire like that."

"She'd break her neck."

"She can go on after the countess," said Fabio, "and before Stranski."

"The Human Gorilla," suggested Umor.

"The Wolf-child of Cádiz."

"The Pocket Yeti," said Gila.

"I'm not going on as anything," interrupted Little. "Doctor Tau-Tau says it will all fall out in a couple of days. I used his Bearded Lady lotion."

"Oh," said Gila, sounding disappointed.

"Are you sure?" said Fabio.

"We could apply some more," said Umor.

"I used the whole bottle," said Little, "and I don't like being hairy. When it falls out I'll go back on the wire, as myself."

"Well, you're turning your back on a long and hirsute career," said Fabio.

"On your own head be it," said Umor.

"And all over the rest of you," said Gila.

Miles and Little took their place by the fire, and Umor passed them battered tin plates piled high with steaming food. The circus performers resumed their laughter and talk as though there was nothing remarkable about sharing their supper with a fur-covered four-hundred-year-old girl. Indeed it was no more remarkable than the lives that many of them had led, lives so rich and strange that they could fill a hundred books and still leave secrets untold. For the first time in days Miles began to feel warm, and content, and full.

"Well, Master Miles," said Fabio quietly, when Miles had cleaned his plate, "are you going to tell us where you got to?"

"I went looking for my father," said Miles.

"Your father," repeated Fabio. He was silent for a while. "And what did you find?"

"Nothing, so far," said Miles. He refused to allow the sinking feeling to overtake him again. "It was a false trail," he said, "but I'll keep trying."

"You went with Tau-Tau?" said Fabio. Miles nodded. It was on the tip of his tongue to tell Fabio about the Fir Bolg, but he was weary from his adventure and did not want to have to tell the entire story to the assembled company. Fabio did not ask him where they had gone, but instead he asked, "Did he come back with you?"

Miles suppressed a smile. "He'll be back anytime now," he said.

"He fell behind," laughed Little, and Fabio looked at her with curiosity in his hard black eyes.

A moment later the fortune-teller himself wandered in from the surrounding darkness and threw himself down on the nearest log with a theatrical groan. As no one paid him much attention, he groaned louder.

"I'm sure you're all wondering where I've been," he announced to the company in general.

"Well?" said Etoile politely.

"I've been tramping around the countryside, looking after young Miles and his little friend.

Excitable kids, could have got into a lot of trouble if I hadn't been watching over them. They fell back a little on the road home, but my second sight tells me they'll be along shortly. The pace was too . . ." At that moment he spotted Miles and Little, sitting quietly on the far side of the fire, and his voice trailed off in midsentence. He sat forward on the log and rubbed his eyes with the back of his hands. "Well, well," he said. "How did you . . . wait, don't tell me." He closed his eyes and placed his fingers to his temple, as though waiting for a telephone call from the world next door. "Yes, I see now. You took the shortcut. Ingenious, I must say."

"That's right," said Little. "We took the shortcut you suggested."

"Of course, of course," said Doctor Tau-Tau doubtfully. A grin lit up his face suddenly, and he waved his hand proudly in Little's direction. "What do you think of the Bearded Lady, eh?" he asked the assembled audience. "One of my many potent preparations, that is. A brilliant disguise for traveling around the countryside unnoticed, wouldn't you say?"

"I think I'd notice," said Umor.

"It all depends," said Fabio.

"On what?" said Umor.

"On whether she's traveling with a herd of minia-ture bear-weasels," suggested Gila.

"I never thought of that," said Umor.

"I'm going to bed," said Little, a yawn extending her matted beard.

"I'll walk with you," said Miles. They set off between the trailers, their way lit by the occasional lamp hanging from the eaves. Miles felt as though he could sleep for days. They reached the Toki sis-ters' wagon and sat on the step for a while, their breath fogging the air, until Little broke the silence. "Do you think they really would have eaten Doctor Tau-Tau?"

"I don't know," said Miles, "but I'm glad you got us out of there before they had a chance."

"It was lucky I came across that fox," said Little. She turned to Miles, and her clear blue eyes regarded him from the matted hair that sur-rounded them. "Remember when we heard the bees singing the flowers?" she said.

Miles nodded.

"The flowers would never open if they couldn't hear the bees," she said, "and the bees would starve without the flowers. The One Song has tied us together too, Miles. We can't look after each other if we keep secrets, can we?"

Miles shook his head. "I suppose not," he said.

The Circus Bolsillo, flagged, bagged, horse-shoed and hobnailed, meandered slowly southward in the weeks that followed Miles's encounter with the Fir Bolg. The frost began to thaw and the days to lengthen as the circus brought the spring to each town it visited. In fields and on village greens they pitched their big top, and every night they filled the tent with people, and the people filled the tent with laughter and gasps of wonder as Little's music and the genius of the brothers Bolsillo worked their peculiar magic. In the mornings, as they packed up their show to take to the road again, Miles would see that the spring in the air was matched by a new spring in the step of the people passing by, and he would smile to himself as he hosed down the elephants, or fed enormous steaks to the haughty lions.

There was little time in the bustling rhythm of his traveling life for Miles to discuss his visit to the Fir Bolg with anyone, but he turned the strange adventure over and over in his mind as he worked. Doctor Tau-Tau would say nothing more on the subject, and he became so despondent whenever Miles tried to bring it up that Miles would feel sorry for him, and let it drop. He wouldn't hear of Miles mentioning his meeting with the Great Cortado, pointing out only that the Bolsillo brothers had worked for Cortado at the Palace of Laughter for some time, a point with which Miles found it hard to argue.

The circus had not been raided again by the Fir Bolg since leaving Nape, and Miles wondered whether they were relying on him to find the Egg and fulfill his mother's promise, or simply living in fear of the stranger with the blinding light. He felt sure that the Bolsillo brothers knew more about the hairy little cavemen than they liked to admit, though he knew from experience that getting the brothers to talk could be like eating jelly with chopsticks.

On a fine spring afternoon Miles sat, weary from hard work and an early start, on the box seat of the Bolsillo brothers' wagon. Little sat beside him, humming to herself as she stitched sequins onto a new outfit with tiny, invisible stitches. She had indeed returned to her normal appearance, although it had taken longer than Doctor Tau-Tau had predicted. The hair had gradually fallen out in clumps, which had rolled around their various campsites and snagged themselves on corners and on ropes for several weeks, while Little herself had hidden away during the daylight hours, looking like a small yak with a severe molting problem.

Miles looked at Fabio, who sat on the far side of Little, talking and chucking softly to the horses. The little ringmaster's mood was always lightest when the tent was packed away and they were on the open road, and it seemed a good opportunity to try and wring some information out of him.

"Fabio," said Miles, "have you ever heard of the Fir Bolg?"

"Of course, Master Miles," said Fabio.

"Furry fellas, live in old stories," came Umor's voice from inside the wagon.

"Who's been telling you about them?" asked Fabio.

"I've met them," said Miles, "that time when I went off with Doctor Tau-Tau, and Little grew her beard."

"Is that so?" said Fabio, his gaze fixed on the road ahead.

"They kept us in a cave for two days," said Miles, "and they said they were going to eat Doctor Tau-Tau."

"Nobody could be *that* hungry," said Fabio.

"Probably just those hairy kids again, playing at

cavemen," said Umor.

"They let you go in the end, then," said Fabio.

"Little helped us escape," said Miles. "That's why she needed the Bearded Lady lotion."

The great cart horses plodded on, their hooves thumping a soft tattoo on the dusty road. Eventually Fabio spoke. "What did they want with you?"

"They were looking for a Tiger's Egg," said Miles. "Doctor Tau-Tau thought I had swallowed one."

There was a loud crash from inside the van. Fabio reined in the horses, and the wagon came to a halt. He turned to Miles, leaning forward in his seat. "That fool has been filling your head with nonsense," he said. "Tigers don't lay eggs."

"And chickens don't hunt antelope," said Umor from inside the wagon.

Fabio cracked the reins, and the wagon creaked as the horses ambled forward. He talked to them softly for a while. Little continued sewing, as though she had heard nothing. Miles sighed. The Bolsillo brothers' reaction made him almost certain that they had also heard of the Tiger's Egg, but he would have to choose his moment to find out what they knew. "There's something else that puzzles me," he said after a moment.

Fabio rolled his eyes, but he gave Miles a look of faint amusement. "Life is a puzzle, Master Miles," he said.

"And some of the important bits are lost under the sofa," said Umor.

"Why did you say 'well done' to me," said Miles, "after Dulac had his accident?"

"Because it was you who set him back on his feet," said Fabio.

"But I didn't do anything," said Miles. "I felt dizzy and had to sit down."

"You have the touch, Master Miles," said Fabio.

"Your mother left it to you," said Umor.

"Tau-Tau guessed it," said Fabio.

"Must be the only thing he's ever got right," chuckled Gila from inside the wagon.

"The boy's life had all but run out."

"You lent him some of your own."

"Which came as a surprise to us."

"And to you, it seems."

Miles thought about the feeling of hollowness that had come over him, as though he might have blown away like a dried leaf. It was not a very nice sensation, but with the Bolsillo brothers' explanation it seemed to make a certain sense. Little glanced up at him and smiled, then returned to her stitching. Miles leaned his head back against the painted wood of the wagon, and as the sun created swirling patterns on his closed eyelids he slipped into a light doze.

"Have you ever seen the sea, Master Miles?" said Fabio, his voice coming from somewhere far away.

Miles opened his eyes. It seemed as if he had awakened into a new world, and for a moment he could not remember where he was. The wagon had stopped on the crest of a hill and there, spread out before them, was the sea. It was still and broad and blue, and it stretched to the very edge of the world. On the far horizon lay a pale suggestion of a distant coast. Miles had seen the sea in pictures, but they could no more paint the vastness of the ocean than they could bring to him the salt tang that hung on the air, or the unfamiliar cries of the seabirds, urgent and wild, that set his heart beating faster. He sat up straight and took in a deep breath, and though he did not know it at the time, that breath of sea air filled him with a wanderlust that would be with him to the end of his days.

Below them the hills swept down to the clear blue waters, and there nestled the port of Fuera like a handful of sugar cubes emptied into the curve of the bay. In the port Miles could see the rust-colored sails of the schooners that came from the east, and the funnels of the steamships with their cargoes of coal and sugar and diamonds and silk. As the wagon started down the winding road that led toward the port, Miles looked at Little. Her sewing was forgotten and a smile lit her face as she gazed out on the ocean, and although the sky was no longer hers he thought he could see some of its boundless freedom reflected in her eyes.

CHAPTER SEVENTEEN

CHASING GHOSTS

Miles Wednesday, salt-lipped and sea-struck, drank in the smells and the sights of far-away places as he wandered with Little through the crowded market of Fuera. The tops of the schooner masts swayed gently above the surrounding roofs, and the palm-shaded square was packed with stalls selling goods that had arrived by sail or steam from every point of the compass. There were silks and spices, turtles and tea chests, macaws, monkeys and incense and pearls, rope, sailcloth and brass chandlery, coffee and cinnamon, oils and unctions and strange carvings of grimacing faces, knives and pots and enormous seashells that nature had decorated with the colors of a tropical sunrise. From the surrounding countryside, too, there were eggs, geese, buckets and barrels, salt meat and vegetables, and fresh fish landed that morning from the trawlers whose masters lived by the water's edge.

They passed a stall selling rough woven robes in white and cream, with embroidered cuffs and collars, and from the back of the stall a flash of red caught Miles's eye. A single crimson fez stood at the table's edge, and the stall holder, following Miles's eye, picked it up and placed it with a flourish on Miles's head. The hat sank slowly over his eyes. "It is big, young sheikh, but you will grow. Thirty shillings, my special price for you," said the man, his pointed beard wagging as he spoke.

"It's not for me," said Miles, "and I don't have nearly that much."

"It is of superior quality, and will last you a lifetime," said the stall holder, and he leaned forward as though imparting a valuable secret. His breath smelled of something sweet and spicy. "Because I like you, for you I give it for twenty shillings."

Miles removed the hat and shook his head. "I'll have to leave it, thank you," he said.

The stall holder threw up his hands. "Eighteen shillings, and I am robbing myself. Tell no one!" he said at the top of his voice.

Little took the hat from Miles and turned it in her hands. "It is a beautiful hat," she said as she handed it to the man. "You must be as clever as you are generous, but we really can't take it. It would not be right to give you so little money for this."

The stall holder looked at Little and his dark eyes softened. "You are right, little princess," he said at last. "It is too small a price, so instead I will make to you a present. Please take the fez. It is yours." He dropped a handful of sugar-dusted sweets into the hat, and handed it back to her with a bow.

"Thank you," said Little, and she popped a sweet into her cheek and handed one to Miles.

As they wandered on through the crowd they came across the Bolsillo brothers, arguing loudly with a bony man who sat in the center of a miniature city of wicker birdcages. The cages were filled with a screeching, scratching rainbow of brightly colored birds. There were parrots and macaws and cockatoos and budgerigars, and between them they kept up a riot of conversation in the borrowed tongues of men and birds, punctuated now and then by a deafening screech or a cackle of laughter.

"You bare-faced brigand!" Umor was saying to the man as they approached.

"That's five times what they are worth," said Fabio.

"And they're half starved," said Gila.

"We'll take them off your hands for four shillings apiece," said Fabio.

"You'll have five less beaks to feed," said Umor.

The bird seller threw back his head and laughed. No more than half his teeth remained in his head, and most of those were gold. "No no, my little friends," he chortled. "These magnificent birds were bred by the emperors of the Indus themselves. Each is more precious than the finest jewels, and they will talk like a harem on holiday."

While Gila and Umor haggled on over the birds, Fabio winked over his shoulder at Miles and Little. "All the animals fed and watered?" he asked. Miles nodded. "Time to feed ourselves, so," said Fabio.

They reached a price with the bird man and left him shaking his head with a woebegone expression, as though he had just sold his grandmother for a handful of seed. Gila carried a cage almost as large as himself, in which five bedraggled cockatoos shifted nervously on their perches. They found a sunlit courtyard filled with café tables, and Gila set the birds down in a shaded corner. The waiter seemed to know the Bolsillo brothers, and soon their table was filled with an assortment of rich spicy foods, clustered around a tall silver coffeepot.

The Bolsillo brothers were in a buoyant mood. There was to be no show that evening, and the three off-duty ringmasters became progressively merrier as Umor tipped brandy from a small hip flask into their thick black coffees. Gila produced his harmonica and played a tune that made everyone laugh. A pale moon rose in the evening sky, not content to wait until the sun had gone.

"You're very quiet, Master Miles," said Umor.

Fabio showed his pointed teeth in a smile. "Still chasing ghosts, I think," he said.

"Whose goats?" said Umor.

"Ghosts," said Fabio, pouring Miles a coffee. "He's chasing the ghost of his father."

"Ah, that ghost," said Umor.

"Bigger than most," said Gila. He had stopped playing his harmonica, though his tune seemed still to echo from the courtyard walls.

"That, and the ghost of a Tiger's Egg," said Fabio quietly.

"Does it really exist, the Tiger's Egg?" asked Miles.

"Who knows?" said Fabio. "Your mother brought with her a fine tiger when she joined Barty Fumble's Big Top, and rumor grows in the circus like mushrooms in a basement."

"My mother had a tiger too?" said Miles in surprise.

Fabio shook his head. "There was only one tiger," he said.

"Varippuli," said Gila, and Miles thought he saw him shudder slightly.

"The tiger joined the circus with Celeste," said Umor, "but it was Barty Fumble who showed him in the ring, and they gained a certain respect for each other."

"Where did my mother come from?" asked Miles. He had never known the Bolsillo brothers so willing to talk, and he wanted to learn as much as he could while their tongues were loosened.

"Celeste came from across the sea to the south," said Fabio.

"With a wagon full of books," said Umor.

"And the far eyes."

"And the healing hands."

"Too many gifts for one person to carry, perhaps," said Fabio.

The three men sat in silence for a while. A gecko crept up the wall behind Gila's head, and froze at the edge of a circle of lamplight, waiting for his dinner to land.

"She joined Barty Fumble the same month that we did," said Gila.

"And before long she had won his heart."

"Yeurgh!" said Umor.

"I'd rather win a gold watch," said Gila.

"Or a set of copper-bottomed saucepans," said Umor.

"People whispered that she had a Tiger's Egg," said Fabio, "but it was just a story."

"A tall story," said Gila.

"Not one of ours," said Umor.

"We only do short stories."

"The Fir Bolg believed in it," said Miles cautiously. "And Doctor Tau-Tau thought I had one because—" He paused, glanced at Little and took a deep breath. "Because I meet a tiger now and then, and he said that usually only happens when you own a Tiger's Egg."

The Bolsillo brothers fell silent, and Fabio's eyes narrowed.

"You meet a tiger?" he said.

Miles nodded. "I've spoken to him several times. We've even ridden on his back," he said. "Me and Little."

Fabio looked at Umor and raised his eyebrows. "A tiger that talks?" he said.

Umor shrugged. "Never heard of such a thing."

"Stressful thing, meeting a tiger," said Gila.

"Makes your imagination work overtime," said Umor.

Fabio stroked his chin. "Who else have you told about this?" he asked.

"Only Doctor Tau-Tau. It sort of slipped out, but I didn't think he would believe me anyway."

"Better you keep it to yourself, from now on, Master Miles," said Fabio.

"Button your lip," said Umor.

"Tie a knot in your tongue," added Gila.

Miles nodded. The gecko on the wall had caught a crane fly, whose trailing legs twitched as the lizard munched it with a pop-eyed stare that reminded Miles of Doctor Tau-Tau himself. The evening air was becoming chilly, and he thought about his warm bed, and the prospect of his first early night since leaving Partridge Manor.

"Maybe Celeste really did have a Tiger's Egg," said Little, "and that has something to do with Miles meeting this tiger."

Fabio shrugged. "Beats me," he said.

"It's not the kind of thing you ask of a lady," said Umor.

"Maybe it's just a big, furry pussycat," said Gila.

"In that case," said Miles, "I'll bring him to meet you next time, and you can give him a tin of cat food."

Gila showed his pointy teeth and chuckled, but his smile did not quite hide an anxious look as he poured another round of coffee.

CHAPTER EIGHTEEN

THUNDER AND EGGS

The Circus Bolsillo, steel-boned and canvas-skinned, remained in the port of Fuera for almost a week, filling the big top to bursting point every night, and twice on Saturday. It seemed that everyone from miles around saw the performance at least once, and some of them came two or three times. Miles and Little worked even harder than usual so that they could complete their tasks by midday and spend the afternoons exploring white-washed alleyways and shady courtyards, ending up at the bustling docks where whistling seamen trotted up and down gangplanks with bales and barrels on their shoulders, the weight bending the planks beneath their feet. By the week's end Miles and Little knew every corner of the town, and still they felt there were a thousand stories waiting to be told.

The weather broke as the circus packed to leave on the Sunday morning. Miles had been up since before daybreak, helping Gila to prepare the animals for the road, and lending a hand to the tent boys wherever he could. They could see the thunderclouds roll in as the deflated canvas lay flattened on the ground, and they worked with redoubled speed to pack the tent away before the rain. The first fat drops began to fall as the last of the folded canvas panels was stowed away in the truck and the circus people scurried about like ants over the vacated ground, checking that nothing had been overlooked.

Overhead the seagulls cried forlornly, wheeling like slender ghosts against the heavy clouds. Miles stood tall on the back of the tent truck and looked down toward the port. The schooner masts were swaying wildly in the gathering storm, and he could see the agile figures of the sailors who clambered around the rigging, making sure that every line was fast and the sails properly secured. He felt a sudden urge to grab Little's hand and run straight to the docks and up the gangplank of one of those stately schooners, just to see where chance and the restless winds would take them.

"Time to go, Master Miles," called Fabio, and Miles turned and jumped down from the truck.

"Someday we'll go sailing on one of those. What do you think?" he said to Tangerine, but what Tangerine thought we will never know, as he was hiding in Miles's pocket from the summer storm.

The Circus Bolsillo wound out of the port of Fuera like a multicolored snake, as the skies above split with blue lightning and a deafening downpour hammered on the wagon roofs and streamed from the broad backs of the cart horses, who lowered their heads and plodded at their usual steady pace along the muddy road.

Miles and Little sat with Umor and Gila in the Bolsillo brothers' wagon. The rain flung itself like gravel against the small windows and the china rattled in the cupboards as they jolted and swayed along the potholed highway. Gila played quietly on his harmonica, and something about his tune reminded Miles of the song that Fuat had sung as they made their way through the great cavern to see the Shriveled Fella. He thought of the Fir Bolg, scratching a living in the darkness and yearning for the return of the Tiger's Egg that his own mother had borrowed from them.

"Did the Fir Bolg always live underground?" he asked Little. He leaned close to her to be heard over the din of the rain and the ceaseless rumble of thunder.

"I don't know," said Little. "I didn't ask them that sort of thing. I was mainly trying to find out where they were keeping you, and when they would sleep."

"The stories say that the Fir Bolg once ruled this land from sea to ocean," shouted Umor, whose sharp ears could hear a gnat's burp in a bell factory.

"They fought a great battle with the people who came from the east, and most were killed or driven into the sea."

"But some took to the hills and hid in the caves there."

"The smaller fellas fared better."

"And the hairier ones stayed warmer."

"And the smallest, hairiest ones were the badger's bootlaces altogether."

"At least that's what the stories tell us."

"But how did Celeste come to borrow the Tiger's Egg from them?" asked Miles.

"Speaking of eggs," shouted Umor, "it's way past breakfast time."

"My guts are rumbling like thunder," said Gila.

"I suppose you're making all that lightning too," said Umor, taking down a frying pan from its hook on the ceiling. "Carve up some of that bread, Master Miles, and don't lose hold of any fingers."

Miles carved thick slices from a loaf of bread while a clutch of eggs sizzled and spat in Umor's frying pan.

"Did my mother ever mention the Tiger's Egg to you?" asked Miles.

Gila took down a stack of plates and dealt them onto the table with a clatter, like round playing cards. Umor deftly flipped an egg onto each one, and Little piled the bread that Miles had cut into the basket in the center of the table.

"Celeste had great powers of healing," said Umor.

"And she could read the future like the morning papers," said Gila.

"Some said that her powers were greatly enhanced by a Tiger's Egg."

"She never told us, Master Miles."

"And we never asked."

"She did say that her grandmother had the far eye."

"And her mother could heal the knots out of wood."

"Are they still alive?" asked Miles. Finding out about his parents was something that had occupied his mind a great deal in the months since he had first met the Bolsillo brothers, but he had not even begun to think about the possibility that he might also have grandparents, aunts and uncles.

"Nobody knows, Master Miles."

"Celeste never returned to her home."

"There was a falling out, I think," said Umor, "though I only heard her speak of it once."

"She did have a twin sister who used to visit once a year," said Gila.

"But after Celeste died she never came again," said Umor.

"A twin sister? How come you never told me that?" asked Miles, though he knew what the answer would be before the question had left his mouth.

"You never asked," said Umor simply.

Miles sat down to his breakfast, his mind racing. Somewhere in the world there was a woman who could help fill in the blank space in Celeste's photograph, who might share her laugh or the gleam in her eye, and who knew her heart perhaps better than anyone. He did not think to wonder why his mother's relatives had never returned to rescue him from Pinchbucket House. He had grown up there with many other orphans who had been forgotten or abandoned by their families, and as far as Miles was concerned there was nothing unusual about that.

He thought over the things he knew and tried to fit them together in a way that made sense, and if you have ever tried to assemble a jigsaw puzzle wearing mittens, with half of the pieces missing and your head in a paper bag, you will have some idea of how frustrating a task it was. He knew that his mother had died and that his father had left soon afterward. He also knew that Celeste was rumored to have borrowed a Tiger's Egg from the Fir Bolg, and that this stone, if it had ever existed, had not been seen since Barty Fumble's disappearance. His parents had had the friendship of a tiger named Varippuli, who had been shot by the Great Cortado after Barty left, and a tiger had walked uninvited into Miles's own life less than a year before. But why had his father left him behind? Had he taken the Tiger's Egg with him, and if so, why had he not returned it to the Fir Bolg? What was the deal that his mother had struck with the hairy little people?

"If I can find the Tiger's Egg," he said aloud,

"then maybe I can find my father. Or if I can find my father, maybe I will find the Egg."

"What you might call a father and egg situation," said Gila.

Umor shook his head sadly. "You heard what Fabio said. Your father is dead and gone, Master Miles, and you have a life to live."

"Your shoes are pointing forward and your face to the past," said Gila.

"You need to turn around," shouted Umor, "before we tie your shoelaces together."

"That's all very well," said Miles, "but the past kept me in a cave for two days, and still thinks I owe it a tiger's soul."

A deafening crash of thunder sounded overhead, and the inside of the wagon was lit with a blinding light. The Bolsillo brothers winced, and Little got up to look out of the window. "There's trouble in the Realm," she said, and she shook her head. "I hope Silverpoint isn't at the hard end of it."

"I hope he puts a sock in it soon," muttered Gila, but his words were lost in the noise of the storm.

CHAPTER NINETEEN

HORACE AND PAGI

The Circus Bolsillo, tusked, top-hatted and belching fire, wound its way along the summer coast, tracing a route that circuses have followed since your grandfather's grandfather was a child. They stopped at Whelk and Carrig and Twelve Bells, and though Miles could not get enough of the sea, none of these towns left such an imprint on his heart as the port of Fuera. He learned about every aspect of the show, until he knew each animal's favorite treat and every performer's likes and dislikes and every nut and pulley of the mighty tent's skeleton. He knew how to cure a sick parrot and fix the ticket machine and clip a lion's claws and check the trapezes, and how to take care of a hundred other details that made the difference between a circus and a shambles. The sun darkened his skin and hard work made him wiry and strong and popular with everyone, until Gila commented that if he could double in size and grow a beard he would be Barty Fumble himself. Miles pretended to laugh the comment off, but inside it made him light with pride.

By the time they left the coast and turned northward again, Miles and Little were so at home in the circus that they felt as if they had spent their whole lives on the road. Fabio showed them how to juggle and Umor taught them to cook. By night Miles stood against a wooden board painted with his own silhouette while Stranski—crusty and mute—flung knives at his outline with deadly accuracy, and Hector the monkey picked wallets from the pockets of unsuspecting punters. Afterward he climbed into the star-painted box and the audience gasped as he was neatly sawed in half, and Miles himself was still surprised, by the end of every act, to find that his legs were still his own. Little danced like thistledown on the high wire, and flew through the air with such grace that it would be easy to believe her strapped-on wings were real if you had never seen the shimmering pair she had lost. In the daytime she seemed to be everywhere at once, and the music she made sweetened the circus like honey in warm milk, though not a note of it could be written on paper.

They passed through Hamba and Shelduck and Sevenbridge, following the river Volte upstream, and turned west (somewhat to Miles's relief) before it could bring them to the city of Smelt. The strange caravan made its way back along the road by which the tiger had brought Miles and Little to the Palace of Laughter the previous autumn, and one hot afternoon, as the apples ripened in the orchard, they saw ahead of them the town of Cnoc perched on its round hill.

"That's where old Baltinglass lives, isn't it?" said Gila, who was driving the wagon while Fabio took a siesta inside.

Miles nodded, shading his eyes to search for Baltinglass's house among the jumble of red roofs that covered the crown of the hill. He hoped to surprise his old friend by turning up on his doorstep unannounced, although he knew from experience that surprising the blind explorer was not nearly as easy as it sounded. "I'd like to visit him while we're here," he said.

"Better still," said Umor, "you can invite him to the show."

"I don't know if he'd want to come," said Miles, "not being able to see the acts."

"He might enjoy the music," said Little.

"No doubt about it," said Umor.

"We'll find him a seat behind a pillar," said Gila.

The tent boys had already started unpacking the big top into an empty pasture at the edge of town as Miles and Little walked up the winding road toward Baltinglass of Araby's whitewashed house.

They reached the hobnailed door and Miles pulled the bell rope, bringing the jangle of pots and pans from somewhere inside the house. They heard the thump, thump, thump of a walking stick on a terra-cotta floor, then the door flew open and Baltinglass's wrinkled face was thrust through the gap, his eyes staring out into eternal fog from under his black knitted hat.

"Well?" he shouted before Miles or Little could say a word. "Whatever it is, I've already got half a dozen of 'em, and they bring me out in hives. Come back Tuesday when I'm feeding the crocodiles. They'll be needing something to chew on." He reached out and made a quick low swipe with his stick as he spoke. Little jumped nimbly over the cane, but Miles was not quick enough to avoid a crack on the ankle. "Ouch!" he said.

A toothless grin split Baltinglass's wrinkled face. "Master Miles!" he said in delight. "Why didn't you say? You've grown half a head taller by the sound of it, unless you're wearing high heels. No doubt you have Little with you, but she's too quick for me, eh?"

"Hello, Mr. Baltinglass," laughed Little. "Can we come in?"

"Do that thing," said the old man. "Doorstep's no place for a powwow." He flung the door wide and waved his stick dangerously in the air to usher them inside. The house was cool and semidark as usual. Carved faces grimaced from the walls, and blades of every shape and variety glinted between them. Baltinglass led them along the hallway and into the living room. "What brings you to an old nomad's doorstep on an autumn afternoon?" he barked.

"We were passing through," said Miles. "We've been on the road with the Circus Bolsillo all summer."

"Ah, the circus!" said Baltinglass. "That explains the grunting of wildebeest that I heard in the wee hours. Thought the river madness was coming back to me."

"But the circus doesn't ha—," began Little, but

Miles nudged her and put his finger to his lips.

"Did you ever finish making your apple jelly?" asked Miles, as Baltinglass flung open the French windows.

"There was no point," barked Baltinglass. "It was too late for that batch. I went off gallivanting with Gertrude Partridge at a crucial moment, and when I got back the whole batch was fizzing in the sun. Gave it to old Julio for his pigs. They were drunk for a month, and now they all call me Uncle. Least they would if they could talk."

"I doubt it," whispered Little in Miles's ear. "Pigs call everyone 'Mum.'"

"Anyway, these blasted crocodiles have kept me too busy to be thinking about apple jelly." They had emerged into Baltinglass's sunlit garden, and he headed for a wooden bench that sat in the dappled shade of an apple tree. The old man reached out for the arm of the bench, and when he found it he sat down with a sigh, propping his cane beside him.

"What crocodiles?" asked Miles with interest.

"Those ones," said Baltinglass, picking up his stick and waving it over his shoulder. "Horace and Pagi. Hungry devils, and you have to keep your wits about you when you're feeding them. Their favorite food is thumbs."

Miles got up from the bench and looked in the direction that Baltinglass had indicated. There was a freshly dug pond at the edge of the garden, and half submerged in the pond was a cage of bamboo, lashed together with an assortment of different-colored string. He could see no sign of any crocodiles.

"Probably underwater," said Baltinglass without turning around.

"Where did you get them?" asked Miles.

"They were a present from the sultan of Abyssinia on his golden jubilee. I once helped him out with a small camel problem, but that was back when I had eyes and teeth. In any case he never forgot the favor."

"They don't have a lot of room in that cage," said Little.

"'Course they don't!" said Baltinglass. "That's why they need to be taken to the circus. You've got crocs in that outfit, haven't you?"

"We have," said Miles, "but they live in cages too."

"Ah," said Baltinglass, "what's a few bars when you're on the road? In the circus they'll get to see a bit of the world. Broaden their scaly little minds. If people would pay to see me rear up and snap my jaws I'd put *myself* in a cage and join the circus faster than a lizard's lick."

"That reminds me," said Miles, "the Bolsillo brothers asked me to invite you to tonight's show. If you'd like to come, that is."

"Count me in, Master Miles," shouted Baltinglass. "The song of the trapeze! The swish of the popcorn! The smell of the hurdy-gurdy!" He got to his feet and pointed his walking stick more or less in Miles's direction. "How about a spot of lunch first? I'm sure I've got a jar of whelks gathering dust somewhere."

"Thanks," said Miles, "but we have to get back. There's a lot of work to be done before the show."

"Off you go then," said Baltinglass. "Ask your masters if two enraged reptiles will cover the price of admission, and you can come back later with your crocodile handler and a cart." He set off with a purposeful stride toward the house. "You can let yourselves out, eh?" he called over his shoulder. "The door is where we left it, I suspect, and the sooner you go the earlier you'll be back."

Baltinglass of Araby, white-caned and milk-eyed, marched down the center of the road, his stout cane knocking obstacles out of the way rather than directing him around them. He headed a procession that brought the people of Cnoc out of their windows to stare with open curiosity. Behind the blind explorer came a cart that was pulled by Tembo the elephant, and on it was a cage from which the two crocodiles, Horace and Pagi, leered with their crooked grins and slow yellow eyes. On either side walked Gina and Jules, the crocodile handlers, and Miles and Little brought up the rear, handing circus flyers to the mesmerized spectators.

By nightfall the big top had been raised, anchored, checked and checked again. The banked seats were filling up with the people of Cnoc, as the Circus Bolsillo's thousand lights flickered on and the band began to warm up their instruments. Baltinglass of Araby had installed himself in a ring-side seat, where he sat cracking his knuckles as though readying himself to take on a lion or two if the need arose. Behind the starry curtain the Zipplethorpe family made final adjustments to the tack of their horses, who stamped and snorted nervously as they waited to open the show.

The band struck up with a fanfare, and Fabio Bolsillo boomed his introduction through an enormous megaphone as the Zipplethorpes galloped into the ring and the night's entertainment began. Miles was kept busy backstage, helping the tent boys with a well-rehearsed routine that was now second nature to him, and left him little time to worry about his upcoming performance with Stranski the Magician. Before he knew it the second half had begun, and he was helping Hector the monkey into his little waistcoat with the secret pocket, while Countess Fontainbleau and her lions held the audience in thrall.

Miles gave Tangerine a quick squeeze for luck as he prepared the props for his performance with Stranski. A strange feeling came over him as he waited for the knife thrower to stride in through the tent flaps. It was a feeling he had had before, that everything he could see and hear had happened already in precisely the same way. He knew from Lady Partridge's encyclopedia that this feeling was called déjà vu. He closed Stranski's star-painted box with a snap that sounded like an echo of itself, and at that moment Perseus the lion emerged from the ring and into the tunnel of netting that led to his cage outside. The lion glanced at Miles, as he knew it would, in a way that seemed to say "we've been here before, haven't we." A trumpet squealed and a man's loud cheer rose above the crowd, and he was sure he had heard the same squeal and the same cheer on another night just like this one.

The sensation grew stronger as he stood against the board in the floodlit ring, feeling the swish of air from the knives as they thumped into the painted wood on either side of him. The knives thumped into the same board almost every night, but that did not explain it. Even Baltinglass of Araby, who had never been to the show before, seemed to have sat forever in that same seat at the ringside.

As he climbed into the star-painted box and Stranski locked the enormous padlock, Miles became convinced that if he just concentrated a little harder he could make the echo in his mind pull ahead of what was happening around him, and he would know what was going to happen next. It was a strange feeling, like perching on the edge of a high platform, waiting for the trapeze to reach him. The roar of the saw began, and he pulled his knees tightly to his chest. As he did so he grasped at the slippery images in his mind, and in a sudden flash he knew what he was about to see. Seated in the semidarkness, behind and above the snowy figure of the blind explorer, would be a man who looked disturbingly familiar. He peered past Stranski's polished head into the gloom, his stomach tightening, and sure enough the man was exactly where Miles expected to find him. He was staring at Miles intensely from deep-set gray eyes, and with his stubby nose and blue chin he looked for all the world like the Great Cortado, but without the fabulous mustache to cover up his mean little mouth.

CHAPTER TWENTY

A BETTER MAP

Miles Wednesday, spotlit and box-locked, lay trapped as Stranski's saw rattled and coughed through the fresh plywood. He knew that any movement he made might be his last, ingenious though Stranski's contraption might be, and he could not have felt more helpless. His view of the man in the audience was blocked now by Stranski himself, who stood in front of him and sawed like a demon. Stranski glowered at Miles with a deeper frown than usual, and Miles tried to relax his muscles as he had been taught, but with little success. When Stranski wheeled the box halves apart and stepped to one side there was only an empty seat where the blue-chinned man had been.

"Are you sure it was him?" said Little when he told her afterward.

Miles shook his head. "It was hard to tell without the mustache. It's not that I could see him very well, it's just . . ." He searched for the right words.

"What is it just?" asked Little, folding her goose-feather wings carefully and putting them away in the cloth bag that Delia Zipplethorpe had made for them.

"I felt like I already knew he would be there. Like I'd lived the whole thing before, or dreamed it."

"Then you probably did," said Little.

"I don't remember dreaming about it. It just all seemed so familiar when it happened."

"What do you think he was doing here, if it was him?" asked Little.

"I don't know," said Miles, "but I'm sure Tau-Tau does, and I intend to ask him as soon as I get a chance."

The sound of applause and a strangely muscular music drifted across from the big top. "That's K2," said Little. "They'll be finishing up soon."

"We'd better get back over," said Miles. "I told Baltinglass I'd collect him after the show."

The evening was warm and filled with the chirping of crickets. Moths spun dizzily around the light-bulbs, and the monkeys chattered softly in their cage. Gina smiled at Miles and Little as she passed them, stepping carefully over the uneven ground in her stiletto heels. She led a pair of ostriches on long gold ribbons. They looked as though they were imitating her walk. The flaps on the big top were pulled back, and the people began to stream out into the night. Miles and Little slipped in against the tide, keeping a sharp eye out for anyone who looked like a clean-shaven Cortado, but they found only Baltinglass of Araby waiting for them in his ringside seat, a broad grin on his face and crumbs of popcorn on his shirt.

"A spectacular spectacle!" barked Baltinglass. "An excellent extravaganza! I could see what was happening just by listening to the music, and not a cranium hit the ground from start to finish." He grasped his cane and levered himself out of his seat. "What happens next, Master Miles?"

"Supper happens next," said Miles, "once the last few things have been stowed away and Umor has a good fire going."

They made their way toward the open space in the midst of the trailers where Umor was preparing supper. As they rounded the corner of the Toki

sisters' wagon, Doctor Tau-Tau appeared, muttering
to himself as had become his habit, the fez that
Little had given him perched on his cotton-candy
hair. He tripped over Baltinglass's cane and would
have fallen headlong in the grass if Miles had not
reached out and steadied him.

"Lucifer's laundry!" spluttered the fortune-teller.
"Watch what you're doing with that stick. Are you
blind?"

"Of course I am!" shouted Baltinglass. "Are you?"

"Don't be ridiculous!" huffed Doctor Tau-Tau,
straightening his fez. "I happen to be gifted with a
second sight so powerful that it sometimes inter-
feres with my first."

Baltinglass snorted. "What did I have for breakfast then, Mystic Ming?"

"Bacon, eggs and mushrooms, a pile of toast and
a bucket of strong tea," said Tau-Tau without hesita-
tion.

"Lucky guess!" barked Baltinglass. "What's my
mother's maiden name?"

Doctor Tau-Tau stared closely at Baltinglass's
wrinkled face. He closed his eyes and rubbed his
temples in a circular motion with his fingertips.
"Begins with C . . . ," he muttered. "Curt . . . Cuss . . .
it's coming to me from a great distance. . . ." His eyes

snapped open suddenly. "Cousteau!" he said. "It's Cousteau, isn't it?"

"How should I know?" said Baltinglass. "I can barely remember my own name on a good day." He made a sweep with his cane before resuming his path, and Doctor Tau-Tau had to skip back to avoid having his shins rapped. Baltinglass took one step forward, then he stopped dead as though he had run into an invisible tree. His eyebrows shot up and disappeared into his woolly hat. "Well, tilt me backward!" he exclaimed. "It *was* Cousteau. Elisabeth Lucy Cousteau was my mother's full name. It's just come back to me like a siren in the fog." He turned toward the fortune-teller. "I've never had much time for mumbo jumbo," he barked, "but your mumbo jumbo seems to be of superior quality. Maybe you should give me the entire package."

"Ah, well," said Doctor Tau-Tau, eyeing Baltinglass's cane nervously, "a bit busy this evening, you know. Perhaps another time. . . ."

"Busy?" shouted Baltinglass. "What's the matter—you have to wash your hair?" He turned to Miles. "I don't smell any supper yet, Master Miles. Do we have time for some mumbo jumbo first?"

"We certainly do," said Miles. He was keen to know how Doctor Tau-Tau had plucked Baltinglass's mother's name from the air, and the fortune-teller's reluctance to continue only made him more curious.

"Yes, well . . . if you insist," said Doctor Tau-Tau doubtfully. "If you'd like to follow me, I will see if my bird is prepared."

"What's that?" shouted Baltinglass, his hand cupped behind his good ear. "What do you do, pluck the fortune out of a roast turkey?"

"She's not a turkey," said Miles. "She's a Java sparrow. She picks out a card and Doctor Tau-Tau reads your fortune from it."

"Is that so?" said Baltinglass. "With any luck I'll get the queen of hearts. Not that luck has paid much attention to me so far. I've been struck by lightning twice, and I haven't seen a blue sky or a plump barmaid in thirty years."

Miles led Baltinglass up the stairs of Tau-Tau's wagon, as the fortune-teller fumbled with his oracle cards and lit his incense with a shaking hand. "Come in, come in," said Tau-Tau grandly, as though the invitation had been given freely in the first place.

Miles and Little sat themselves on the end of Doctor Tau-Tau's bunk and watched as he lifted his birdcage down from the top of the cupboard and placed it in front of the red and gold envelopes that were spread out on the circular table. The small bird hopped from her cage and along the row of overlapping envelopes. She pulled one out with her beak and hopped onto Doctor Tau-Tau's waiting hand. "Well done, Satu," said Tau-Tau quietly. While the bird ate colored seeds from his palm he shook the card from the envelope with his other hand and held it up in front of him.

Doctor Tau-Tau peered at the card in the dim red light. "Mmm-hmm," he said, sounding more like a dentist looking at a cavity than an interpreter of hidden meanings. He put the card down on the table and rubbed his temples with his fingertips. Baltinglass drummed his fingers on the arm of the chair. "I see mountains," said Tau-Tau eventually. "There is a town . . . no, a village in their shadow. White houses. Red roofs. There are three poplar trees on the edge of town, and beside them a small house. There are little girls, several of them, playing around the house. I see, wait a minute. . . ." His voice trailed off as though he were a radio going out of tune, then came back a moment later. "I see an enormous pig, with a small boy sitting on his back. A boy with bare feet . . ."

"Rosie!" interrupted Baltinglass, in a quieter voice than usual. Miles gave Little a puzzled look, and she shrugged. Doctor Tau-Tau was massaging his temples again.

"Rosie was a fine pig," said Baltinglass. His stared past the fortune-teller, his blind eyes fixed on the past. "Wiser than many a person I knew. She had eight litters of eight. Sixty-four children in all, and enough grandchildren to crew an ocean liner. She died a natural death and was buried under the poplars, which was unusual for a pig, as they have the misfortune to be made of rashers." He sighed deeply, and scratched the back of his head. "A fancy trick," he bellowed at Doctor Tau-Tau, "and I haven't the foggiest notion how you did it, but I already know about my barefoot, pig-riding past. What's on the road ahead for these restless old bones, eh? Can you do that one?"

"Patience," said Tau-Tau. "The veil of truth is not . . ."

"Patience is overrated," shouted Baltinglass. "There's no point asking about the future if I'm going to spend it sitting in this armchair while your second sight looks for its glasses."

"I . . . see a journey—," Doctor Tau-Tau began hastily.

"Long one?" interrupted Baltinglass.

"Yes," said Tau-Tau, fiddling with the sleeves of

his silk dressing gown. "Very long. With camels, or maybe horses. And wait a moment . . . I see . . ." He glanced sideways at Miles, then quickly returned his gaze to Baltinglass's wrinkled face. "I see another large animal. Perhaps . . . a tiger," he said.

Baltinglass snorted. "You're living in a circus, man. You'd have to be blindfolded not to see large animals. And there are no tigers here—those are lions. Totally different smell." He took a pipe from one pocket and a worn leather pouch from the other, and began to tug strings of tobacco from the pouch and cram them into the bowl of the pipe. "You should stick to the past," he shouted, as he rummaged in his pocket for matches. "You seem to have a better map for that."

Doctor Tau-Tau's face turned a deeper shade of red, and his eyes bulged. He scooped the red and gold envelopes from the circular table angrily and stacked them in a pile. Miles half expected to see steam coming out of his ears.

"In the land of my birth," he said heatedly, "our childhood companions were tigers, not pigs. Perhaps *you* should stick to what you are familiar with."

Baltinglass of Araby sat up straight in the armchair. His ropy neck extended from his old sweater until it was twice its usual length, and his blind eyes stared straight at the fuming fortune-teller.

"And what land might that be?" he asked.

Doctor Tau-Tau cleared his throat nervously and straightened his fez. "It's nowhere you'll have heard of," he said.

"No place has been planted on this earth that I haven't heard of," said Baltinglass. "And I've bunked or bartered in two-thirds of them. Try me."

"Ma . . . Malabar," said Tau-Tau. "I was born in Malabar."

"You told me it began with a 'Z,'" said Miles, "the place where you came from."

Doctor Tau-Tau's face took on a hunted look. "That's right," he said. "Zanzibar, I meant. It was Zanzibar."

"Ha!" barked Baltinglass. "Malabar, Zanzibar. You sure it wasn't Hotel Bar?"

"It was a long time ago," said Tau-Tau weakly. "I don't remember being born."

Baltinglass of Araby turned his head slightly. He seemed to be listening intently. "Say that again," he shouted.

"Say what?" said the fortune-teller. "I don't remember being born?"

"Borrrn," mimicked Baltinglass. "Let me tell you

something, Doctor Tea Towel. I've traveled the length and breadth of this country and many others besides, and I know every dialect there is. I don't know what kind of accent you've tried to paste on over your own, but it's been bothering me since you fell over my stick, and now I know why. I can hear what's hiding underneath it."

Doctor Tau-Tau stumbled to his feet and picked up the birdcage. "Well," he said hastily, stretching up to replace it on top of the cupboard. "I don't know about you, but I'm hungry." He turned to Miles and Little and attempted a smile. "We'd better get ourselves out to that fire before all the supper is eaten, don't you think?"

Baltinglass slammed his cane on the table, making everyone jump. "I may look like an old blind fool," he bellowed, "but I'm only old and blind. I know how you could describe my childhood home. You were born within spitting distance of it yourself. That's a Grubwater accent if ever I heard one, and for the first ten years of my life I heard nothing else. You're a fraud, Tau-Tau, and if I still had my eyes I'd have your proper name pinned on you before you could lace up your boots."

CHAPTER TWENTY-ONE

CELESTE'S APPRENTICE

Doctor Tau-Tau, unmasked and aghast, sat down heavily in his chair as though some of the air had been let out of him. "That was a long time ago," he said quietly, "and a different life. I suppose you're going to march out there now and tell everyone."

"And what if I do?" said Baltinglass. "Will the stars stop spinning overhead?"

"For you, no," said Tau-Tau. "But for Doctor Tau-Tau they will. It has taken me many years to change my appearance and create a new life for myself, and I don't believe anyone would recognize me now, though I keep a low profile when I'm nearer to home. Who would want their future revealed by Noel Dank of Grubwater New Street?"

"Dank," said Baltinglass to himself, "of Dank Haberdashers and Discontinued Items? Next to the undertakers on the corner?"

Doctor Tau-Tau nodded, evidently forgetting that Baltinglass couldn't see him. The blind explorer puffed on his pipe for a minute, a frown of concentration on his face. "Then you must be old Phelim's youngest boy. The chubby kid. If I remember rightly he was grooming you to take over the business. How did you come to be a roving swindler instead? Did you buy a kit?"

"I am a leading clairvoyant and a healer of note," said Doctor Tau-Tau, taking on some air again. "Fate apprenticed me to this boy's mother, who had a fine reputation in the divining arts."

Baltinglass of Araby turned toward Miles. "You hear that, Master Miles?" he shouted. "If this fraud is besmirching your mother's good name I'll be glad to give him a taste of my sword stick on your behalf. Just say the word."

"It's true, I think," said Miles. "I don't know a lot about my mother. She died when I was born."

"Well that's a damn shame!" said Baltinglass. He turned back and jabbed his cane in Doctor Tau-Tau's direction, almost poking him in the eye. "I trust you've painted the lad a true portrait of his mother, whom he never had the good fortune to meet."

"Yes, yes, I'm sure I have," said Tau-Tau.

"No you haven't," said Miles. "I don't even know what she looked like."

"Ah, really?" said Doctor Tau-Tau. He got up and lit the stove under his copper kettle. The smell of masala tea filled the air, and he breathed in deeply. "That smell always reminds me of the first time I met Celeste, in this very wagon as it happens."

Miles sat forward on the bunk. He tried to picture his mother sitting on the upholstered stool that now creaked under the bulk of Doctor Tau-Tau, while his father's laugh boomed out from somewhere else in the camp. He could almost feel Celeste's presence, dark and serene, but her face was beyond his imagination's grasp.

"Did you come to have your fortune told?" Miles asked.

"Not exactly," said Tau-Tau. "I was working for the tax office at the time, and with my natural diligence I had risen swiftly to be head of my department. When the circus came to town I was sent to make an undercover investigation into how much cash was changing hands, especially through these sideshows. I suspected they were not paying a fraction of the tax they should have been."

"So you were a tax collector before you became a fraud!" shouted Baltinglass. "I see what you mean about rising up the career ladder."

"What was my mother like?" asked Miles.

"Celeste," said Doctor Tau-Tau, pouring the masala tea into small china cups, "was not what I imagined. I expected big gold earrings and a knotted scarf, all those trappings, but she wore a plain white dress and a necklace of shells. She had no crystal ball, just an incense burner and a silver pot of this fragrant tea on the table before her. Her hair was very dark, I remember, but try as I might I can't bring her face to mind, though I knew her for several years after that first meeting."

"Did she tell your fortune?" asked Little.

"That she did, and I was astonished at her insight. She spotted right away that I was an uncommon man, and within moments she had outlined my various strengths more accurately than I could have done myself. She seemed almost amused that I should feel the need to come and see her at all."

Baltinglass snorted, but his head was nodding and Miles could not tell if the snort was a comment on Tau-Tau's story or the beginning of a snore.

"Then she must have seen the real reason you were there," said Miles.

"Ah," said Doctor Tau-Tau, leaning across to hand him a cup of tea. "I have no doubt that she would have rumbled a less-experienced investigator in an instant, but I was an expert at undercover work. I had perfected a way of making my mind a blank in order to make my cover more convincing." He leaned over again and handed a cup to Little, then he placed his fingertips to his temples. His eyes bulged dramatically. "It's like a wall of iron inside my mind. My profession was an unknown quantity to her. She said so herself, and she was certainly no amateur. She said she could see in me the makings of a great clairvoyant."

"Then you were able to find out what she charged?" asked Little.

Doctor Tau-Tau sat back on his stool. "That was the strange thing," he said. "She told me she never charged a single penny for her services. That came as a great surprise to me, and in fact it even came as news to her husband, who had just barged into the wagon to get something at the moment she revealed this startling fact. I could see that she must have kept it a secret from him as well."

Miles thought about this for a moment, and

smiled to himself. It was the same smile that always crept across his face when he came across a clever plan, a smile he had inherited from Celeste, though he did not know it. Indeed it was the very one she had worn as she told the tax investigator that she had no interest in money all those years ago.

"How did you become her apprentice?" asked Little.

"That happened in the years that followed," said Doctor Tau-Tau. A long, rumbling snore escaped from Baltinglass's wrinkled lips, and Tau-Tau had to raise his voice to be heard above the noise. "I returned to my work, but I could not get Celeste off my mind. The power of her uncanny insight remained fresh in my memory, and by the time the circus came again I had made up my mind where my true path lay. I went to see Celeste once more, and asked her to teach me everything she knew about second sight and the healing arts. She refused outright at first, but eventually she realized, I suppose, that it was pointless trying to ignore my latent powers, and that at least she could be the one who set me on the path to greatness. Alas, I was not apprenticed to her for long. When she died I had only completed my initial training, which consisted of learning to care for her horse and to repaint her wagon. Still, one can't mope forever, and her death only increased the need for my talents. I took the name of Doctor Tau-Tau from a previous life that I had lived on the island of Sulawesi, and took her place at the Circus Oscuro. Since Barty Fumble's mind had snapped like a twig and the baby . . . and you were just a baby, it fell to me to inherit her diaries. With the help of these I continued my studies."

"But then you lost them," said Miles.

"Alas, yes," said Doctor Tau-Tau. His voice dropped to a whisper, and he looked over his shoulder as if someone might be lurking outside the window. "Such was the Great Cortado's murderous rage that I fled the circus with nothing but the clothes I stood up in. The diaries had been handed down through Celeste's family and contained the knowledge of generations, and their loss was a great tragedy to me. In the course of my long travels I sought to collect again as much of that knowledge as I could, and I dared to hope that someday I would return and find the diaries safe in the trunk where I had left them." He sighed deeply. "It was a forlorn hope. I have never found a trace of them since."

Miles opened his mouth to ask Doctor Tau-Tau about his sighting of the Great Cortado in the circus audience, but before he could say anything

Baltinglass's eyes snapped open. "And if you do find those diaries," barked the explorer, "they belong to the boy, and don't you forget it, or you'll be Noel Dank the ex-taxman again before you can swallow twice." He planted his cane in the blood-red carpet and hauled himself to his feet. "Now what about that supper?" he said. "Something out there smells sweet as a nut, and if we don't get moving quickly these old teeth might just jump out of my mouth and go without me."

CHAPTER TWENTY-TWO
SHAKY GUANO

Baltinglass of Araby, fortified and unfooled, sat by the fire and mopped up the last of his gravy with a chunk of bread. When his plate was clean he belched contentedly and rummaged in his pocket for his pipe. "I've feasted with moguls and supped with sovereigns," he announced to anyone who would listen, "and I can't remember having a better feed than that one. My compliments to the chef, and may his pot never cool."

"My pleasure," said Gila.

"I'm the chef!" said Umor. "You can't even cook."

"True, but I can accept a compliment," said Gila. "You stick to what you're good at and I'll do the rest."

"Where we come from," said Fabio, "a fine meal calls out for a good tale."

"Not sure I can help you there," said Baltinglass. "The stories crawl around my head like maggots in an apple, but they've been jumbled up in there so long they've all swallowed each other's tails, and separating one from the next would be tricky work."

"Let them all out!" said Umor.

"We'll round them up if they get out of hand," said Fabio.

Miles thought about the yellowed newspaper clippings on Baltinglass's wall, and all the wealth of stories that must be hidden behind them. There was Baltinglass at the mouth of the emperor's tomb, Baltinglass perched in the rigging of a schooner, Baltinglass shaking hands with a dignified man with a long pointed beard. There was one small faded photo that had intrigued Miles the most. It showed a much younger Baltinglass standing at the foot of an enormous tree, soaked to the skin and with his left leg heavily bandaged. His face wore an odd grimace, but what really aroused Miles's curiosity was the bizarre hat perched on the young explorer's head.

"Tell us the one about the hat with the spike," said Miles.

Baltinglass turned sharply to Miles. "What hat?" he said. "What spike?"

"There's a picture on your wall," said Miles. "It shows you standing by a tree, wearing a sort of helmet with a long spike on it."

"There's no such picture," barked Baltinglass.

"There is," insisted Miles, more curious than ever. "It's in the corner, above the wooden man with the grass skirt."

Baltinglass rubbed his stubbly chin with yellowed fingers. "Above the wooden man, eh? That's not a photo of me crossing the Yukon on a husky sled, then?"

"No," said Miles. "That's on the opposite wall, next to your doctorate in painful swellings."

"Well fry me in whale blubber!" muttered Baltinglass. "That's the trouble with pictures—you can't feel what's in 'em. I thought that one had gone out with the potato peelings years ago."

"Tell us about the funny hat then," said Gila.

"We like a story with a point to it," said Umor.

Baltinglass grunted. "You have a knack for picking the ones with the sharpest teeth, Master Miles. And it's not a funny hat, it's a unicrown. I'll tell you how I came by it, but don't blame me if you find your pillow crawling with nightmares."

He lit his pipe and puffed on it in silence for a while, as the circus performers made themselves comfortable and waited for him to begin. Everyone loves a good tale, and those who count the road as their home value stories more than most.

"When I was young and full of beans," began Baltinglass, "there was a fellow lived in our town named Shaky Guano."

"Strange sort of name," said Umor.

Baltinglass turned his blind stare to the little clown. "You're allowed one interruption each," he shouted. "Any more and you'll get a lesson from Ingrid."

"Who's Ingrid?" asked Umor.

Baltinglass reached out with his cane, quick as a lizard, and rapped him sharply on the shins. "This is Ingrid," he said. Umor opened his mouth to say something, then changed his mind and closed it again.

"Shaky Guano's real name was Seamus Baltinglass," continued Baltinglass. "He was my father's younger brother, and from an early age it was obvious that he had no interest in pig farming. He ran away from home as a young lad, and was gone for fifteen years. Whatever happened to him in that time scrambled his wits like an egg, and he returned a changed man. He wore on his head the strangest hat; a round metal cap like half a melon, with a spike sticking out of the top. He would not say what it was or how he came by it, but if anyone tried to remove it he would scream like a train whistle, and pretty soon people gave up trying and left it where it was. He had developed a mortal fear of being indoors, and instead he roamed the streets under moon and hail, shouting and flailing like he was under attack from invisible bats. Before long people began to call him Shaky."

"What about the Guano bit?" asked Miles.

"That came from the smell," said Baltinglass. "He gave off a powerful stench of bat guano that was resistant to soap or scrubbing of any kind. It was no bad thing all the same, as it prevented him sneaking up on anyone unawares. Shaky was mad as a spoon, and people liked to have some warning of his approach.

"A lot of folk in the town were afraid of him, but not me. I was only a little lad, but it seemed to me that his fight was with himself and nobody else. On his quieter days he loved to talk, and I was happy to listen. The stories Shaky told had no rhyme or reason to them. He would always begin by promising to tell me about the Lake of Gold, but somehow he never arrived at that story, though I tried to steer him to it many times. Once he told me of being pursued by eight men dressed entirely in copper, and another time that monks in yellow robes had taught him to make paper from smoke. But however garbled his tales were, they opened my mind to the strange and wonderful world that awaited me beyond our narrow valley, and I too began to think of pig farming as a future I would be happy to leave to someone else.

"I joined the navy on my fourteenth birthday and left Grubwater without a backward glance. It was three years before I came home on leave, and Shaky died the day before my return. I knew that he was gone as I approached Grubwater, although I can't say how. It just seemed there was a gap like a missing tooth in the landscape of the village. He had been hiding up a tree from the madness that pursued him, and there between the land and the sky he had given up the ghost. I went to see him laid out, and the undertaker, old Roger Murtice, took me aside. 'You were the only one who had any time for the old fruitcake,' he said, handing me a filthy bundle, 'so I kept this for you.' He looked relieved to be rid of it."

Baltinglass paused for a while to gather his story.

"I suspect," he said to no one in particular, "that somewhere in this circus there is a bottle of gin. I can feel the old malaria coming on, and a medicinal drink may just keep the beast in the basement, if it's not too late."

"But of course," said Countess Fontainbleau. "Little, be a dear and fetch a bottle from the cabinet in my trailer. And don't let Eunice out. She has a slight chill and I left her on the bed to keep warm."

Little slipped away into the darkness, and Baltinglass resumed his story.

"I remained with the navy for several years. It was an adventure that sailed me to almost every corner of the world, and I collected memories like more timid folk collect stamps."

Miles cleared his throat, keeping a wary eye on Ingrid. "You didn't tell us what was in the bundle," he said.

"You didn't ask," barked Baltinglass.

"I'm asking now," said Miles.

"It was the unicrown, of course, the strange hat that Shaky Guano had worn night and day, and the only thing he possessed to leave behind. On closer inspection it seemed to be made entirely of copper. It was decorated with a fine pattern and looked like a lot of work had gone into it, but I had no idea what it was for, and I felt slightly disappointed." Baltinglass turned his sightless gaze to Miles. "Little did I know then that it would save my life on two occasions," he said quietly, "nor that it would demand the sight of my two eyes in payment."

CHAPTER TWENTY-THREE
THE UNICROWN

Baltinglass of Araby, dry-tongued and tobacco-browned, held a match to his pipe and vanished for a moment behind a cloud of smoke. A baby cried in the darkness, and a woman's voice sang to him softly. The air was warm and thick and carried the smell of approaching rain.

"How did the unicrown save your life?" asked Gila.

Baltinglass sighed. "I carried the thing in my kit bag for years, and after a while I no longer noticed it was there. One night I was in a tavern named the Old Tar Barrel, on the waterfront in Fuera, playing cards with a retired professor who was a regular there. He was a man of great learning and I enjoyed his company, but to tell the truth I was more interested in his daughter. She was a fine young girl named Gertrude, strong-willed and well-built. She would often collect her father from the tavern in the wee hours, and I believe she had taken a shine to me also."

"Gertrude?" said Miles. "Was that Lady Partridge?"

"Who else would it be, Master Miles?" answered Baltinglass, giving him a rap on the shins with his cane in an almost absentminded fashion. Miles tried to picture the young Lady Partridge who had caught Baltinglass's eye, but without much success.

"I had no luck at cards that particular night, and I played until I hadn't a farthing left," continued Baltinglass. "I rummaged for stray coins in my kit bag, and up came Shaky Guano's unicrown instead. When the professor saw it he asked me at once for a closer look. 'I don't know where you got this, my friend,' he said to me eventually, 'but it's a greater treasure than you realize, or it would not be rattling around in your kit bag.' He insisted we return at once to his apartment, a place piled to the ceiling with books and manuscripts, and there he placed the unicrown under a strong lamp and spent the night searching through old volumes and muttering to himself, while I talked with Gertrude into the early hours and eventually fell asleep in an old armchair.

"The professor shook me awake in the first light, hopping like a cricket on a griddle. He showed me symbols and patterns in his own books that closely matched the ones on the cap, and told me that the unicrown was one of the only surviving artifacts of the Dagat people."

"The who people?" said Countess Fontainbleau.

"The Dagat were a people who lived in the port of Al Bab more than a century ago. They had built the port into a wealthy trading center over many generations, but eventually they came under attack from seafaring barbarians. Their defenses were overrun, and those who were not slaughtered fled with all the wealth they could load onto a single schooner. The fate of these last few Dagat was lost to history, but it so happened the professor had studied the Dagat culture in some depth. He recognized the symbols on the unicrown at once, and realized that the lines and crosses that swirled around them were a kind of map. The professor believed that the Dagat had fled up the coast from Al Bab and hidden themselves in the mangrove swamps of the Sindhu Delta. Here their ship had sunk, or they had deliberately scuttled it, and the unicrown itself had been made to help the surviving Dagat to find their lost wealth, if indeed any of them survived at all."

"Why the spike?" asked Fabio.

"The professor wasn't so sure about that," said Baltinglass. "He thought the spike might act as a sort of sundial to help with navigation. Personally I thought it would make a handy weapon, although on balance a good saber would be more useful for trimming the corners off barbarians. In any case the professor felt he had enough information to mount an expedition without delay. My stint in the navy had just expired, and the thought of searching for untold wealth appealed to me more than signing up for another ten years under the lash. I dreamed of returning, encrusted with gems and glory, to sweep the lovely Gertrude off her sturdy feet.

"Neither the professor nor I had the money to finance such an adventure, but the professor had a plan. It seemed that a young dandy named Lord Partridge of Larde was staying in the Regal Hotel in Fuera. He was rumored to be an easy touch for anyone with a scheme that could swallow money like quicksand. The rumors were accurate. We found him on his balcony with a face full of toast and marmalade, and within half an hour he had his checkbook out and was producing zeros like bubbles from a goldfish's backside.

"I hired a couple of old salts I knew who would be handy in a tight corner, and I chartered a small schooner with Partridge's money. Before the week was out I had it stocked to the gunwales with food and equipment, and helped the professor to lug on board a chest full of books and maps. A reporter from the local paper somehow got wind of our plans. Fresh-faced boy named Tenniel, with ears like jug handles—I can see his face like it was yesterday. The day before we left, the local paper published a front-page story on our quest, and the following morning the crowds were so thick on the quayside, there wasn't room to spit.

"Gertrude was there to see us off, of course. We made a proud sight as we cast off and sailed into the dawn. Our party numbered just five. There was myself, the professor with his books and maps, the two hired hands, Gannet and West, and young Tenniel from the paper, who persuaded me that the trip should be documented and photographed, and who I reckoned could double as an extra hand along the way.

"We sailed before a brisk breeze and by midday on the third day we could see the mangrove swamps like a gray-green smudge on the horizon. The channels were wide and clear where we entered the delta, but they soon became so shallow and choked with roots that we had to anchor the schooner and continue in the small lifeboat. We rowed slowly among the twisted trees, where every ripple in the brackish water might be a hungry crocodile. The professor pored over his books, and examined the unicrown with an eyeglass. Every now and then he would point down one channel, or turn us back the way we had come to try another. He had developed a worrying fever, and I began to doubt whether he knew any better than I did where we were.

"By the third day in among the mangroves the professor's fever had worsened, and our supplies were almost exhausted. I believed all our luck had been squeezed out, and I cursed myself for being ill prepared for so long a search. I spotted a broad tree that stood on an island of drier ground, and there we landed to rest. The professor was shaking like jelly. The unicrown dropped from his hand and rolled toward the water, and I picked it up and tucked it into my belt for safekeeping. I felt it wise at this stage to ask the professor exactly what he was looking for, as I doubted he would live to see it." Baltinglass leaned forward and lowered his voice, and every head around the campfire leaned in also, like beads shifting in a kaleidoscope.

"The professor just smiled, and said that if he had the strength to stand up he could probably throw a stone that would land right in the middle of the the sunken hoard. He told me to look around the far side of the tree. I did so, and to my astonishment I was greeted by a vision of paradise. Right there, in the midst of all those reeking channels, was a lagoon of cool, clean water. The sun laid a trail on the water like a necklace of diamonds, and snowy white wading birds stepped carefully around the shallow edges. I thought about my uncle Seamus, wondering if he had stood as a young man at this very spot, and what could have happened to turn him from that proud adventurer into the demented soul I had known as a child.

"I set Gannet and West to keep watch for crocodiles, then I waded out into the water without further delay. The lagoon was not very deep, and at any moment I expected to stub my toe on a gold brick or a priceless goblet. When the water reached my chin I put on the goggles I had brought and took a deep breath. I could see at once that the professor had steered us right, and my heart leaped with excitement. On either side of me I could make out the rotting beams of the ancient boat, curving up out of the mud like the ribs of a giant beast. I bent down and dug carefully in the soft mud, knowing that if I stirred it up too much I wouldn't be able to see a thing. I found nothing, not a coin or a cup or a set of dentures. I dived and I dug several times more, but there was no carpet of gold among the timbers of the ship, no gemstones hiding in the weeds, and my spirits sank as I kicked my way back to the surface for the last time. It was obvious that the wreck had been visited before us, perhaps many times, and not a brass farthing of the Dagat's legendary wealth remained.

"I heard Gannet shout something to me, but before I could make out his words something grabbed my left leg below the knee and gave it a mighty twist. I was flipped like a pancake and dragged under the water. A big scaly foot planted itself on my chest, and the air left me in a stream of bubbles. A crocodile had my leg clamped in its jaws and was staring at me with its yellow eye. I thought my goose was cooked for sure, but suddenly I remembered the unicrown that was tucked into my belt."

Baltinglass paused and massaged his left shin for a minute. "Strange thing was, I felt sorry for the beast as I poked him in the eye with that spike. I was on a fool's errand, and he was only looking for an honest lunch. I knew a well-aimed poke would be enough to send him packing, and sure enough he let me go at once, though he had made dog meat of my leg. I still have the scars. Looks like I was attacked by a mad can opener."

Baltinglass of Araby rolled his trouser leg to the knee. The twisted scars on his shin glinted in the firelight, and his audience sucked in their breath in unison. Miles leaned forward and stared. He reached out to touch the old man's maimed leg without knowing why, and he felt the earth begin to spin beneath him. The distant rumble of thunder faded and died, and the murmur of the circus folk became a thin buzzing in his ears. He felt light and full of air, just as he had when he wiped the blood from Dulac Zipplethorpe's face. He could hear Baltinglass's voice as though it came from a great distance.

"... has never stopped aching from that day to this. Morning, noon and—" Baltinglass stopped suddenly. Miles withdrew his hand and sat up straight, afraid that he would topple off the log in his dizziness. He opened his eyes to see Baltinglass running his fingers over his shin. "Well I'll be bleached and bottled! Blasted thing's gone numb now. Never did that before." He rolled his trousers back down and stretched out his leg. His knee joint cracked like a distant rifle.

"It would have been better if I had killed the beast outright, as it turned out," the old man continued. "Gannet and West helped me out of the water, and Gannet fetched the medical box and began to bandage my leg. When Gannet was done with my leg, young Tenniel insisted that I stand by the tree for a photo. As he set up his camera I felt a strange urge to put the unicrown on my head. The thing had just saved my life, and I was in need of all the luck I could get. To my surprise it fitted like a second skin. The pain in my leg was intense, but I stood by the tree, still wearing the unicrown, while Tenniel made his photograph."

The thunder growled and Baltinglass growled back, like a dog facing down a wild boar. "How the photograph found its way into the paper is a mystery to me," he said, "for none of my companions, including Tenniel himself, ever made it home."

CHAPTER TWENTY-FOUR

LIGHTNING STRIKES TWICE

Miles Wednesday, shin-rapped and story-
lifted, felt Tangerine wriggling as he tried
to poke his threadbare head out into the night air.
Miles knew that he liked a good tale as much as
anyone, and he put his hand in his pocket to make
sure the bear did not climb out altogether in his
excitement. With every word of Baltinglass's tale
Miles could feel his own appetite for adventure
grow stronger, a wanderlust inherited from the
blind explorer himself and sharpened by the salt air
of Fuera. Already it had carried him far from his
barrel on the side of the hill, and he knew somehow
that it would sweep him and Little to places that he

had barely begun to imagine.

"I decided we'd camp where we were for the night," continued Baltinglass, "and begin the return journey in the morning. We built a small fire to keep the night at bay, and West took a pot to fill at the water's edge. That was a mistake. The wounded crocodile was waiting in the shallows, and it burst from the water and took him in the space of a heart-beat. Gannet snatched a rifle and put it to his shoulder, but there were only ripples to aim at, and we never saw hide nor hair of West again.

"No one wanted to sleep on the ground that night. We carried the professor up into the tree, and found perches for ourselves among the branches. Gannet was silent, and the professor slipped in and out of reality as his fever rose and fell. I didn't sleep a wink all night, and as dawn broke I climbed to the highest point in the tree to take a look around.

"Thunder rumbled overhead and the sky hung low above us, but it never crossed my weary mind to question the wisdom of wearing a copper hat in a tall tree during a thunderstorm. Rain swept toward us like a smoky curtain, and I looked up at the purple clouds at the very moment they split open and sent a rope of lightning down toward me. I knew then that the unicrown demanded a high price for the good luck it brought to its wearer."

Miles glanced at Little. She was looking into the fire as though she did not want to hear what came next. Tears glinted in her eyes.

"The lightning hit me like a burning sledgehammer and left me hanging upside down in the smoking tree, my body humming like a bee. My surviving companions were all blown clear into the swamp and were relatively unhurt, but I had taken the full wattage through my copper hat. My senses were shuffled like a deck of cards, and for a long time after that I traveled the lands that Shaky Guano had described in his wildest ramblings. I heard the howling of the rocks buried deep beneath my feet, and I didn't know days from hours, or seconds from weeks. I became aware that I was blind in one eye, and still I considered myself lucky to be alive. Our dinghy had been pulverized by the lightning, and without maps or compass we wandered further from the sea into the trackless jungle. The professor died in that soggy place, thin as a rail and eaten up by fever. Our supplies had long since run out, and we were forced to drink the moisture that had collected in leaves, and eat whatever had drowned in it. After some time I became dimly aware that we were no longer in a jungle at all, but in a scrubby desert that stretched to the horizon. How long we tramped through dust and sand I can't say, but a mighty sandstorm overtook us one day, and when it had passed I could find no trace of Tenniel or Gannet.

"I wandered alone through a world that would make the devil tremble, and forgot my purpose and my road. At night I stuck the unicrown upside down in the sand and by morning I would have a cup full of dew. I stumbled from oasis to scrub and gnawed on whatever root or nut I came across. Once I killed a stray goat who had been frightened by a sudden squall, but in the desert there is no greater crime, and when its owner caught up with me he told me with great courtesy that he would remove my head as soon as he had given his camel a drink. I took out the unicrown and placed it on my head. I had a desperate idea that I could convince him I was some class of ragged royalty with goat-killing privileges. That move saved my life, but not in the way I intended, and the unicrown took my remaining eye in payment."

Baltinglass reached into his pocket for his pipe, but his hand shook so much that he dropped it in the long grass. Little picked it up and handed it to him. She laid her hand on his knotty wrist, and his shaking eased a little.

"They say that lightning never strikes twice, but I'm not one to stay within the rules. The squall had grown stronger, and no sooner had I placed the uni-crown on my head than I was blasted by lightning again. It blew the shoes off my feet and turned the sand around me to glass, but oddly enough it unscrambled my wits this time around. For the first time in months I could remember my name and where I came from, but my good eye had been poached like an egg, and now I could see nothing but whiteness on every side.

"The goat owner had a loud and urgent discussion with his god, who told him, apparently, that I had been taught my lesson. From that moment the laws of desert hospitality took over. The man became my host and my protector, and took me all the way back to the port of Al Bab, though it was hundreds of miles from his road. He booked me a passage to Fuera and paid for it from his own pocket. The moment my feet were back on dry ground I stumbled straight to the professor's house to bring Gertrude news of her father's death, and ask her forgiveness for my part in it."

Little squeezed Baltinglass's hand, and wiped her eyes with her sleeve. "It wasn't your fault," she said. "It was the professor's expedition as much as yours."

"He was in my care nonetheless," said Baltinglass. "I should have brought him back alive to his daughter, but there were more ugly surprises in store for me. I found that I had been gone for three years, and we had all long since been given up for dead. Gertrude had married that buffoon, Lord Partridge, and retired to his mansion in Larde. I sent her my apologies in a letter, and I took to the road again, eyes or no eyes, because I knew no other life. I never saw Gertrude again until she came to my door many years later with a gaggle of policemen and we took to the road to find out what had become of you two. It was only then that I learned Partridge had blown himself to bits with an exploding pudding several years before."

"It must have been much harder to travel without your eyes," said Little.

"That's what I believed at first, but I was wrong. I found a whole other world behind the one I had known before. What you smell and hear and feel tells you more than your eyesight ever will. I've heard the beating heart of a deer that no one else could see, and felt the darkness on my tongue. Sometimes, when the night is still, I can hear the moon sliding through the sky. The world comes alive when you can no longer see it, little girl."

"What happened to the unicrown?" asked Miles. "Do you still have it?"

"Maybe I do," said Baltinglass, sticking out his jaw, "and maybe I don't. To tell the truth I'm in no hurry to see it again. One end is sharp enough to put your eye out, and the other end seems to do the job just as well."

"Weren't you afraid to put it back on after you were struck the first time?"

Baltinglass reached out, quick as a snake, and grabbed Miles by the wrist. He leaned forward until his nose was inches from Miles's face. "Sometimes you can only win by reaching right into the jaws of what scares you the most. If I hadn't put that blasted hat back on my head I wouldn't have had a head left to put it on, and I wouldn't be sitting on this log telling you stories, would I now, Master Miles?"

CHAPTER TWENTY-FIVE

A KNOT OF PITCHFORKS

Little Sky Beetle, mountain-bound and sun-striped, poured thick coffee from a dented silver pot in the cluttered wagon of the Bolsillo brothers. The wagon shook and swayed on the bumpy road, but Little swayed with it and did not spill a drop. Baltinglass had stayed at the circus overnight, and in the morning Miles and Little had walked him to the door of his whitewashed house. "Tell me this," he had yelled, turning to Miles and Little as the door swung open, "did my little bed-time story give you nightmares?"

"A few," said Miles, "but they were good ones."

Baltinglass chuckled. "It didn't take the wheels

off your wanderlust, then."

"It didn't stop you exploring, and you were the one with the crocodile chewing your leg," said Miles.

"You've got a point there, and that reminds me . . ." He leaned forward and lowered his voice. "I don't know what you did to my old leg last night, Master Miles, but the pain that's dogged me for forty years has vanished without a trace."

"I didn't do anything, really," said Miles, although he knew the Bolsillo brothers believed otherwise.

"Have it your own way," said Baltinglass, "but I've got the leg of a twenty-year-old, and it will have to take many a step to catch up with the rest of my old bones. In fact I'm starting to think I might have one last trip left in me. Maybe we'll all take to the road together once you're finished gallivanting with the circus, eh?"

"I'd like that," said Miles.

"You might even take a look at these old eyes sometime," the old man said. A worried look crossed his wrinkled face. "On second thought, maybe not," he added. "I'd be afraid I might come across a mirror."

Miles sat now in silence, lulled by the rocking of the wagon on its iron springs, and thought about the touch that he had inherited from his mother. The words of the Shriveled Fella came back to him: "*The bright hands are on you,* buhall." That must have been what he meant. He wondered if it was possible to lend someone so much of his life that there was none left for himself, and he shivered at the thought. The weather was turning colder now, and for the first time since they left he found himself looking forward to the soft beds and warm food that awaited them in Partridge Manor. "Not long now," he whispered to Tangerine, and felt his little head nod silently in the warmth of his jacket pocket.

The circus rolled on through the hills and wound its way slowly up the mountain slopes. Miles had taken over the reins while Fabio dozed in his bunk. He sat in the box seat, trying to imitate the soft clucks and whistles that Fabio used to speak to the horses. They reached the mountaintop in the late afternoon, and Miles realized that it was nearly a year since he and Little had traveled this road the other way in search of Silverpoint and Tangerine. He could see below them the stepped vineyards and the yellow sea of sunflowers through which they had ridden on the tiger's back, and beyond that the dark green of the forest that stretched back along the road to the hamlet of Hay. He wondered if the tiger was somewhere in that landscape, pacing silently through the shade of the trees, or standing in the clear waters of the stream waiting for a fat fish to swim by.

Fabio and Gila joined him on the box seat and they started down the mountainside with the evening sun shining in their eyes. From time to time they passed small groups of farmers in the fields, fanned out and carrying pitchforks and stout sticks, and marching through the vines and the sunflowers with a purposeful air.

"A lot of farmers abroad this evening," remarked Fabio.

"What do you expect," said Gila, "bank clerks?"

"Scarecrows," said Fabio. "Farmers should be at their dinner."

The road snaked through terraced vineyards that gave way to sunflower fields, and the circus ambled between the ranks of enormous flowers, their heads drooping like tattered grandmothers nodding off in the fading light. Ahead of them the dark line of trees grew gradually nearer, and at length the sunflowers ended and a small pasture opened out to their left, just before the start of the woods.

"This is where we stop for the night," said Fabio.

"Good," said Umor. "The horses are tired."

"And the tires are hoarse," said Gila.

They pulled into the field, and the other wagons and trucks followed, arranging themselves in a ragged circle. The circus people dropped down into the soft grass, yawning and stretching the journey from their tired bones, and the cart horses sighed deeply and flicked at swarming midges with their tails. Little sang like a blackbird, and Tangerine wriggled in his sleep, dreaming whatever stuffed bears in warm pockets dream. Umor lit a small fire in a circle of stones, while Fabio uncoupled the horses and Gila filled their nosebags from the hay wagon.

"I wonder what all those farmers were searching for," said Miles, bending down and blowing on the fire while Umor added more kindling.

"Their lost childhood," suggested Umor.

"Or a lost potato," said Gila.

"Why don't you ask them?" said Fabio.

Miles turned to see a knot of men approaching them warily, bristling with farm implements.

"Identify yourselves," said a squat bald man, holding a pitchfork longer than himself.

"If you wouldn't mind," added a taller man behind him.

Fabio looked pointedly at the words THE INCOMPARABLE CIRCUS BOLSILLO spelled out in enormous colored letters on the wagon beside him.

"I am Fabio Bolsillo," he said, "and this is the incomparable Circus Bolsillo."

The man with the pitchfork grunted. "There's a devil on the loose," he said. "Have you seen it on your travels?"

"It's not a devil, it's a giant baboon," said his tall companion. He had tangled orange hair and a beaky nose.

"I heard it was a yeti," said a third man. The others turned and glared at him. "Or something," he mumbled.

"What does it look like?" asked Miles apprehensively. He had a feeling he already knew the answer.

"We've not seen it," said the beaky man, "but they say it's big and hairy with teeth like fence posts."

Miles cleared his throat loudly. "Where was it last seen?" he asked.

The squat bald man turned to look at him. "Ate a whole coop of chickens in Hay this afternoon, then took off into the trees. They say it's headed this way," he said. "If it shows up in our fields it'll be sorry." His companions didn't look so sure as to who would end up the sorrier.

"It's just scared," said Miles. There was only one creature he knew of that fit the nervous farmers' description, and he was worried that they would provoke it into doing something terrible. He was sure that if The Null hurt someone else he would not be able to save it a second time.

"Wasn't too scared of the chickens, was it?" said the tall beaky man. "If you don't mind me saying so," he added.

"What do you know about it anyway?" asked the bald man, scowling suspiciously at Miles.

"It used to be with our circus," said Fabio.

"But it took early retirement," said Gila.

The bald man surveyed the brightly colored trailers that filled the field, as though he was obliged—as chief pitchfork-carrier—to check that it was indeed a circus. His inspection was interrupted by the rumble of an approaching engine, and he turned around irritably. A battered blue police van came barreling along the road and screeched to a halt in a cloud of beige dust. The dust was so thick on the windshield that it was hard to imagine how anyone could see through it. The driver leaned out of his side window, and Miles recognized him at once. It was Sergeant Bramley, and he wore an official police frown that put the bald man's petulant scowl in the shade.

"Now then," said Sergeant Bramley, addressing the farmers. "Aren't you supposed to be combing the fields and ditches?" He spotted Miles and raised his eyebrows in surprise. "Master Wednesday," he said, giving him a curt nod. He ducked back into the dusted cab, and reappeared a moment later. "Lady P. would like a word with you, young man," he said. A ginger cat poked his head out from below the sergeant's double chin. Miles ran around to the other side of the van and there, sure enough, was the monumental figure of Lady Partridge, beaming down at him from the battered cab as though she were in a gilded carriage. She wore the same Chinese dressing gown she had lived in for years, but since moving back into her stately home she had taken to wearing ornate hats that would once have snagged in the tangled branches and bric-a-brac of her cluttered tree house. The one she wore now was crested with peacock feathers, making her look like some kind of prehistoric tree decorated with red dragons.

"Hello, Lady Partridge," grinned Miles.

"I'm *so* glad to see you, Miles!" boomed Lady Partridge. "You look quite the part! You must tell me all your adventures as soon as we have the chance to sit down together, but I'm afraid we have a more pressing matter at hand. I suppose you've heard that our hirsute guest has escaped?".

"You mean The Null?" said Miles. He was sure he should know what "hirsute" meant, having reached the letter "Q" in Lady Partridge's encyclopedia, but it seemed that much of his book learning had been pushed out of his head to make room for the kind of education gained from running through pitch darkness with cave dwellers and having knives thrown at you by a man who never washed.

"I'm afraid so," said Lady Partridge. "The creature went missing sometime in the night, and I very much hope we are the ones to find it. There's no knowing what damage a scared man with a pitch-fork might cause, especially to himself."

"Can I come with you?" asked Miles.

"By all means," said Lady Partridge. "If we do find the creature there's a chance it might recognize your voice, if it has any memory at all. We shall have to be very careful, of course, but there are several sturdy policemen in the back of the van, and they may come in useful if they have managed to disentangle themselves from their net on the way here."

"I'll just get Little," said Miles.

"Don't be too long," said Lady Partridge. "Night will be falling soon, and we should press on."

Miles ran back through the field, looking for Little. He could not see where the Toki sisters had parked their trailer, but as he passed Doctor Tau-Tau's wagon he was startled by the red-faced fortune-teller himself, who stepped out from the wagon's shadow like a dressing-gowned jack-in-the-box. Miles had not seen Tau-Tau since they had left Cnoc, and had assumed that the fortune-teller had returned to skulking in his wagon as they approached his home turf. "Ah, Master Wednesday!" said Tau-Tau in a strained voice, "a quick word, if you please."

"It'll have to wait, I'm afraid," said Miles. "I'm in a hurry. Have you seen Little?"

"Never mind Little!" said Doctor Tau-Tau, grabbing Miles's arm. "You *must* show me where the Tiger's Egg is hidden."

Miles shook himself free. Doctor Tau-Tau was acting even more strangely than usual. "You know I don't know anything about it," he said. "I only have your word that it even exists!"

"It will be better for you if you tell me," said Tau-Tau. "It will be better for both of us." He sat down suddenly on the wagon steps and put his head in his hands. "My head hurts," he said despondently. "I need to lie down."

"You do that," said Miles. He had spotted Little walking along the top of the wire fence that separated the field from the forest, and he turned on his heel and ran toward her. "I can't tell you what I don't know," he shouted over his shoulder as he crossed the field.

When he returned with Little, Sergeant Bramley had just finished discussing search strategy with the pitchfork platoon. It was decided that the farmers should retrace their steps, as their homes lay in the direction from which the circus had come, and that Sergeant Bramley and his men would turn back toward Hay and make another sweep of the road that ran alongside the forest.

"You take care, both of you," said Fabio, his ears wagging as he placed more firewood on the campfire.

"That beast's no teddy bear," said Umor.

"As you well know, Master Miles."

"We'll be okay," said Little.

The sergeant stubbed out his cigarette and sent the farmers on their way, and the police van took off once more along the road, with Little and Miles wedged on the bench seat between Lady Partridge and Sergeant Bramley. The sergeant squinted through the dusty windshield and drove as though he were being chased by a pack of starving wolves, while Miles searched the trees as best he could through the open side window and Little listened to sounds that no one else could hear above the roar of the engine. They had not gone far when Little laid her hand on the sergeant's arm. Without further signal he stood on the brakes and the van screeched to a halt with the sound of several half-entangled policemen piling up against the bulkhead behind the cab.

"What is it, my dear?" asked Lady Partridge.

"Listen," said Little.

The cloud of beige dust gradually settled around them, and they could all hear a sound that the roar of the engine had hidden moments before. It was a sort of terrified bleating, coming from somewhere in the woods. Sergeant Bramley straightened his cap and took his truncheon from its clip above the windshield. "Sounds like it's got itself a sheep," he said.

CHAPTER TWENTY-SIX

SHADOWS AND TEETH

Doctor Tau-Tau, suspended, upended and bleating like a sheep, hung by his belt from a tall tree. The Null sat brooding over him like a shadow on an X-ray. The light had all but gone from under the trees, but even so the creature seemed to radiate darkness, and only the red rims of its eyes showed in its hairy silhouette.

"It's Doctor Tau-Tau!" whispered Miles. "What's he doing here? I thought he was sick in his wagon."

"Someone should call the police," whispered a nervous voice behind him.

"We are the police, Constable Wigge," said Constable Flap.

"Someone should call the army," said Constable Wigge.

Lady Partridge huffed up behind them, her dressing gown trailing twigs and leaves along the forest floor. "There it is!" she whispered, as she arrived at the edge of the clearing where the search party crouched in the bracken. "What on earth has it . . . ?"

The Null shifted on the branch, causing the dangling Doctor Tau-Tau to bounce in the air. He whimpered loudly.

"It's all right, Doctor Tau-Tau," said Miles as loudly as he dared. "We'll get you down somehow."

The Null bared its teeth and growled. The fortune-teller, whose broad backside had been facing the search party, managed to twist himself around and peer over his shoulder.

"There you are, and not a moment too soon!" he said in a trembling voice. "Get my sleepwater, boy. Don't forget how I saved you from those underground barbarians, eh?"

"Sleepwater?" said Miles. The name rang a bell.

"In my leather case, boy," said Doctor Tau-Tau, pointing to the ground below him. "A small yellow bottle, if the brute hasn't smashed it."

"Be very careful, Miles dear," said Lady Partridge.

Miles crept forward slowly, never taking his eyes from The Null. An old doctor's bag lay on its side below the tree, its mouth open and its contents scattered in the moss. Miles was directly below The Null now, and its eyes followed him unblinkingly. He could smell the musty odor of the beast, a smell that had always reminded him of rotten bananas, and he could almost feel the crushing embrace with which it had once tried to squeeze the life out of him. He sank down slowly on his hunkers, and the beast suddenly opened its mouth and let out an eerie cackle that froze him to the bone. His hand shook as he rummaged among the spilled contents of Doctor Tau-Tau's case. He felt notebooks of some kind, a small wooden figure, a coin with a square hole cut from its center. His fingers found a bottle, and he straightened up carefully. He wished that the tiger was there beside him.

"What now?" he whispered.

"Climb up here and make it drink the stuff," said Doctor Tau-Tau.

"Do no such thing!" called Lady Partridge from the edge of the clearing.

"Just throw it up to him, Miles," said Little. "I'm sure Doctor Tau-Tau has already thought of a way to make The Null drink it."

"I have?" said Tau-Tau in a strained whisper. "I have, of course," he added. "But you won't be able to throw it high enough. Better if you climb up here yourself. Boys like to climb trees, don't they?"

"Put your hand out," said Miles, who had been learning all summer how to throw daggers and was now almost as accurate as his teacher, Stranski, "and keep still!"

Doctor Tau-Tau stretched out his trembling hand. Miles sized up the distance for a moment, then he drew back his arm and threw the small bottle. It arched up through the gathering gloom, straight to the outstretched fingers of the fortune-teller, who almost forgot to catch it in his surprise.

"Right . . . ," said Doctor Tau-Tau, but before he could do anything The Null suddenly came to life. In a whirl of tangled hair it swept out along the branch, grabbed the collar of the terrified fortune-teller's jacket with its curved yellow nails and hauled him upright, freeing his belt from the branch that supported him. It snatched the bottle from the air as it fell from the terrified Tau-Tau's hand, and let him go. The fortune-teller dropped unceremoniously to the ground twenty feet below, where he landed with a soggy thump in a carpet of moss. There was a collective gasp from the edge of the clearing. Constable Flap, who had earned a diploma in first aid from a course in *Modern Constable* magazine, crawled across the moss toward the crumpled figure of Doctor Tau-Tau, peering nervously up into the branches as he came. Miles, who had stepped backward in the nick of time, looked up, too, at The Null. The creature bit the neck clean off the bottle with a crunch, and much to everyone's surprise it emptied the contents down its throat. There was a moment's silence while the stout lady, the four-hundred-year-old girl, the boy, the sergeant and his constables all held their breath, and The Null crouched against the trunk with its eyes closed and its great jaw hanging open. The only sound was the soft counting of Constable Flap, who held Doctor Tau-Tau's wrist in his fingers and marked out his pulse like a whispering metronome.

Miles was just beginning to hope that the sleep-water had worked on The Null, when the creature's eyes snapped open and it let out a cackling howl that made Constable Wigge break cover and bolt for the safety of the van. It swung down from the branch and hung there for a moment, its great fangs bared and its wild black eyes staring down at Miles, who backed slowly away from the tree. The creature's hollow eyes stared straight at him, and they seemed to suck in the last of the failing light. "Maybe," thought Miles hopefully, "it remembers all those mornings I read to it from the newspaper." He thought about all the gossip and tattle that filled the *Larde Weekly Herald* from cover to cover. "Maybe it's better if it doesn't," he muttered to himself.

The Null let go of the branch and dropped to the ground, and the mossy earth jumped beneath Miles's feet. It leaped over the cowering constable and came toward Miles at a run. Time slowed, and Miles saw in sharp detail the swirling motion of its long black hair, the flaring nostrils and the red mouth open in a hideous grin. He felt rough bark at his back. From the corner of his eye he saw the open mouths and white faces of his friends, and he heard Sergeant Bramley shout "Halt in the name of the law!" from his hiding place in the bracken.

If you have ever found yourself backed against a tree with a nightmare charging at you like a hairy locomotive you have probably found yourself wishing, as Miles did, that something would happen in the nick of time to save you from a grisly end. A sudden flash flood. An intermission with popcorn. Sixteen stern nurses with folded arms. Miles, of course, wished for a tiger, and so fervently did he do so that when he heard a rumbling growl from the undergrowth to his left he almost forgot to be surprised. The tiger burst from the bracken and crossed the clearing in a single leap, his great front paws landing with a double thud right in front of Miles and skidding in the loose leaves as he recovered his balance. The entire forest held its breath.

The tiger and the beast faced each other, no more than a tail's length apart, their labored breathing loud in the deathly stillness. They looked like two halves of a dream, black and gold, circling slowly in the dim clearing. The Null crept on its mighty knuckles, and the tiger moved as slowly as a rainy afternoon, low to the ground with his tail switching from side to side. Miles glanced across at where the search party crouched in the undergrowth. Little's eyes were fixed on the beast and the tiger. Lady Partridge was motioning frantically to Miles to get behind the tree, and Sergeant Bramley held a whistle to his pudgy lips, though he knew the only reinforcement was Constable Wigge, hiding in a van with nothing but a wheezy siren and one working headlight.

The Null stood upright and its hair rose until it looked twice its normal size, an inky shadow that threatened to swallow everything around it. Even the flaming orange flanks of the tiger seemed to grow dull, as though he had moved from sunlight into cloud. The great cat looked suddenly tired, his ribs heaving and his baggy stomach swaying beneath him. The Null bared its yellow fangs and cackled, then in the space of a heartbeat it broke from the circle and leaped at Miles.

The sudden move took Miles by surprise, but the tiger reared up and took a swipe at the flying beast with his mighty paw. Miles threw himself sideways and felt The Null's straggling hair whip the backs of his legs as it collided with the tree trunk. The enraged beast's howl scattered the crows from the treetops. It spun around, clutching a bleeding shoulder, and found itself inches from the tiger, who had drawn himself up to his full height. The tiger seemed to make an enormous effort to meet The Null's desperate stare. The tiger bared his teeth, but to Miles's surprise he did not attack, but spoke to the gibbering beast instead.

"You have lost yourself," he said, and his rich voice seemed to bring some of his strength back with it. The magnificent tiger took a deep breath, and the glow began to return to his flanks. His gaze grew steadier, and The Null seemed to deflate before him. It turned to Miles, a haunted look in the black voids of its eyes. It was there one moment, then suddenly it was gone, bounding away through the trees and shedding its desolate cackle like a trail of shadows, with the mighty tiger on its tail and night falling softly through the trees like the curtain at the end of a play.

CHAPTER TWENTY-SEVEN

A DOSE OF DARKNESS

Lady Partridge, dragon-wrapped and feather-crowned, sat in a high-backed cane chair on the lawn of Partridge Manor, beaming over a table set with a white cloth and a lavish breakfast served on fine bone china. The china was old and slightly chipped around the edges, like its owner, and was piled with eggs, bacon, sausages and mushrooms, fresh raspberries, and enough toast and marmalade to feed a small village. Miles and Little sat to her left, piling breakfast onto their plates as though they had not eaten for a month. The autumn sun shone on the lawn, and a fresh breeze tugged at their hair and flapped the corners of the tablecloth.

"I trust you slept well after all that excitement?" said Lady Partridge.

Little nodded, butter dripping from her chin.

"Not really," said Miles. "It was nice to be back in my own bed, but I couldn't sleep for thinking about The Null."

"I think you're quite safe from the poor beast for the moment. Our trusty policemen have continued the chase, and with luck they will track The Null down before any harm is done." She looked at Miles with a curious expression. "What really interests me," she said, "is how a tiger appeared from nowhere just in time to save your skin. I have never seen anything quite so astonishing, but I can't help feeling it came as less of a surprise to you."

Miles felt his face flush. "I just hope they don't kill each other."

"Or anyone else," said Lady Partridge. "But who knows, they might have tired themselves out galumphing around the countryside and decided to sit down for a friendly chat. Pass the butter, Little, there's a dear." She peered again at Miles over her glasses. "I could have sworn that tiger said a few words to The Null, though I may have imagined it in the heat of the moment."

"The tiger is our friend," said Little, "but Miles

doesn't like to talk about it."

"I don't mind, really," said Miles. "I suppose I never expected anyone to believe me."

"With good reason, Miles dear," said Lady Partridge. "It would certainly sound like a tall story if I hadn't been there myself. Isn't a tiger rather a dangerous sort of friend to have?"

"Maybe," said Miles. "He can be quite frightening, but he has helped us out of a few tight spots, and he's had plenty of chances to eat us if he wanted to."

"How on earth did he learn to talk?" asked Lady Partridge.

"I never asked him," said Miles. "It would seem like a rude question. Anyway, you get used to it after a while."

The conversation was interrupted by a small boy who ran up to Lady Partridge and tugged on the sleeve of her dressing gown. "What is it, Marcus?" she asked.

"Lady P., Baumella says that Mr. Tau-Tau is awake."

"Is he indeed?" said Lady Partridge. "Well you run back in there, young man, and ask Baumella to escort Doctor Tau-Tau out here so that he may join us for breakfast."

The boy stood where he was, looking up at Lady

Partridge's feathered hat.

"It means 'bring,'" said Miles. "Ask Baumella to bring Doctor Tau-Tau here."

"Quite so," said Lady Partridge, and the small boy ran back across the lawn and disappeared around the corner of the mansion.

"Well," said Lady Partridge. "Now perhaps we'll find out how this fellow managed to have himself hung from a tree by his trousers."

"He does seem to have a knack for getting into trouble," said Miles.

Doctor Tau-Tau appeared a moment later, and trod an unsteady path toward the breakfast table, the looming figure of Baumella the giantess gripping his shoulder firmly.

"Please join us, Doctor Tau-Tau," said Lady Partridge. The fortune-teller slumped into a chair at the end of the table. His face was closer to peppermint green than its usual brick red. Lady Partridge fixed him with a stern gaze. "We haven't been properly introduced, since you were suspended from a tree when we met," she said. "I am Lady Partridge, and you are a guest in my house. You've been unconscious for some twelve hours, but I trust a little breakfast might help revive you."

"Much obliged, Lady Parfait. I am . . . Doctor

Tau-Tau," said Tau-Tau, straightening his fez. "Or did you just tell me that?" He picked up his fork and speared a sausage on his third attempt.

"We were just discussing how a person might find himself hung in a tree by an unidentifiable beast, when he was last seen taking to his bed with a headache," said Lady Partridge politely, pouring tea into his cup.

"I was called from my sockbed on urgent business," said Tau-Tau. "My bicksed. My sickbed. Are those eggs?"

"Please pass Doctor Tau-Tau an egg," said Lady Partridge to Little.

"In any case," said Tau-Tau through a mouthful of sausage, "I am a renowned clairvoyant. I think." His forehead wrinkled. "Yes, that's me. Doctor Tau-Tau. I'm often called on urgent business, and I have a perfect right to be escaping through the woods."

"Escaping?" echoed Miles. "What were you escaping from?"

"Who said I was escaping?" said Doctor Tau-Tau, washing down his food with a gulp of tea.

"You did," said Little. "Your second sight must be very clear if you knew The Null was on its way. You probably even know why it was heading for the circus."

"It's a fr-freak. I mean a curiosity. The circus is its home," said Doctor Tau-Tau, looking at Little as though trying to remember who she was. "Its home," he added, "is the circus."

"And why, one wonders, did you not want to be there when it arrived?" asked Lady Partridge.

"I would have thought that was obvious!" said Tau-Tau. "It would have had me for supper if I hadn't overpowered it with my sleepwater. It takes a potionful power to make a monster like that. A powerful potion. And a great degree of skill to subdue it." He looked over his shoulder at the bright lawn and the children clambering around in the tree house. "I hope you've got the beast under lock and key again."

"Unfortunately not. Your sleepwater seemed to be a tonic to the creature, and it was last seen cantering away through the woods without so much as a stifled yawn," said Lady Partridge.

"Your sleepwater *is* very strong," said Little. "I know, I was given it once and I slept for a day and a half. Still," she said, mopping egg yolk from her plate with a piece of toast and looking at Tau-Tau with her clear blue eyes, "the potion that made The Null what it is must have been much stronger. Perhaps the person who made *that* potion could teach you how to make a better sleepwater."

Doctor Tau-Tau plonked his cup back in its saucer with a rattle. "Sleepwater is designed to be injeedled. I mean injected. With a needle. It's ten times more potent when it's used properly. And besides, there's no one else alive who could make a brute like that, nor was there ever." His chest inflated like a balloon. "Only Doctor Tau-Tau has the knowledge to make a potion that can transform a hell into a man from baboon! I mean a man into a baboon from hell!"

"*You* made The Null?" said Miles in astonishment.

"How extraordinary!" said Lady Partridge. "So the poor creature really was once a man?"

The fortune-teller looked from one face to another. The red was returning to his cheeks, but his face still wore a puzzled frown. "Doctor Tau-Tau," he muttered. "That *is* me, isn't it?"

"I think you should tell us more about this creature," said Lady Partridge. "It may help us to find it. Perhaps we may even find a cure someday. With your help, of course."

A hunted look came over the fortune-teller's face. "I don't think so," he said. "It was a long time ago. I don't remember so well. I think I need to lie down."

"A long rest will undoubtedly do you good," said Lady Partridge, "but we do urgently need to find out more about this beast before it can do any more damage. Perhaps another cup of tea might perk you up enough to tell us more before you go for your sleep."

Little poured more tea for Doctor Tau-Tau, who shifted uncomfortably under Lady Partridge's steady gaze. His hand shook as he lifted the teacup to his lips. "A skill such as mine involves a certain amount of risk," he said. "In my work I use powers that would terrify the average man out of his wits. When I joined the Circus—the Circus Whatsisname—I still had much to learn, but it wasn't long before my skills were tested to their limits. The Great Cortado was angry. He had lost a popular fortune-teller in Celeste. His perform wouldn't tiger . . . his tiger wouldn't perform, not without Bumble. Fumble. Barty Fumble." Doctor Tau-Tau mopped his brow with a table napkin. "Where was I?" he asked.

"The tiger wouldn't perform," said Little.

"You know this story already?" said Tau-Tau.

"You were just telling us," said Miles. He had heard this story before, deep under the ground in the caves of the Fir Bolg, but it seemed that Doctor

Tau-Tau had more to tell.

"Of course," said Doctor Tau-Tau. He frowned for a minute, then continued. "The Great Cortado called me into his trailer one night and asked me how much Celeste had taught me about the healing of the mind. I told him the extent of my talent, and that I was making a detailed study of Celeste's notebooks. He cut me short and demanded that I restore Bumble Fumble to his wits at once. He had a whottle of biskey in his hand, and his blunderbuss lay across his lap. He threatened to shoot me there and then if I refused."

Doctor Tau-Tau began to slice a sausage carefully on his plate. "It's not easy to work under such a threat, and I may have exaggerated my skills slightly. Celeste had allowed no one to see her notebooks while she lived, and I was only beginning to try to decipher them. It was tricky work, and mistakes were inevitable. With no time to make a detailed study I prepared a . . . a remedy from bitter herbs and rare ingredients that I found in her wagon, following Celeste's notes as best I could. I took the remedy in to Bumble Fumble, who sat in a darkened wagon staring out of the window as he had since . . . since whatever it was had made him like that."

Miles stared at Doctor Tau-Tau as he spoke. A feeling of dread was rising up from the soles of his feet, making the fortune-teller's words slippery and hard to grasp. He felt Little's hand on his, and he realized he was gripping the tablecloth tightly. Doctor Tau-Tau rambled on, his poppy eyes concentrating on his sausage.

"Of course, I didn't realize the full power of those ingredients when prepared by a master healer such as myself. The remedy was supposed to lift the spirits of the desolate, but I must have misread the quantities of some key ingredients. The light was bad, of course, and the handwriting . . ."

"What happened?" said Miles. His voice was little more than a whisper.

Doctor Tau-Tau looked up, and for the first time he seemed to realize what he was saying. "Ah yes . . . m-most unfortunate," he stammered. "The remedy was a hundred times too strong. Or was it a thousand? It drove the man mad with unbearable joy. He leaped from his chair and bounced around the wagon like a ball bearing in a pinball machine. Broke some fine pieces that Celeste had . . . but never mind. Where was I? Ah yes. Fumble. He was crazed with delight. He bellowed with laughter and embraced me so tightly that he nearly broke my ribs. I was afraid the Great Cortado would hear the commotion and judge this spectacular remedy a failure. It hadn't yet reached its full potential either, as Bumble had fallen to the floor and was rolling with hysteria.

"I knew that I had to make things right and quickly, so I locked him in and ran to my own wagon as fast as I could. I rifled through Celeste's notebooks in a desperate search for oaty-dants to the herbs I had used. Antidotes, I mean. I looked out of the window and I could see Cortado weaving through the darkness with his gun. I made the best mixture I could improvise and ran back to Barty's wagon, shaking the bottle as I went."

Lady Partridge cleared her throat. "Perhaps it would be better not to hear the gory details. I take it that the antidote was not a success."

Doctor Tau-Tau nodded, avoiding Miles's eye. "Alas, no," he said. "No one should have to work under that sort of pressure of course, especially—"

"I want to know," said Miles, "exactly what happened."

"Are you sure, my dear?" asked Lady Partridge. Miles bit his lip and nodded.

"There's not much to tell," said Tau-Tau. "The ingredients I used were correct, of course, but the mixture had never been tried, and I wanted to be sure it was powerful enough to counteract the initial reddy-me . . . remedy. I managed to pour some of the antidote into his mouth as he laughed hysterically, and it seemed to work. He calmed down at once, but unfortunately it did not stop there. His mood darkened by the second, and he became morose and then enraged."

Doctor Tau-Tau seemed lost for a moment in unpleasant memories. He picked up the salt and shook some into his tea. Miles stared at the pop-eyed fortune-teller. His chest felt tight, as though The Null had him in a stranglehold once again. He found it hard to breathe.

"Barty . . . Fumble's skin mottled and began to turn black," said Doctor Tau-Tau in a whisper. "His beard seemed to expand as I watched. His unbearable happiness was gone forever, and everything else went with it. He began to cackle then, a nightmare laugh unlike any sound a man ever made. I could see the light leaving his eyes, and a morning funster . . . a monster forming before me. I could see my reputation suffering unfairly. I saw the Great Cortado at the door with his blunderbuss raised. He fired a blast of the gun, but he was so drunk that he missed me entirely, and shattered the window instead. I pushed past him and out into the night. The little man had lost all perspective, and I had to flee for my life. I had no time to pack anything, not my clothes, not my herbs, not even Celeste's precious notebooks."

"You mean these notebooks?" said Miles. He reached into his pocket and held up two battered notebooks for Doctor Tau-Tau to see. He was numbed by the fortune-teller's dark story. He could feel Lady Partridge's eyes on him, and Little's too, but he fixed his stare on Doctor Tau-Tau's puzzled face. This bloated, blustering man had led him to believe that his father was alive, when all along he knew exactly what had become of Barty Fumble, because he himself had turned him into a living nightmare.

The crushing weight in Miles's chest seemed to grow even heavier, and he could almost smell The Null's rotten banana smell. He felt dizzy, and closed his eyes for a moment, the notebooks shaking in his outstretched hand. A terrible thought that had been growing in his mind as Tau-Tau described his father's fate suddenly came to the surface. Perhaps The Null had not been trying to kill him as it squeezed him in a rib-cracking embrace at the top of a pillar in the Palace of Laughter. Maybe, thought

Miles, when the beast had bowled through Silverpoint and made straight for him it was following some distant echo of the blood. Maybe it had a blind instinct to fill the howling emptiness it felt inside. Maybe, in a bizarre sort of way, that deadly bear hug was nothing more than a lost father hugging his lost son. It was too much to think about now, at the breakfast table on Lady Partridge's lawn, and he pushed the thought down with an effort and opened his eyes.

Doctor Tau-Tau was still staring at him with his mouth open. "Those are mine!" he spluttered. "Where did you get them?"

"They fell out of your bag when you dropped it from the tree," said Miles, forcing himself to breathe. "I've seen them before, on the floor of your wagon. The name Celeste is written inside the covers."

"Celeste? No it isn't!" said Doctor Tau-Tau, his face turning an unhealthy puce. Miles opened the notebooks. "Of course it is," said Tau-Tau. "But they were blank apart from the name. All that writing is a result of my research, made while I traveled through foreign parts in search of knowledge. And money, of course, but mostly knowledge. I . . ."

Miles put the notebooks back in his pocket. The

more he learned about this red-faced windbag, the more he found their lives were entangled. It seemed there were some ties that could never be cut. "Remember what Baltinglass said," said Miles to Doctor Tau-Tau. "The diaries are mine."

Doctor Tau-Tau deflated at the mention of Baltinglass's name. "You have a lot of things to put right," said Miles, "and the first thing is your promise to help me look for my father. You may have forgotten it, but I haven't."

CHAPTER TWENTY-EIGHT
A CHIME IN TIME

Sergeant Bramley, red-eyed and road-dusted, blinked wearily as he drove the police van over the stone bridge and up Broad Street toward the police station. The sergeant avoided working overtime whenever he could, but it seemed that every time he became entangled with Lady Partridge he was sure to lose a night's sleep. He and his crack search team had spent the night combing the countryside for The Null without success, but having dropped off the other constables in the surrounding villages and hamlets he decided that reporting to Lady Partridge could wait until he had spent a few hours in his comfortable bed. Fate, however, had other ideas.

An unexpected commotion was waiting for him when he turned into the small square at the top of the street. Some fifty or sixty people were milling about in front of the police station, and the mood looked ugly. You may wonder how Sergeant Bramley could tell this at a glance, but he had many years of policing behind him, and he knew that when several of the people present have their hands wrapped around the throats of their neighbors it is seldom a good sign. Add to that several black eyes, at least two bandaged heads and a great deal of finger-jabbing and there is no longer any doubt that trouble is afoot. Sergeant Bramley groaned. He considered trying to do a U-turn before he was spotted, but he could see a couple of people that he had recently fined for doing just that, and they had spotted him already. He parked right in the middle of the square, and stepped down from the cab, brushing the dust from his uniform.

"Now then," he said in a commanding croak. "What's all this? Obstructing the public thoroughfare. Causing an affray. Who's in charge here?"

"You are!" shouted Piven the baker, who had a firm grip on the sleeve of a pasty-looking boy with a worried expresssion. "And I want this delinquent arrested."

"I didn't do nothing," protested the boy. There were shouts from other members of the crowd, who were pressing forward to air their complaints. Sergeant Bramley held up his hand and glowered at them.

"You haven't done much work, maybe," said Piven, "but you've managed to clean out the cash-box behind my back, and I only hired you a fort-night ago. And then—" He turned back to Sergeant Bramley. "Then he has the cheek to ask me for an advance on his pay."

The worried-looking boy held his hands out, palms upward. "I needed me bicycle fixed, else I'd have to walk three miles to work. He docks me wages if I'm late."

The sergeant took out his notebook and reached behind his ear for a pencil. He had no intention of writing anything down, but it was an old habit and it helped him to think.

"Now let's get the facts straight," he said to Piven. "You say this lad's been pilfering from you?"

Piven nodded. "I picked up the cashbox yester-day to take it to the bank, and there wasn't a penny left in it."

"If the lad has cleaned you out," Sergeant Bramley pointed out, "he'd have to be a bigger fool than he looks to ask you for more money, wouldn't he?"

"That's what I told him," said the boy, "and I'm certainly not a bigger fool than I look, Sergeant sir."

A small man broke through the crowd at this point and planted himself in front of the sergeant. He had a nasty black eye and his arm was in a sling. "Never mind that," he interrupted angrily. "What about that lying toe-rag who lives next door to me? Says I shinned up his ladder and stole a watch from his bedroom, when he's the one who's been helping himself to our silverware."

More shouts came from the crowd, and the people pressed forward. It seemed that everyone had a theft to report, and it was clear that the resulting investigations would last until Christmas and beyond. Sergeant Bramley placed his whistle in his mouth and blew with all his might. The piercing shriek had the desired effect. The people shrank back automatically, as though they expected a cordon of highly trained policemen to appear on cue and surround them.

"Now then," said the sergeant hoarsely, "all complaints will be dealt with in due course. The police station will reopen this afternoon at four o'clock sharp, and all allegations must be written in triplicate and signed by the allegator." He was not sure if that was a real word, and for a moment he pictured sixty irate reptiles clutching crumpled papers and hammering on his door.

An old lady stepped forward and poked the sergeant in the chest with her green umbrella. "Due course is no good to me, young man!" she shouted. "I need my money returned this afternoon. I've got cat food to buy, and the coal man comes first thing in the morning."

The shouting and jostling began again, and the sergeant was just wondering whether a second blast on the whistle would work as well as the first, when twelve o'clock came to his rescue. Now if you think that the arrival of midday is too ordinary an event to save a lone policeman from sixty feuding neighbors, you have not taken into account the strange phenomenon of the Pinchbucket clocks. The ugly clock that Fowler Pinchbucket had presented to Lady Partridge had spent the summer on the sideboard by the open window, and although it only chimed twice a day, everyone who heard it was captivated by its beautiful melody. Before long the Pinchbuckets were doing a brisk trade in the clocks, which sold for a remarkably low price. Every chime was different, but so skillfully were they made that each one joined with the next to create a spectacular symphony that floated and whirled through the narrow streets like the summer breeze itself, and for a short while work would cease and coffee would be brewed, and people would remember just what it was they liked about their day, even if they could not give it a name.

It was this feeling that swept through the crowd as midday struck and the Pinchbucket clocks worked their spell. For a moment the urgency left their complaints, and they felt sheepish at having leaped to assumptions about their neighbors and friends. A moment was enough for Sergeant Bramley, who set a course for his bed and slipped through the crowd with the stealth of a much thinner man. The crowd began to drift away so that they could put their complaints in writing, which suddenly seemed a perfectly reasonable suggestion, and the sergeant breathed a huge sigh of relief as he turned his key in the police station door, leaving his dusty van right where it was in the center of the square.

Miles Wednesday, breathless and mission-bent, slowed for a moment as he neared the police station despite the urgency of his task. A tinkling chime that seemed to come from everywhere and nowhere was sweeping through the air. It was almost as beautiful as the music Little coaxed from the circus orchestra, and for a moment it seemed to lift the terrible chill that Doctor Tau-Tau's revelations had laid on his heart.

Little smiled as she caught up with him, and together they let the music wash over them as they paused to wait for Lady Partridge and Doctor Tau-Tau, who puffed and panted behind them in a tide of cats. "Do you hear that?" said Miles.

Little nodded. "I heard it last night too. It sounds like the chime from many clocks like Lady Partridge's. The tunes dance together like the stars. It's very clever."

"Isn't it beautiful?" said Lady Partridge as she caught up. "I sometimes wonder if that Pinchbucket man was just totally unsuited to working with children. He's become quite popular since he started dealing in clocks, though they're no prettier to look at than he is."

"It sounds like there are a lot of them," said Miles, who was not ready to forgive Fowler Pinchbucket for the years of brutish treatment he had suffered in Pinchbucket House.

"They're being snapped up faster than the Pinchbuckets can import them," said Lady Partridge. "A small foreign gentleman arrives every week or so with a new batch, and they're usually sold out by the next day. They do tend to break down rather frequently, in fact my own clock hasn't chimed since Tuesday, but I suppose such an airy sound must require a delicate mechanism, and Mr. Pinchbucket runs a very reasonable repair service. He does it for a song, in fact." Lady Partridge bellowed with laughter at her own joke.

"Fowler Pinchbucket repairs the clocks *himself*?" Miles asked in disbelief. Fowler Pinchbucket had taken care of all the repairs at Pinchbucket House, and the grim building had grown steadily more dilapidated until it seemed that only the paint was holding it together.

The music of the clocks faded away, and Miles tried to quicken the pace again as they approached the police station. He was not prepared to rest until The Null had been found, and he was relieved to see that Sergeant Bramley appeared to be opening up for the day. The square seemed much busier than usual, and Miles noticed a number of rather bruised and battered-looking people milling about. They seemed in general to be dispersing, as though they had come for a riot and then changed their minds.

"Sergeant Bramley!" boomed Lady Partridge's voice across the square. The sergeant froze on the steps of the police station, and Miles distinctly saw his shoulders sag as he turned around to face them.

"I'm so glad we've caught you," said Lady Partridge. "We've had some news that makes it doubly important that we find The Null before it gets itself into trouble, unless of course you've got the creature in the back of the van already." She glanced curiously at the stranded van in the center of the square.

Sergeant Bramley, standing at the top of the police station steps, took a deep breath and folded his arms. "The investigation is ongoing," he stated in his best spokesman voice. "You may be sure we are working around the clock to follow all lines of inquiry. The station will be closed until four P.M."

"You mean you've lost The Null," said Lady Partridge, "and now you're going to bed."

"Yes," said Sergeant Bramley. "I mean no. The beast has slipped through the net for the present. I will be regrouping until four o'clock." A pleading tone had entered his voice, but Lady Partridge showed no sign of noticing it.

"I'm sure you're in need of a cup of tea," said Lady Partridge, who was convinced that tea held the answer to everything, "and we shall be happy to join you, while we discuss the best way to continue our search."

"Very well," sighed Sergeant Bramley. He was too tired to argue. He slouched into the small police station and filled the kettle. The interior of the station was stuffed with loose papers, beige files, paper clips, faded posters of missing pets and desperate criminals, old raffle tickets, full notebooks, empty cigarette packets, used carbon paper, rubber stamps and ink bottles. Lady Partridge removed a pile of papers from a swivel chair and sat down, while Sergeant Bramley brewed tea in a battered pot.

"Well, Sergeant," she said. "What's the plan of attack?"

Sergeant Bramley shuffled the papers on his desk in a random sort of way, until a yellowed map came to the top. He opened it out carefully. The map had been folded so many times that it had almost separated along the creases into a pile of long rectangles. "We have conducted an intensive search of the area between Larde, Hay and Shallowford," he said, stabbing at the map with a blunt finger. "And as yet have not managed to apprehend the suspect."

"The Null is not a suspect," said Lady Partridge, "until he does something illegal."

"Not a suspect?" said Doctor Tau-Tau indignantly. "The beast kidnapped me and hung me in a tree!"

"Yes, well . . . ," said the sergeant, looking distinctly as though he sided with The Null on that one, "be that as it may, I will make a detailed study of the region to decide which way the beast is likely to have gone. He smoothed the tattered map on his desk and leaned forward on his elbows, pulling his cap low over his eyes.

Miles and Little collected an assortment of enamel mugs and chipped teacups from around the cluttered office, and poured the tea. Doctor Tau-Tau swallowed his tea in two gulps, and stood for a moment staring into the teacup, which he had placed on the counter in front of him. He began to massage his temples with his fingertips. "I see something in the tea leaves," he said. "A picture of the beast is emerging. It is somewhere not too distant, but where we have not searched as yet."

Miles peered curiously into the cup. "I can just see a blob," he said.

"Of course you can," said Doctor Tau-Tau shortly. "You need a keen second sight to be able to read the leaves." He went back to rubbing his temples. "The creature has gone south. It is near—just a moment—it is nearing the town of Iota as we speak."

"Are you seriously suggesting that we should follow the tea leaves to search for a frightened and dangerous beast?" asked Lady Partridge.

Doctor Tau-Tau sniffed loudly. "You may take my advice or leave it," he said. "As for me, I will come with you to Iota, if only to have the opportunity to test my extra-strength sleepwater."

"What would you say, Sergeant?" said Lady Partridge. "Sergeant?"

The sergeant gave a little start and began to fold the map hastily.

"Were you asleep, Sergeant Bramley?" said Lady Partridge.

"Of course not, ma'am," said the sergeant, and Miles heard him mutter under his breath, "No such luck."

CHAPTER TWENTY-NINE
MISSING PERSONS

Miles Wednesday, jolted, bounced and Iota-bound, stared at the little wooden dog that sat on the dashboard of Sergeant Bramley's paddy wagon. It was the kind of dog that has a spring for a neck and is supposed to nod happily at each bump in the road, but the combination of the sergeant's lunatic driving and a van without viable suspension had the little wooden beast in such a frenzy of nodding it seemed his head would fly off at any moment.

Miles barely noticed. He was thinking of the monstrous creature that had once been his father, and try as he might he could not shake off the feeling that somehow he had let the beast down by not guessing its true nature before. Nonetheless he had stared into the empty eyes of The Null from much closer than he would have wished to, and when he thought of the howling void that he saw there it seemed that the hope of finding his father was more remote than ever.

He peered through the dusty windshield for any sign of the town of Iota. It was the place of his birth, according to the story the tiger had told him by their campfire the year before, which meant it was also the town where his mother had died. In his mind's eye he could see a place of storms and statues and strange gateways, and as he watched the road ahead the dim outline of a church spire came into view, rising above the trees. The van swerved suddenly into a small picnic area beside the road, and skidded to a halt. Sergeant Bramley jumped down from the cab and disappeared around the back of the van. He returned a moment later with Doctor Tau-Tau, who looked as though he had spent a couple of hours in a cocktail shaker. "I should have been traveling up front," the fortune-teller was grumbling, "especially as I'm the one who knows the whereabouts of the beast."

"That remains to be seen. Besides, space in front

is limited to authorized personnel, and I'm the one who does the authorizing."

Doctor Tau-Tau stood by the van massaging his temples with a wounded expression. A column of steam rose from the engine, adding atmosphere to the proceedings. "We are close now," he intoned, "but the danger is great. The beast is enraged by the chase, and it must be approached with great care. It will be best if just I and the boy go on from here."

"I'm afraid that's out of the question," boomed Lady Partridge. "Isn't it, Sergeant Bramley?"

"Er . . . quite," said the sergeant. "Constables Flap and Wigge will accompany the boy and the oddball. As senior officer I will remain here in a command and control capacity."

"You are far too modest, Sergeant," said Lady Partridge. "I shall stay here and look after the van. Your steely nerve will be needed if the creature is found, and your constables will be looking to you for leadership."

Sergeant Bramley, who had already pulled the peak of his cap low in preparation for a spot of quiet command and control in the cabin of the van, sighed deeply. "Well, if you put it that way . . . ," he said. He tucked his truncheon into his belt with a resigned air.

"Where do you believe the suspect to be?" he asked Doctor Tau-Tau.

"The beast will be in the churchyard," said Tau-Tau.

"How can you be sure it's there?" asked Miles.

"Because my second sight tells me so," said Tau-Tau, "and anyway, if it can't get to you it's bound to end up here."

"But why?" asked Miles. A sudden thought came to him. "Is this . . . where my mother is buried?" he asked.

"It's the most likely place," said Doctor Tau-Tau. "I've never been here myself. Except," he added, "in my travels of the mind, you understand."

"Never mind all that," said Sergeant Bramley. "Which way is the churchyard?"

"That way," said Constable Flap before Doctor Tau-Tau could reply. The constable had done a course in orienteering in *Modern Constable* magazine and knew that the churchyard was sure to be a stone's throw from the spire that rose above the trees ahead of them.

"Lead the way then, Flap," said Sergeant Bramley. The search party set off along a narrow path that wound through the trees. At the front were Constable Flap, carrying the rolled-up net, and Constable Wigge, who was quaking with fear.

Sergeant Bramley followed with Miles and Little, and Doctor Tau-Tau brought up the rear. The fortune-teller carried a long black case and glanced about him nervously. They came to the edge of the trees and Constable Flap motioned them to stop, using internationally recognized hand signals. Ahead of them was a church of dark stone, its narrow steeple rising from a green copper roof. The shadow of the steeple lay like an exclamation mark across the churchyard, ending in a circle of deep shade under an enormous yew tree.

"It's there, all right," whispered Constable Flap, pointing at the yew tree. At first Miles could not make out anything unusual among the crooked gravestones in the tree's shadow, then all at once he noticed that one of the silhouettes was considerably shaggier than the others. When he shaded his eyes he could make out the shape of The Null, hunched and motionless by the mighty trunk. Miles could not tell if the beast had seen them or not. It seemed to be looking straight at him, but it neither moved nor uttered a sound. Miles began to creep forward, but Constable Flap reached out and gripped his elbow. At least, thought Miles, it was a step up from the Special Ear Pinch Arrest Method.

"Not so fast, lad," whispered Sergeant Bramley from behind him. "The suspect didn't seem too pleased to see you before, and what's more it was last seen in the company of a dangerous and probably unlicensed feline."

"A *Panthera tigris*, in fact," added Constable Flap.

"I won't get too close," said Miles. "Anyway," he lied, "I think it's asleep."

Sergeant Bramley cleared his throat. "Very well. Flap, Wigge, accompany the boy with the net extended."

Miles stepped out into the sunlight. The grass was dry and scrubby beneath his feet, and somewhere high above him a skylark sang. He walked slowly toward the yew tree, and the closer he got the more certain he was that The Null was watching him. He expected at any moment to hear its insane cackle, or to see the beast unfold from the shadows and charge toward him, but The Null did not move a muscle. Miles risked a glance over his shoulder. Constable Flap seemed to be trying to keep abreast of him, but Constable Wigge, white-faced and gripping the other end of the net, was acting as a brake. From the edge of the trees Sergeant Bramley watched them with a frown, his whistle clamped between his fleshy lips, while Doctor Tau-Tau knelt on the ground, fumbling with the long black case he had brought. Little sat in the low branches of a tree, like a white bird among the dark green foliage.

Miles reached the low stone wall that surrounded the churchyard. He could see The Null clearly now. It sat hunched on an overgrown grave, brooding and black, and staring straight at Miles with its red-rimmed eyes.

"Hello," said Miles quietly. "Do you remember me?" He forced himself to meet The Null's eyes. It was as though the creature were hollow, containing nothing but all the empty space in the universe. Miles felt as he had when he looked into the mouth of hell, deep in the caves of the Fir Bolg. The hair stood up on the back of his neck, yet at the same time he was sure somehow that The Null was listening to him.

"Why don't you come home?" he asked the creature. The Null gave an immense sigh, and turned its massive head slowly away. At that moment there came a sound from behind Miles that sounded like a cork being drawn softly from a bottle. He felt something whistle past his right ear, and a small yellow dart appeared as if by magic in The Null's neck. The beast stiffened and let out a deafening howl. Its clawed hand scrabbled in the thick hair on its neck, but before it could find the dart it keeled slowly over and lay still among the weeds.

Miles gasped with shock. He turned sharply to the two policemen behind him, but they were staring openmouthed at the slumped figure of The Null, looking as surprised as Miles himself. Over Constable Wigge's shoulder he spotted Doctor Tau-Tau emerging from the trees with a long blowpipe in his hand and a smug look on his face.

"Is the monster out?" shouted the beaming fortune-teller. A wave of anger flooded through Miles, mixed with a terrible disappointment. Doctor Tau-Tau approached cautiously. "Just as I thought," he said, peering into the yew tree's shadow. "You're safe now, boy. Nothing on earth can withstand my full-strength sleepwater, especially when it's administered properly. When administered properly," he repeated, "my sleepwater is overwhelming."

Miles's knees felt suddenly weak. He could see Little drop from the branch where she perched and run across the grass toward him, and he sat back heavily on the stone wall. "What did you do *that* for?" he said to Tau-Tau.

The fortune-teller gave him a puzzled look. "What did I . . . ? The beast would have torn you limb from limb, boy. What do you think I did it for?"

Miles shook his head. "No it wouldn't. It's the first time it's ever let me get close. I don't know what it was going to do, and I'll probably never know now, thanks to you!"

Doctor Tau-Tau's face turned a darker red. "Nonsense, boy. You don't know what you're talking about. If I hadn't subdued the beast you'd be hanging from a tree at this moment, or worse. The creature is clearly deranged. When you get over the shock of being menaced you'll thank me for my prompt action, don't you worry."

"Not if I live to be a thousand," hissed Miles. "That creature used to be my father, and if it hung you in a tree it was no more than you deserved." At that moment Sergeant Bramley arrived from the far side of the clearing, his notebook in his hand and his pencil retrieved from its perch behind his ear. "Mr. Tau-Tau," he said, "I'm afraid I'm going to have to arrest you for possession of an offensive blowpipe."

"Arrest me?" spluttered Doctor Tau-Tau. "For saving the boy?"

"Constable Wigge," said the sergeant, "you will relieve the oddball of his weapon, conduct him back to the police vehicle and lock him in the back, then you will drive the van back here so we can load the suspe . . . The Null onboard before it comes around."

Constable Wigge needed no further urging to put some distance between himself and The Null, sleepwater or no sleepwater. He took the blowpipe from the rapidly purpling fortune-teller and snapped a pair of handcuffs on his wrists, then he grasped him by the elbow and steered him back the way they had come.

Doctor Tau-Tau shook himself free of Constable Wigge's grip for a moment and turned to Miles. "Boy," he said in a trembling voice, "you will regret your ingratitude. I have seen death stalk you through the cards, and only I know how close it is." Constable Wigge gripped his elbow again, more firmly this time, and marched him toward the trees. "Your death I have seen," shouted Doctor Tau-Tau over his shoulder, "and it is not far behind you, boy."

Miles Wednesday, dust-caked and sleepwater-thwarted, knelt in the weeds by the inert monster that had once been his father. Despite its size The Null looked helpless, its mouth hanging open loosely and its sightless eyes half closed. He leaned forward and looked closely at the creature's hairy face, trying to make out any trace of the man in the bleached-out photograph that he kept in his inside pocket.

"Do you think you will get your father back?" said Little quietly, making him jump.

Miles shrugged. "I don't know if there's anything of him left in there," he said. "What do you think?"

"I don't know either," said Little. "I never saw a thing without a name in the One Song before. But the name of Barty Fumble must be somewhere, because it has not ceased to exist."

"How do you know, if you can't find it?" asked Miles.

"I can't find its place in the One Song," said Little, "but if it was not there, the name Barty Fumble would sound more . . . hollow. It would not have a color. It's difficult to explain."

"What if I do get him back," said Miles, "and I don't like him? What if he wasn't as nice as everyone says?"

Little thought about this for a minute. "I never had a father or a mother," she said, "so I don't really know much about it. But I don't suppose everyone would have liked him so much unless there was a good reason."

"Tau-Tau didn't like him at all," said Miles.

"Doctor Tau-Tau likes himself a lot," laughed

Little. "I don't think there's much room left in his heart for anyone else."

Little's laughter seemed to sweep some of the gloom away, and Miles felt himself smile. He sat back on his heels and looked around him. The Null showed no sign of awaking from its stupor, and Sergeant Bramley and Constable Flap had found a comfortable seat on a stone vault a little distance away. The constable was showing the sergeant a deadly choke hold that he had learned from *Modern Constable* magazine. As he thought it unwise to lay deadly hands on the sergeant, he was demonstrating the hold on himself. Sergeant Bramley, who did not want to appear too interested, was taking his time lighting a cigarette as his constable turned slowly blue. Somewhere in the distance a motor roared to life and buzzed for a while before fading into the autumn air.

Miles and Little sat by The Null, as though they were babysitting an enormous hairy infant. It lay at the foot of a simple granite headstone that was half obscured by tangled weeds, and it was some time before Miles noticed a name carved into the stone in plain, unpainted letters. He reached across The Null and pulled the weeds apart. The inscription read:

Celeste Mahnoosh Elham
What time has stolen
Let it be

Miles read the inscription several times over. So this is my family, he thought, together at last. My mother deep underground, my father no more than a shadow, hollowed out and covered in hair, and a four-hundred-year-old sister whom my parents never knew. He supposed this odd family reunion should seem strange to him, but it did not. He had never known any other life, so what was there to compare it to?

"There's just you and me, really," he said to Little. He felt Tangerine scrambling around in his pocket, and his grubby orange head poked out into the afternoon air. He looked at the sleeping monster, and quickly disappeared back into the safety of his pocket. "And Tangerine, of course," said Miles.

Little smiled at him. "We've done okay so far, haven't we?" she said.

"I suppose so," said Miles.

The sound of the police van came from the direction of the road, and a moment later it jerked into view. The van chugged and bounced along beside the green and pulled into the gravel drive-way of the church, where the engine promptly died.

Miles watched in surprise as Lady Partridge squeezed herself from the driving seat and stepped down into the gravel. "I'm afraid I'm rather out of practice with driving, but I got tired of waiting," she called. "Did you find any trace of The Null?"

"We found more than a trace, Lady P.," said Sergeant Bramley. "We have in fact located and subdued the entire suspect. Didn't Constable Wigge fill you in on the details?"

"Constable Wigge?" said Lady Partridge. "I thought he was with you."

"I sent the constable back to the van some time ago," said the sergeant, pulling out his notebook without even noticing, "to place the oddball with the red hat under lock and key. Do you mean to tell me they never showed up?"

"Not a sign of them," said Lady Partridge. "We had better search for them right away."

Sergeant Bramley flipped open his notebook. "Constable Flap and I will form a search party," he said, as he wrote in fat round letters: Missing persons, 2.

CHAPTER THIRTY

THE LIE DETECTOR

Miles Wednesday, egged, baconed and armed with a screwdriver, sat in the dining room of Partridge Manor with Lady Partridge's black Pinchbucket clock on the table in front of him. The breakfast things had been cleared away and Lady Partridge had asked Miles to see if he could repair the clock, which had not chimed for several days. She said she was tired of calling on Fowler Pinchbucket, but in truth she knew that Miles liked to tinker with anything mechanical, and she was looking for something to take his mind off the events of the day before.

They had found Constable Wigge alone and face

down in the bracken, not far from the churchyard. He had a large lump on the back of his head and was sleeping like a baby. There was no sign of a struggle, which seemed to indicate—in the sergeant's expert opinion—that Constable Wigge had somehow managed to knock himself out and let the prisoner escape. A search of the vicinity had found no further sign of the fortune-teller, and no one had been keen to hang around until The Null woke from its slumber. They had backed the van up to the yew tree and loaded the creature, with great difficulty, into the back.

They had returned to Larde to find the Circus Bolsillo already setting up camp in the long field at the bottom of the hill. Constable Wigge had been placed under the care of Baumella, who was becoming an expert in looking after the comatose, and Little had been sent to the circus to enlist the help of K2 in lifting The Null back into its fortified home.

Miles had hardly slept during the night, and he had dressed himself quietly before sunrise and gone to the gazebo to look in on The Null. He found the beast still groggy from Doctor Tau-Tau's powerful sedative, but he had sat in the old armchair beside the bars until breakfast time to keep it company. Now as he examined Lady Partridge's clock he wondered if The Null's life would ever consist of anything more than sullen brooding and fits of hysterical rage. He had no idea if it would be possible to retrieve his father and restore him to his former self, and indeed he seemed to be the only one who believed that Barty Fumble might still be lost somewhere in that hairy hulk.

The Bolsillo brothers had said that Celeste's powers of healing were greatly enhanced by the Tiger's Egg, and if that was true then the Egg held his only hope of bringing his father back. He was no closer to finding where it might be, however, and even if he found it he knew that the Great Cortado held the key to its use. He thought of the inscription on his mother's headstone: "What time has stolen, let it be." Had she chosen this epitaph herself? Was this a message for her son, that he should not waste his life searching for a father who was dead and gone, as Fabio Bolsillo had said?

"Have you figured out how to open it?" asked Little, sitting down beside him and examining the plain face of the clock.

Miles blinked his thoughts away, and turned the clock around so that it faced away from him. It was far heavier than he had expected, and he had needed all his strength just to lift it from the sideboard to the table. It sounded like all the insides had come loose and were sliding around inside the heavy black case. There was a small door of some sort in the back of the clock, but he could not see any lock or catch that would enable him to open it. Near the base of the clock were four large screws, two on either side, and a small brass plaque with the words QUALIFIED REPAIR PERSONNEL ONLY engraved on it. He removed the screws and placed them carefully to one side, then he stood up on his chair so that he could lift off the outer case more easily.

What spilled out of the case was not what you would expect to find inside any clock. An avalanche of coins poured across the table, along with an old pocket watch, several spoons, a porcelain thimble, a saltcellar, an assortment of jewelry, a silver gravy boat, two napkin rings, a gold locket with a tiny photograph of a boy in a sailor suit, a silver cigarette case, an opal hatpin, a single cuff link and a number of other shiny items, but by far the most surprising thing was a pair of white rats with pink eyes, who sat in the middle of this hoard blinking in the sudden light. They seemed surprised to find themselves on the table in Lady Partridge's dining room.

Miles stared at the white rats in astonishment. Little laughed, and the music of her laughter set the chimes dancing within the intricate mechanism of the clock. "Hello!" she said to the rats. She squeaked a question at them, and the two rats looked at each other. Their whiskers twitched, and the smaller of the two turned to Little and squeaked something back. Miles placed the case down as gently as he could, but the rats seemed in no hurry to go anywhere, as though their natural habitat were a pile of coins and assorted silverware. Little squeaked at them again, and they made a great show of curling up and closing their eyes, though Miles distinctly saw the larger rat was peeking.

"What did he say?" Miles asked.

"He said that it was nice and dark in the clock, and they were just resting."

"Ask them how they got in there," said Miles. With the case lying on its side he could see that the little door in the back had a simple catch on the inside, which struck him as odd. Little squeaked at them again, but they made no answer, and one of them gave a tiny snort that sounded a little like a snore.

At that moment Lady Partridge sailed in through the door on a tide of cats. "Miles?" she said.

"Sergeant Bramley would like . . ." The sight of the small pile of spilled treasure stopped her in mid-sentence. "What on *earth* . . . ?" she said, and she moved forward for a closer look. "Why, that's Dartforth's cigarette case . . . and my pearl earrings. I've searched everywhere for those. There's my locket. What *is* all this stuff doing here?"

"That's just what we were wondering," said Miles. "Little was just asking these two." He pointed at the curled-up rats. "I think they must be Fowler Pinchbucket's. He's always bred rats."

Lady Partridge took her spectacles from her dressing-gown pocket and balanced them on her nose. "My goodness! They *are* rats. I though it was a pair of gloves. Do you mean to tell me they were inside the clock too?"

There was a soft thump as a large gray cat landed on the table. He, too, seemed very interested in the rats. Little said something to him, and he shot her a disappointed look and began licking his paws, as if a pair of tasty white rats were the last thing on his mind.

"They appear to be asleep," said Lady Partridge, peering closely at the rats.

"I think they're just pretending," said Miles. "They said they liked to sleep in the clock because it's nice and dark inside."

"That would hardly explain how a selection of my valuables and a mountain of cash got in there with them," said Lady Partridge. "Although I suppose you could say their money has made them comfortable!" Lady Partridge guffawed with laughter, giving the rats such a start that they were unable to keep up the pretense of sleeping, and instead sat up in the middle of the hoard, blinking sheepishly.

"Sergeant Bramley," called Lady Partridge, "I think you should come in and see this."

Sergeant Bramley sidled in through the door, stepping carefully to avoid the cats that swirled around him, followed a moment later by Constable Flap. "Master Miles. Miss Little," said the sergeant, touching the peak of his cap. He surveyed the pile of valuables and the two white rats, who were looking more uncomfortable by the minute.

"Well, well," said Sergeant Bramley. "What have we here?"

"I opened the clock to see if I could fix it," said Miles, "and we found all this stuff inside. The rats were in there too."

"Rats, eh?" said Sergeant Bramley.

"*Rattus norvegicus*," said Constable Flap.

"Thank you, Constable," said the sergeant, without

turning around. "Now why would anyone hide a couple of rats and a pile of money in a clock, do you suppose?"

"I think it was the rats who brought the rest of the stuff into the clock," said Miles. He upended the heavy clock case so the policemen could see inside. "Look. There's a kind of door here, but the catch is on the inside."

Sergeant Bramley looked at Miles and raised an eyebrow. "Best leave the detective work to the professionals, Master Miles," he said. "What would a rat want with a pocket watch, eh?"

"That's just what we were asking them," said Miles.

"Asking them?" repeated the sergeant.

"Little has a way with animals, Sergeant," said Lady Partridge. "She can speak to them."

"Is that so?" said the sergeant, a look of mild irritation creeping across his face. "I'm afraid interrogation of a suspect must be carried out by a police officer. It will never stand up in court otherwise."

Constable Flap's face brightened. "We could always swear the girl in as a special deputy," he said. He was thinking of the door-to-door inquiries that might be avoided by questioning the rats directly, and he knew that with Constable Wigge on sick leave and the sergeant on important desk duties it would be his own shoe leather that would be worn out in any such investigation.

"Special deputy?" said Sergeant Bramley. "You can't just go swearing people in willy-nilly. It's against procedure."

"No it's not, sir," said Constable Flap. "As senior officer you have the authority. I read about it in—"

"Yes, yes, no doubt," said the sergeant.

"I've got the wording here, sir," said the constable, pulling a folded paper from his breast pocket. "I keep it about my person in case of emergencies." He handed the paper to the sergeant.

Sergeant Bramley put on his glasses and cleared his throat. "Raise your right hand, young lady," he said.

"Which one is that?" whispered Little to Miles.

"The one you write with," said Miles.

"I write with both of them," said Little, and she raised both hands at once.

"I do solemnly swear . . . ," said the sergeant, reading from the paper. He paused, and Miles nudged Little with his elbow.

"So do I," said Little.

"Just repeat what I say, miss. I do solemnly swear to uphold and protect the laws of the land . . ."

"I do solemnly swear to uphold and protect the laws of the land . . . ," said Little, in a voice that sounded remarkably like the sergeant's own. Sergeant Bramley frowned at her, then returned to his paper.

"With the utmost . . . Pah!" He folded the paper again and gave it back to Constable Flap.

"With the utmost pah," said Little, both hands still raised. She enjoyed these rituals that people occupied themselves with. They reminded her of the way she used to zigzag between the cirrus clouds, trying not to touch any of them, instead of just flying directly to where she was supposed to be.

The sergeant began again. "I promise to uphold the law without throwing my weight around, and to give back my badge when asked for it," he said.

"I don't have a badge," said Little, "but I promise anyway."

Sergeant Bramley turned and unpinned one of several silver badges that Constable Flap wore on his uniform, and pinned it to Little's shirt. It was his Criminal Mastermind Outsmarting badge, second class, and the constable was particularly proud of it. He bit his lip and said nothing.

"Thank you," said Little. "Can I put my hands down now?"

The sergeant nodded. "Now," he said, tapping his pencil against his chin, "ask these here rodents how they came to be napping in a clock on a pile of money."

Little had a brief conversation with the smaller of the two, who seemed to be the spokesrat. "They said they sneaked in for a nap, and the money was already in there."

"I think it's the money that was stopping the chimes," said Miles. "There's no room for the mechanism to work." As if to prove him right, the emptied clock gave a whirring cough, and a series of tiny brass hammers began to strike the chimes. It was well before midday, but the clock was made to chime and it had been silent for long enough. The music cascaded through the room, more beautiful than ever without the heavy black case to contain it. The two policemen, the dark-haired boy, the plump lady and the special deputy were lost for a time in worlds within worlds, and not one of them noticed the rats as they sidled and slid down the side of the money mountain and crept to the edge of the table. The edge of the table, however, was as far as they got. Below them the room was carpeted with cats, and canny as the rats were they had not begun to find a way over that obstacle when the last chimes died away and Constable Flap spotted their escape attempt.

"They're trying to evade justice, sir," he said.

"We'll see about that," said Sergeant Bramley. "Constable Flap, go to the van and fetch my lie detector."

The constable's eyes lit up at the sergeant's request. "Do we have one of those?" he asked.

"You'll find it underneath the driver's seat," said the sergeant, keeping his eye firmly on the rats. The constable cleared the cats in one athletic leap and disappeared through the door.

"What's a lie detector?" asked Little.

"It's a device that can tell whether or not you are being truthful," said Lady Partridge. "I must say I didn't know myself that they were standard issue in local police stations."

"I issued this one to myself, Lady P.," said Sergeant Bramley, winking at Miles. Miles looked at Lady Partridge and shrugged.

Constable Flap reappeared with a puzzled expression on his narrow face. He handed the sergeant a large wooden mallet. "This is all I could find under the seat, sir," he said.

"That's my lie detector," said the sergeant. He reached out and grasped the tail of the smaller rat, and raised the mallet in the air. "Now," he said to Little, "ask these here rodents if they can remember anything further about how they came to be in that clock."

Before Little could repeat the question, the rat let out a flurry of frightened squeaks.

"He says the Treat Man put them in there," she said. The rat squeaked some more.

"The Treat Man teaches them to find shiny things and bring them back to exchange for treats. Then he teaches them to open the little door in the clock, but only when it's dark. Once they've got the hang of that he puts two of them in each clock and sends them out. They leave the clock every night to see what they can find, and they fill it up until the bells stop singing. After that they wait and wait, then the Treat Man opens the door and they get a day off and as many treats as they can eat. He empties out the shiny things from the clock and then they go back out on a new mission."

Sergeant Bramley put down the mallet, but did not let go of the rat's tail. "Can the suspect give us a description of this Treat Man?" he said.

"The Treat Man smells like the mushy stuff under the washing machine," Little translated. "His fingernails are dirty."

"That's Fowler Pinchbucket all right," said Miles.

The sergeant released the rat and handed the mallet back to Constable Flap. "Good work, Constable," he said. "And you, Miss Little. You can hold on to that badge for the time being. I may need you to testify in court, once I've decided if these here rodents are suspects, witnesses or evidence."

"Whichever they are," said Lady Partridge, "they've certainly ratted poor Fowler Pinchbucket up a treat," and she dissolved into helpless laughter.

CHAPTER THIRTY-ONE
A RESPECTABLE
ESTABLISHMENT

Sergeant Bramley, sweaty-faced and silver-buttoned, raised his fist and hammered on the door of the Canny Rat. "Open in the name of the law," he bellowed. Constable Flap had suggested that they make use of the element of surprise, but the sergeant did not get many opportunities to shout anything in the name of the law, and he was not about to miss one when it fell into his lap. Windows opened in several neighboring houses at the sound of his command, and the heads of the people of Larde leaned out into the narrow alley. The sergeant raised his fist to knock again, but the door swung open before he had the chance. Mrs.

Pinchbucket emerged from the gloom, a smile pasted on her sour features. "Good morning, Sergeant," she said. "And there's young Miles and his . . . sister. How nice of you all to drop by."

"I have a warrant to search these here premises," said Sergeant Bramley, skipping the formalities. He produced a piece of paper from his pocket and waved it in front of Mrs. Pinchbucket's nose. If she had taken the trouble to read the tiny writing Mrs. Pinchbucket would have discovered that it was just the guarantee on a new sofa that the sergeant had bought the weekend before. The sergeant disliked applying for warrants, which involved driving to Shallowford and climbing the steep driveway of the district judge's house while his suspects generally made good their escape. He found that people tended to believe in official documents without reading them at all, which made it seem doubly foolish to go to all that trouble.

Mrs. Pinchbucket was no exception. She paled slightly, and opened the door wider. "By all means," she said. "There's nothing illegal here. It's a perfectly respectable establishment, and if there was anything illegal here, which there isn't, it wouldn't be ours, and we would know nothing about it. *Fowler!*" she called over her shoulder. "Come up and close that cellar door behind you. There's a terrible draft."

"No can do," came Fowler Pinchbucket's thick voice from somewhere below. "I'm counting the loot. There can't be a draft anyhow, woman. There's no window down here."

Mrs. Pinchbucket's face turned even paler, and her smile more brittle. "Such a hoot, my husband," she said. "We have *visitors*, Fowler," she called in a voice like broken glass.

"No need for introductions, ma'am," said Sergeant Bramley. He marched past Mrs. Pinchbucket in the direction of the cellar door, followed by Miles and Little. Constable Flap closed the front door of the tavern and stood in front of it with his arms folded, leaving the anxious landlady no choice but to follow the sergeant and his companions.

If you have ever been visited by an officer of the law when your cellar is stuffed with stolen goods you have probably found yourself wishing, as Mrs. Pinchbucket did, that something would happen in the nick of time to save you from a long stretch in prison. A husband who can hide things very quickly. A sudden earthquake. A fully grown Bengal tiger who is on your side. None of these things came to Mrs. Pinchbucket's aid, however. When Miles, Little and the sergeant descended the cellar steps they found Fowler Pinchbucket sitting in the center of an enormous pile of coins, silverware, jewelry and trinkets that must have amounted to half the total wealth of Larde, and certainly cleared up any doubts about the mysterious burglaries that had been sweeping the town. Behind him on a long trestle table were a dozen or so of the ugly black clocks, and behind them an entire wall of wire-fronted cages. Some of the cages were empty, and in others Miles could see pairs of white rats, stuffing themselves with nuts or curled up asleep in nests made of shredded paper.

"Well, well, well," said Sergeant Bramley. "What have we here?"

Fowler Pinchbucket stared at the policeman with his mouth open, his brain struggling to come up with a brilliant idea, or indeed any idea, to explain away the incriminating evidence that surrounded him. "It's a research project," said Mrs. Pinchbucket's flinty voice from the cellar steps. "For insurance purposes. We're employed by a foreign gentleman to survey the town's valuables. All these items will be valued and returned. They're simply on loan, you might say."

"That's right," said Fowler, who hadn't quite followed his wife's explanation but knew it would be wise to back it up.

"Valued, eh?" said the sergeant, his pencil poised over a notebook he could barely see in the dim light. "And who might this foreign gentleman be?"

"We don't know, exactly," said Fowler. "He comes by every week or two. Never gives us notice. He looks through all the loot—the borrowed stuff, every last item—then he goes away again. He says we can keep what we want."

"No he doesn't," said Mrs. Pinchbucket frostily. "He asks us to kindly catalog all the items and return them to their rightful owners."

"Exactly what I meant," said Fowler. He got to his feet and wiped his sweating hands on his trousers.

"It doesn't look very cataloged to me," said Miles. "And how are you going to give it all back? Are the rats trained to replace the stuff where they found it?"

Fowler glowered at Miles. "The Wednesday boy, eh?" he said. "How did you know about my rats?"

"You were ratted up a treat," said Sergeant Bramley, trying out Lady Partridge's joke. Fowler looked at him blankly, and the sergeant made a mental note not to try humor on desperate criminals. Especially not Lady Partridge's humor. He cleared his throat. "I'm afraid I'll have to arrest you both on suspicion of rat-assisted theft. You have the right to remain silent, and for that matter I'd prefer it that way. Run up those steps, Master Miles, and tell Flap to get down here with those extra secure handcuffs he got on mail order."

When Miles, Little and the two policemen emerged with the handcuffed Pinchbuckets the neighbors were still leaning out of their windows. They had been waiting for a little drama to liven up the morning, and the arrest of the Pinchbuckets was just the sort of thing they had in mind, although some felt that a few shots and a scream or two might have made things more exciting. As Mrs. Pinchbucket passed by the window of a balding man in a vest, she called up to him: "You owe us two shillings since last Tuesday, and don't think I've forgotten."

CHAPTER THIRTY-TWO
SOMEWHERE MUCH

Miles Wednesday, circus-savvy and almost twelve, headed for the long field where the Circus Bolsillo would be preparing for the last show of the season. The Pinchbuckets had been locked up in the small cell at the back of the police station, and the Canny Rat had been secured until someone could be appointed to sort out the stolen goods and return them to their owners. Meanwhile there was a big top to raise and there were animals to be tended, and the thought of the familiar work put a spring in his step.

He arrived to find the twin peaks of the big top already hoisted, and sections of canvas being laced into place to make the walls of the tent. Tembo and Mamba, who seemed to enjoy the work at least as much as their performance in the ring, trumpeted loudly as Umor walked them back to their enclosure, their part of the job completed. Miles ducked into the huge cool oval of the empty tent and looked upward. As he expected, Fabio and Gila were perched on the crossbar that joined the two main tent poles, checking the rigging and the trapezes and setting up the colored spotlights. "Master Miles!" called Gila. "Where have you been?"

"Nowhere much," said Miles.

"Then get up here to somewhere much and give us a hand," called Fabio.

"We don't have all day," said Gila.

Miles started up the tent pole toward the distant ceiling. He did not have Little's confidence with heights, and chose his footholds with care, but there was no place in the circus he loved more than to be perched up high under the striped sky of the big top. Up there in the rigging was an oasis of peace from which he could look down on the bustle below as he tightened bolts and checked pulleys, and the nervous thrill in his stomach only added to the attraction.

"Well, Master Miles," said Fabio as he reached the

platform at one end of the crossbar. "Last show of the season tonight."

"Back to your schooling after that," said Gila, handing Miles a wrench with a long handle.

"No more being sawn in half," said Fabio.

"Though you can still come and shovel elephant dung for us."

"Tembo and Mamba would miss you if you didn't."

"And so would your shovel."

Miles set to work tightening the tension on the steel cables that held the rigging in place. He had a question he wanted to ask the Bolsillo brothers, but the thought of it made his stomach tighten like the cables with each twist of the wrench. He decided to ask an easier question first. "Where did Barty Fumble's Big Top spend the winters?" he said.

"All over the place, in the early years," said Gila.

"But later we used to winter just outside Fuera," said Fabio, tapping a fat bolt into place with a lump hammer.

"Your father loved Fuera, Master Miles."

"He called it the heartbeat of the world."

"No he didn't, he called it the cocktail of the continents."

"If you ask me," said Umor, running up the rigging

like a monkey in overalls, "it was the temptation of the taverns."

Miles took a deep breath and tried to make his voice as casual as possible. "Why didn't you tell me The Null used to be my father?"

Fabio's tapping stopped instantly. Gila continued fiddling with the cables at the back of a spotlight as though he had gone suddenly deaf, but his shoulders hunched. Umor, who always climbed the rigging barefoot, stared at his toes and said nothing.

"Who told you that?" said Fabio, staring at Miles with his hard black eyes.

"Doctor Tau-Tau," said Miles.

Fabio spat over the edge of the rigging, without looking to see if anyone was below. "Tau-Tau has a head full of wind," he said.

"Maybe," said Miles, "but I'm sure he's telling the truth. He told us the whole story at breakfast the other day. Lady Partridge was there too."

"What did he tell you?" said Fabio quietly.

"He said that he made Barty Fumble into The Null by mistake. The Great Cortado threatened to kill him if he didn't bring my father back to his senses, and he tried to make a cure from Celeste's diaries, but he made a mess of it."

"Then it's true!" said Gila to his spotlight.

"Poor Barty," said Umor.

"You mean you didn't *know*?" said Miles. "How could you not guess, when The Null arrived on the night Barty disappeared?"

"There's not much of a resemblance," said Gila.

"And everyone said that Barty had left," said Umor.

Miles looked from one to the other of the three little men, searching for clues in their faces. It was hard to believe that they had never questioned the strange events of that night, never searched for their friend Barty Fumble, or asked themselves how such a large man could have disappeared so completely.

"I knew," said Fabio quietly. "To tell the truth, we all did."

Gila opened his mouth to speak, but Fabio threw him a dark glance and he closed it again quickly.

"In the back of our minds, I think we all knew that The Null was what was left of your father," said Fabio. "We just didn't want to admit it."

"Those were dangerous days, Master Miles," said Umor.

"The Great Cortado was a frightening man."

"Even on his deathbed."

"We were afraid he would come back."

"And he did."

"It wasn't just that," said Fabio. "The Null is not Barty Fumble. Not anymore."

"There's nothing in there," agreed Umor.

"How do you know?" asked Miles. "Why has nobody ever tried to reach him?"

Umor stared at his wiggling toes, suspended over the tent boys who were assembling the banked seats far below. "He's too far gone," he said.

"You couldn't put The Null on the couch," said Fabio.

"It would eat any doctor in four minutes."

"And pick its teeth with his stethoscope."

"Maybe I can reach him with the help of the Tiger's Egg. You said that it was the Egg that gave Celeste some of her healing powers."

Umor and Fabio shook their heads in unison. "Don't ever fool with that thing," said Umor, showing his pointed teeth in a nervous grin.

"It takes great skill to handle a Tiger's Egg," said Fabio.

"And years of practice."

"There's no one alive now who could master it."

"Then it does exist," said Miles. "Is it really inside me, like Doctor Tau-Tau says?"

Gila looked over his shoulder at Fabio, his eyebrows climbing into his curly hair. Fabio looked at Umor, then all three unexpectedly burst into laughter.

"That man has a deep well of foolishness at his disposal!"

"And no holes in his bucket."

Miles felt a hot prickling on his skin. He felt as though he were left out of some great joke, and he didn't know whether to be offended or to laugh along.

"The Egg is not inside you, Master Miles," said Umor.

"You are its owner," said Fabio.

"But you might never be its master."

"But if I'm its owner," said Miles, "how come I've never seen it in my life?"

Fabio glanced at his two brothers and sighed deeply.

"I will tell you the whole story," he said, "though you will think less of us afterward."

Umor cleared his throat loudly and shook his head. He looked like a small boy caught near a broken window with a large catapult.

"He has a right to know," said Fabio. "And the secret has weighed on us too long."

"Tell him, so," said Gila. Umor stayed silent, but he would not meet Miles's eye.

"It was not by chance that we first met your mother, Master Miles," said Fabio.

"We were sent to keep an eye on her."

"On her and the Tiger's Egg."

"Who sent you?" asked Miles.

"Our father's people sent us," said Fabio.

"Our father was of the Fir Bolg."

"His name was Fathach of the Nine Toes."

Miles looked at the three little men as though seeing them for the first time. It was true that they were not quite as hairy as the Fir Bolg he had met, but their small pointed teeth and their glittering black eyes were so like those of the little cavemen it was a wonder it had not been obvious to him before. "Our father was not typical of his people," said Umor.

"He had itchy feet."

"He would leave the caves and travel for many weeks."

"Always at night, of course."

"He could no more stand the light than his kin, but to tell the truth he couldn't really stand them either."

"He got work as a circus sideshow."

"The Shrunken Man of Kathmandu, they called him."

"It cost half a shilling to see him by a dim red light."

"And for another half shilling he would play a tune on the pipes that could curl your hair and cure blisters."

"He met our mother there, in Neptune Dangerfield's Three-ring Hoopla."

"She was small, like he was, and a fine horse-woman, and old Fathach could play a woman's heart like the pipes under his arm."

"Or so she told us."

"She wasn't after his money, that's for sure."

"He traveled with the Three-ring Hoopla on and off for several years, though he returned often to his people."

"He always seemed to be off visiting whenever one of us was born."

"I came a year after Fabio," said Umor, "and Gila two years after me."

"Our mother never allowed us to visit our father's people."

"She was afraid she would never see us again."

"Why did she think that?" asked Miles.

"Because it was true, Master Miles," said Fabio. "Our father's eldest sister would have claimed us as her own, and we would not have been allowed to leave."

Miles tried to imagine how it would feel to be kept underground forever, between dim light and darkness on a diet of rabbit and marsh grass. The two days he had spent there with Doctor Tau-Tau had seemed like an eternity. Down below him the tent boys were arranging red-and-gold painted boxes in a broad circle to form the ring, while others filled it with a layer of fresh sawdust. They shouted and joked and whistled snatches of unidentifiable tunes, striped by the afternoon light that entered between the loosely anchored canvas walls. Now and then one of them would glance up toward the striped ceiling, wondering why Fabio was not yelling instructions at them as was his habit, but Fabio's eye was not on them today.

"If you never met the Fir Bolg, how did they send you to keep an eye on Celeste?" asked Miles.

"Our father took us to the Crinnew when we were old enough, and there we met his people."

"What's a Crinnew?" asked Miles.

"It's a meeting that's held the first new moon after midsummer's day."

"The elders of all the Fir Bolg tribes come to Hell's Teeth to attend the meeting."

"The Fir Bolg at Hell's Teeth aren't the only ones?" asked Miles in surprise.

"There are seven tribes who send their people to the Crinnew," said Umor.

"They have to travel at night, and keep hidden."

"Why didn't they capture you once you went there?" asked Miles.

"We went under our father's protection."

"Fathach's sister claimed us, but our father refused to give us up, and disputes that can't be talked out at the Crinnew must be settled by a fight."

"Your father fought his sister?" asked Miles in surprise.

Gila laughed. "It never came to that, but the women of the Fir Bolg are fierce creatures."

"Did you not notice that on your visit?"

"Our father's sister was like a stoat full of wasps."

"But in the end a bargain was made that she would drop her claim on us, and we would look after the Tiger's Egg in return."

Gila mopped his brow as if he still felt the relief.

"She was a fearsome crone, that one," he said.

"And I would not have learned good cooking from her," said Umor.

"We'd be eating half-boiled rabbits with the fur still on," said Gila.

"We'd have had fewer dinner guests."

"And less washing up," said Umor.

"What about the Tiger's Egg?" asked Miles, who was beginning to think the Bolsillo brothers would never get to the point.

"The Tiger's Egg belonged to the Fir Bolg of Hell's Teeth," said Fabio, scratching his stubbly chin. "How they came by it I don't know, but they had had it a lifetime or more."

"They could not get much use from it," said Umor.

"They didn't have the knowledge of it, and in any case a tiger will not venture underground."

"They agreed to lend it to Celeste for twenty-one years."

"She was to do something for them in return, at the end of that time," said Umor.

"Though they would not tell us what that was."

"They had not heard from Celeste in five years, and they were getting worried."

"They wanted us to find her, and keep an eye on her and the Egg."

"Because you could see in the light?" said Miles.

"Of course, Master Miles. And we would not stand out so much as a true Fir Bolg."

"We searched for her for some time, and found

her in Barty Fumble's Big Top."

"We found work there easily, and soon became friends of both Barty and Celeste."

"They got married a couple of years later, and before long they were expecting you, Master Miles."

"Barty had never looked happier."

"But not Celeste," said Fabio quietly, looking at Miles from under his bushy eyebrows. "Not Celeste."

"She must have seen something bad was coming," said Umor.

"But Doctor Tau-Tau says," said Miles, "that a fortune-teller can't read her own future."

"That's what Celeste always said," agreed Umor.

"But she would have been able to read yours."

"Maybe she saw you would grow up without parents."

Miles nodded. He felt suddenly angry at the mother he had never met. If she was a healer, and could read the future, and had the power of a Tiger's Egg at her disposal, how could she let her son fall into the clutches of Mrs. Pinchbucket and her foul husband? The suddenness of this unexpected feeling caught him off guard, and he opened his mouth and blurted out his question. "How could she let herself die?"

Gila flinched as though he had been hit, and Umor continued examining his toes, but Fabio looked Miles straight in the eye.

"She didn't, Master Miles," he said. "We did."

CHAPTER THIRTY-THREE
A STROKE OF GENIUS

Fabio Bolsillo, broad-faced and dark-eyed, watched Miles closely as the boy tried to grasp what had just been said to him. Perched sixty feet above a ring of sawdust is probably not the best place to hear a shocking secret, and the little ring-master was ready to reach out and grab Miles if he seemed about to lose his balance. Fabio could tell that his two brothers were thinking the same thing.

"I don't understand," said Miles at last. "What did you have to do with my mother's death?"

"We borrowed the Tiger's Egg, Master Miles," said Fabio.

"We needed it to save Gila's life," said Umor.

"On the night you were born there was a terrible storm."

"The thunder roared so loud, we thought the earth would crack," said Umor.

"The animals were nervous, and even Tembo took fright," said Fabio.

"She broke out of her pen and crashed her way through the camp."

"Gila tried to stop her, but she was terrified out of her wits."

"She never even saw me," said Gila.

"She crushed him against one of the tent trucks, and when we found him he was close to death."

"We didn't know what to do. Barty and Celeste were occupied with the birth of . . . with you, Master Miles," said Umor.

"I was sure Gila would die," said Fabio quietly, "so I sent Umor to get the Tiger's Egg from Celeste's wagon."

"We knew where it was hidden."

"We knew a little about its use, from scraps of things our father had told us."

"We thought, Master Miles, that we could borrow its power for a few moments, and no one would ever know."

The Bolsillo brothers fell silent. The tent boys

had gone back to their wagons, and a light breeze sang in the cables that anchored the tent. One of the canvas panels flapped and danced in the wind, and little storms of sawdust eddied across the ring.

Umor resumed the story. "I brought the Tiger's Egg to where Gila lay."

"He was the color of marzipan, and he shook like a leaf."

"I held the Egg to his chest, and all at once the thunder stopped."

"We could hear Varippuli roaring in his cage, like he would smash his wagon to pieces, and then we got really frightened," said Fabio.

"I ran back to Celeste's caravan and hid the Egg exactly where I had found it. When I got back, Gila was breathing again."

"But Celeste paid the price."

"We didn't mean it to happen, Master Miles," said Umor.

"We were so busy looking after Gila, we only found out the next morning."

"We never knew exactly how she died."

"But she lost the protection of the Tiger's Egg just when she needed it most."

"So you see," said Fabio, "how a Tiger's Egg might be considered a mixed blessing."

"Or a mixed curse," said Umor.

Fabio looked straight at Miles, his eyes like little black olives in his sun-browned face. "Just supposing you found the Tiger's Egg," he said, "what would you do with it?"

The rigging creaked as the big top stood against the breeze. Suddenly it seemed a very long way to the ground. "You know where it is, don't you?" said Miles.

"No, we don't," said Gila.

"Fried it for breakfast a long time ago," said Umor.

"Yes, we do," said Fabio.

"Don't tell him," whispered Gila.

"It's too dangerous," muttered Umor.

"It's his inheritance," said Fabio. "And it's time he knew."

"I don't know what I would do with it in the end," said Miles, "but it's my only chance of getting my father back, and I'd have to try that first."

"You would never be able to do that," said Fabio.

"It would take a lifetime of learning."

"And there's no one to teach you."

"I have my mother's diaries," said Miles. He did not mention that the diary he needed most was in the possession of the Great Cortado. "She knew how to use it."

Fabio sighed. "We hid the Tiger's Egg many years ago, Master Miles, and we had to hide you too."

"After your mother died and your father . . . left, you were no longer safe," said Umor.

"Varippuli's attack had made the Great Cortado more dangerous than ever."

"With your parents out of the way, he was in sole charge of the circus again."

"And he swore that he would kill you as soon as he recovered."

"Why me?" asked Miles with a shiver. "I was just a baby."

"He believed that Celeste had been a witch, and that Varippuli was her familiar," said Umor.

"He wanted revenge."

"And you were the easiest target."

"We had to get you away from the circus."

"And we had to send the Egg with you."

"Why would you do that?" asked Miles.

"The Tiger's Egg was your inheritance, Master Miles."

"And the promise that went with it."

"Besides, we were afraid the Great Cortado would find it by chance."

"It would be safer with you than it would be at the circus."

"But how to send it with you? That was the question."

"You were only three weeks old."

Gila grinned. "There was one thing you never let out of your grasp," he said.

"Had it with you day and night," said Fabio.

Miles's hand reached instinctively into his pocket, and he felt the threadbare grip of his oldest friend. "Tangerine!" he said.

"Tangerine." Umor nodded. "I took the Egg from its hiding place again and sewed it into the stuffing of the bear's head."

"It was a stroke of genius," said Gila.

"It was good stitching," said Umor.

"Then we wrapped you up in the dead of night and took you to the orphanage in Larde."

"We left you on the doorstep, with the bear tucked up in your arms."

"Afterward we told everyone that you had come down with a fever in the orphanage, and you had died in the night before the doctor could be found."

"But you were supposed to be looking after the Egg," said Miles. "What did the Fir Bolg say?"

Fabio gave Umor a sidelong glance. "Well . . . ," he said.

"We never actually told them, as such," said

Umor. "We just told them that it was safe."

"We meant to go back and fetch you, and the Tiger's Egg, on your eleventh birthday."

"Which was when the Egg was due to be returned."

"But you came and found us instead," said Umor.

"Or the Egg did," said Fabio.

"But you didn't return it to the Fir Bolg then, either," said Miles.

"That's true, Master Miles."

"Returning the Tiger's Egg is only half of the bargain."

"The other is the promise that Celeste made."

"And we still hadn't found out what that was."

"A bargain half fulfilled would not go down well."

"Didn't you know they'd come looking for it?" asked Miles.

"We tried to delay them," said Umor.

"I went to the Crinnew," said Gila, "and I asked them for more time."

"They agreed, and gave us another year."

"Then why were they raiding the circus?"

"Some of the young lads are very keen on raiding parties," said Fabio.

"They would think it a fine thing to come back

with the Tiger's Egg."

"A Fir Bolg agreement is a flexible thing," said Gila.

"Everyone makes up their own mind."

"There are no leaders."

"Two hundred kings and twelve," said Miles.

"That's right, Master Miles," said Umor. "Two hundred kings and twelve."

"What we didn't know," said Fabio, giving Miles a sharp look, "was that you'd go looking for *them*."

"If we'd known where Doctor Tau-Tau was bringing you we'd have been after you like cheetahs on roller skates."

"You were lucky to escape with your life."

"You were lucky that Little was more awake than we were."

"But how can I ever return the Egg if we don't know the other half of the bargain?" asked Miles.

Fabio scratched his curly head and frowned. "You say you have your mother's diaries?"

"Yes," said Miles, "two of them, anyway."

"Well that's simple, then," said Umor, standing up to coil a rope that dangled from the rigging.

"The deal must be in the diaries," said Fabio.

"Otherwise what's the point in keeping one?" agreed Gila.

Miles reached into his pocket, which Tangerine now shared with two of his mother's notebooks. They were still there, and beside them he felt the little bear's sawdust-stuffed head. "It must be very small, the Tiger's Egg," said Miles. He had pictured something about the size of a hen's egg, but it would certainly have to be smaller to fit comfortably inside Tangerine's head.

"It's the size of a man's thumb, from the last knuckle," said Umor.

"Then I suppose it's not so ridiculous that Doctor Tau-Tau believed I'd swallowed it," said Miles.

"'Course it is!" said Fabio. "You have to talk to a Tiger's Egg so that it accepts you as its master."

"You'd have to be talking to your stomach day and night," said Gila.

"What's so odd about that?" said Umor.

"Do you talk to that bear of yours?" said Fabio.

Miles nodded. "All the time," he said.

"Then perhaps you've already made a start, Master Miles."

Little Sky Beetle, waist-deep and water-bound, sat in the hippo tank in Jules and Gina's wagon, holding a newborn pygmy hippopotamus in her arms. The barrel-shaped infant slept peacefully, his belly full with his first feed, while his mother, Violet, lay in the shallows, now and then heaving an enormous sigh. Miles climbed into the darkened trailer and sat on a bench beside the tank. "So this is where you are," he said to Little. "I didn't even know Violet was expecting a baby."

"She's been talking about it for weeks," said Little. "Isn't he cute? He was born just an hour ago."

Miles stood up and looked more closely at the sleeping hippo. He was about the size of a small pillow, the gray-black of his back fading to a delicate pink on his underside and his cheeks. "Has he got a name?" he asked.

"Not yet," said Little. "Gina asked me to look after him while she went to help Jules get the crocodiles ready. She said I could name him if I wanted. Have you any ideas?"

Miles shrugged. He did not feel in the mood for baby naming.

"It was a difficult birth," Little whispered. "We though we would lose Violet at one point."

Miles looked at Violet sleeping in the shallows, her ribs heaving with each breath. "Fabio says it was his fault that my mother died," he said.

"Why does he say that?" asked Little.

"Because they borrowed the Tiger's Egg at the

moment I was born," said Miles. "There was a thunderstorm, and Gila was accidentally crushed by Tembo. They thought they could save him with the Tiger's Egg. My mother died because she didn't have the Egg to protect her."

Little shifted the heavy calf to a more comfortable position. He gave a wriggle and let out a quiet squeak. "Celeste died because her part in the One Song reached its end," she said.

"But the Egg has the power to protect your life, doesn't it?" asked Miles.

"It can be used to hide from the Sleep Angels," said Little, "but that's not the same thing as having a life. Once your part in the Song has been sung, you have no purpose to fulfill. That's when you should rejoin the Song, otherwise you are just blowing around like a leaf in the wind."

"Then it wasn't the Bolsillo brothers' fault that she died?" said Miles. He felt a wave of relief wash over him.

"No," said Little, "and if they've believed that ever since, you should tell them that it's not true."

"But what about Gila?" asked Miles. "Was it the Egg that saved his life?"

Little smiled. "It's hard to be sure. The Fir Bolg are not like other people. They are clever and wise, and they make their own bargains. I don't think they'd have survived all this time otherwise."

The baby hippo began to struggle in her arms. "He's hungry again already," said Little, "and I think I'll call him Puck."

CHAPTER THIRTY-FOUR

PLAYING WITH FIRE

Miles Wednesday, thief-rumbler and Egg-successor, sat by the square hole in the floor of Lady Partridge's tree house with his feet dangling out through the trapdoor. He had time to kill before the circus show, and had climbed the rope ladder to the tree house with his mother's diaries in the pocket of his jacket. Now he was searching through them for any mention of the Fir Bolg, or indeed for anything he could make sense of at all. He was sure that some pages had been lost during the Fir Bolg's search of Doctor Tau-Tau's pockets, and he hoped that none of them were vital.

He turned the thin pages carefully, but he could not concentrate on the dense writing and overlapping pictures, and eventually he gave up and put the diaries back in his pocket. He felt Tangerine cling onto his fingers, and he lifted the bear out carefully and placed him on the carpet, well away from the square hole and the fifteen-foot drop to the ground below. Miles leaned back on his elbow and watched Tangerine as he wandered about the uneven floor of the tree house, kicking at things in his path like a half-stuffed hooligan. The bear wandered back to the boy and flopped down on the carpet, leaning his head against Miles's chest.

"So," said Miles, "there's more to you than meets the eye, after all." Tangerine kept a modest silence.

Miles could feel his own heart beating, and he tried to picture the Tiger's Egg inside Tangerine's head. He closed his eyes and listened to the creaking of the twin beech trunks as the tree swayed gently. A picture of the tiger came into his mind's eye. The magnificent animal was pacing in the distance, appearing and disappearing by turns, as though he were passing through a fog. Miles concentrated hard on the tiger's image. Several times he had dreamed of performing with the tiger in the ring of the Circus Bolsillo, and he always awoke with the feeling that his dream could be pulled into the light and made real, if only he could learn how.

The tiger in his picture turned away and began to fade into the grayness beyond. A sinking feeling caught hold of Miles. He felt as though he would never come close to mastering the Tiger's Egg. He remembered when he and Little had watched the Council of Cats in the moonlit garden the year before, and how he had struggled to understand their speech. "You must stop trying to listen before you can hear," Little had said to him. Maybe, he thought, catching hold of a tiger's soul is a little like grasping a language that seems to have no meaning. He held on to the picture of the fading tiger, but he stopped trying to pull it toward him, and instead he opened his senses and waited.

The heartbeat in his ears grew louder, and suddenly he was no longer sure if it was his heartbeat or that of the tiger. His nose filled with a musky odor, and all at once the tiger was rushing toward him, his mighty paws flashing white and his fearsome teeth bared. Miles gave a yelp of fright and opened his eyes, half expecting to find the mighty animal leaping at him across the tree house. The tree house was silent, however, and except for

Tangerine he was alone. The wind had dropped and a stillness lay on the air. Miles's heart thumped like a frightened rabbit. He picked up the little bear and slipped him into his jacket pocket, then he turned and put his foot on the top rung of the rope ladder. Excitement gripped his stomach as he descended into the garden. He was sure that the tiger would be waiting for him among the trees. He dropped the last few feet and turned to look. The trees around him stood as still as if they were painted onto the sky, and the stern rectangle of the manor house watched over the grounds. Over by the pond a small group of children launched a boat they had made, which left a perfect V behind it in the mirror-smooth water. There was not so much as the whisker of a tiger to be seen.

Miles felt himself deflate as he turned and began to scuff his way through the fallen leaves toward the gate of Partridge Manor. He felt a fool for imagining that he could master the tiger's soul all at once, just because he now knew that it lived in the stuffed head of a small bear in his pocket. He also felt a little relieved. He had certainly not felt in control of the charging tiger that still burned bright in his mind's eye, and it was a sobering reminder that he was playing with fire trying to summon up such a powerful beast. "Maybe," he said quietly to Tangerine, "I'll never have the strength that my mother had. Maybe . . ."

A deep voice sounded in his ear, making him jump. "So it is you, tub boy," said the tiger. "I almost didn't recognize you, since you weren't bleating for help over something."

Miles turned as he walked, a broad smile spreading across his face and warmth rising through him as though the sun had just come out. "Why would I need your help?" he asked. "I've found my father—sort of—and helped to capture a pair of serial burglars since I saw you last." He almost added, "And learned the whereabouts of a tiger's soul," but he bit his tongue in time. He had a feeling that the tiger was no more aware of the Tiger's Egg than a shadow is aware of the tree that casts it.

"I'm pleased to hear you're learning to stand on your own two feet," said the tiger.

"Still, I was glad you turned up when you did, back in the forest," said Miles.

The tiger turned his head away, almost as though he were flinching from a blow. His reaction took Miles by surprise.

"We did get The Null back safely, in the end," he

said cautiously. "It lives in Lady Partridge's gazebo."

The tiger turned his gaze back to the boy, and there was something haunted in his expression. When he spoke it seemed to cost him a great effort.

"There is a blackness in that—thing—that has no place in nature," he said.

"I know," said Miles, "but . . . it's important that it knows it has a friend."

The tiger was silent for a moment. "There is nothing in that darkness that could recognize a friendship," he said at length. "My advice is to steer well clear of it, and a tiger's advice is not something to be discarded lightly."

Miles had no wish to argue with the tiger on that point, so he hastily changed the subject. He was curious to know whether the tiger was even aware of any influence Miles might have over his comings and goings. "What brings you here anyway?" he asked, kicking at a pile of leaves and making his voice as casual as he could.

"I was passing through on the lookout for a snack," said the tiger. "I thought an orphan or two might serve the purpose, if I could find something better than pond water to wash them down with."

Miles looked at the tiger for a clue to what lay behind his answer, but the tiger's face gave nothing away. They stopped short of the wrought-iron gates that led onto the road. "I do have a favor to ask you, as it happens," said Miles.

"Now there's a surprise," said the tiger.

Miles searched for the words he needed. "Remember you told me once that you smelled the circus in me?"

"Vaguely," said the tiger.

"You were right," said Miles. His words came out all in a rush. "Both my parents were circus people and it's a sort of family tradition to show a tiger, and the last performance of the season is tonight and I wondered if you would perform with me, together I mean, in the Circus Bolsillo, tonight, I mean."

The tiger stood in the warm light of the evening sun and fixed Miles with his amber gaze. He said nothing for some time, and the dying light seemed to turn the world to fire as Miles held the mighty animal's stare. He knew somehow that if he looked away he would lose all the ground he had made since first they met, on the side of a hill on a blustery October night.

"I have told you how I feel about the circus," said the tiger.

"You were talking about the Circus Oscuro," said

Miles. He was holding his breath. The tiger had not said no.

"The Circus Bolsillo is different," Miles continued. "It's more like I would imagine Barty Fumble's Big Top to be."

"And why would that make me more inclined to put myself on the playbill?" asked the tiger. His tail flicked behind him.

"I think you used to perform in Barty Fumble's Big Top," said Miles, "as Varippuli."

"Varippuli was shot by the Great Cortado," said the tiger.

"His body was never found," said Miles. "Maybe he just lost his memory. Maybe he just chose to be someone else."

A rumbling growl came from deep within the tiger. "Maybe he just had enough of performing before ranks of people he would rather have found on a bed of lettuce."

Miles laughed. "He used to perform with Barty Fumble. You said so yourself."

"Barty Fumble is dead and gone," said the tiger sadly.

"Not completely," said Miles, quietly glad that he had chosen not to mention The Null's true nature.

"Barty Fumble was my father, and I'm still here."

The tiger stepped closer until his nose was inches from Miles's face. His whiskers lifted as his nostrils flared. Miles stood as still as he did when Stranski was throwing knives at him. "I have no reason to doubt that," said the tiger at last. "But you never had the privilege of being his pupil. Have you ever performed with a tiger?"

Miles shook his head. "I've watched Countess Fontainbleau show her lions, and I hoped you might be able to give me some direction if I need it. I don't think anyone would notice. I'll have to clear it with the Bolsillo brothers, of course."

"Very well," said the tiger. "I will perform with you, just this once, and only because you are Barty Fumble's boy."

Miles felt himself glow like a lightbulb. "Thank you," he said. He opened the gate and turned back to the tiger. "Can I call you Varippuli?" he asked.

"You can call me the queen of Sheba for all the difference it will make," said the tiger.

Miles stood back to let the tiger pass. A trickle of people was already passing the gate on the way to the big top, hoping to arrive before the best seats had sold out. The tiger stayed where he was. "I'm not well suited to mingling with the peasantry," he said. "All that running and screaming makes me want to bite something."

"It's all right," said Miles. "You'll be with me. I'm sort of well-known in this town."

Miles stepped out through the gates, and after a moment the tiger followed. They set off down the road toward the glowing lights of the circus. "I hope you're not thinking of asking to ride on my back," said the tiger.

"Of course not," said Miles. He placed his hand on the tiger's shoulder and they walked along in silence. The Lardespeople stared at them as they passed. Some jumped back in fear, but most seemed to have reached the point where they would not be surprised to hear that the Boy from the Barrel had brought the dinosaurs back from extinction and taught them table manners. They whispered to each other about the capture of The Null and the discovery of the Pinchbuckets' hoard, and Miles smiled quietly to himself, marching through his hometown with a walking, dancing bear in a secret pocket and a Bengal tiger by his side.

They approached the circus gate with its brightly painted signs lit by strings of red and yellow bulbs.

"A word to the wise," said the tiger.

"Yes?" said Miles.

"Remember what I just said about calling me the queen of Sheba?"

Miles nodded.

"I wouldn't put it to the test, if I were you," said the tiger.

CHAPTER THIRTY-FIVE

A SUNDAY ROAST

Miles Wednesday, sparkle-suited and spotlight-blinded, climbed into the star-painted box and lay down while Stranski the Magician closed and locked the lid. A murmur rippled through the crowd as Stranski rummaged in his box of tricks and produced a saw with a long gleaming blade. The magician seemed more taciturn than ever, and Miles wondered whether it was because Fabio had shortened his act to allow an extra slot on the playbill for Miles Wednesday and the Lord of the Monsoon. The tiger had allowed himself to be placed in a cage for dramatic effect, and the knife-throwing part had been dropped from Stranski's act to make time. The mute magician flexed his saw blade, which sang under the lights. The audience held its breath.

Miles readied himself to curl up into a ball. He reached for the lever that operated the flaps and hinges inside the box. The lever seemed to be jammed. He pulled again, but it wouldn't budge. He was still laid out flat, and there was no room for him to bend his legs. "It's not working," he whispered to Stranski. Stranski leaned over the box and positioned the saw to begin cutting. He let out a little giggle. Miles started in surprise. He had never heard a sound of any kind escape the dour magician. He squinted his eyes against the glaring spotlight, trying to make out Stranski's face. The blade began to rasp its way through the box. Something was very wrong. Stranski seemed to have changed somehow, like people in a dream will change into someone else without warning. His face was rounder, and what's more, the badger's bum smell had been replaced by a cloud of cheap cologne. "Stop!" hissed Miles. "The box is jammed. You'll cut me in half."

"What a pity," whispered the Stranski who wasn't Stranski, and he giggled again, a jerky laugh like a machine wound too tight. He wiped his brow with his sleeve, and his face caught the light for a moment. A moment was enough. From this close Miles had no trouble recognizing the impostor in Stranski's suit, mustache or no mustache. It was the Great Cortado, and he was sawing for all he was worth.

"Surprised to see me, instead of that half-wit bell-with-no-clapper?" whispered the Great Cortado. "He's on sick leave." The saw bit deeper. Miles opened his mouth to shout for help, but the Great Cortado was ready for him. Quick as a lizard he tipped the contents of a small bottle into Miles's open mouth and pinched his nose. Miles swallowed involuntarily, and a sour liquid burned in his throat. He tried again to shout, but his voice seemed to have deserted him. His tongue felt thick and numb, like a marshmallow. He sucked in his stomach. "No good trying to make yourself thinner, Selim," said Cortado. "Of course, I do know your real name, but Selim will do fine for me. A backward name"—he giggled—"for a backward child. Who would have thought Barty and Celeste would produce such a snot-nosed little runt?" He paused again to mop the sweat from his forehead.

Miles turned his head with difficulty, trying to see if there was anyone who might recognize the danger he was in. The audience stared open-mouthed, confident that he would be miraculously made whole after he had been halved. Fabio, he knew, was backstage making hasty preparations for Miles's act with the tiger, and Umor and Gila would be settling the elephants for the night. There was never anyone in the ring with Stranski and Miles, so his heart leaped with surprise when he saw some-one sitting on a stool beside Stranski's box of tricks. Miles tried desperately to summon up a shout. Whoever it was sat only a tiger's leap away, but his face—or hers—seemed to be surrounded by a shadow of its own. Miles could not make out who it was, nor could he make a sound. He found it difficult to keep his eyes open.

The Great Cortado resumed his sawing, and Miles felt the shining teeth of the saw begin to snag his sparkly jacket. "I know about your stripy little secret, Selim," Cortado whispered to him. "That bug-eyed fool Tau-Tau finally tracked it down for me, though it took him long enough. And once I've carved you up like a Sunday roast, I'll just reach into the box and see what the tiger has laid. I can wash the cotton candy off it later, or whatever it was you last ate."

Miles's head was swimming with the hot lights

and the numbing concoction he had been forced to drink. It was obvious that the Great Cortado also believed the Tiger's Egg was in his stomach, but he could no more tell him otherwise than he could shout for help, and what chance was there that Cortado would believe him anyway? He turned again to see the figure on the stool. It was a Sleep Angel, he realized now, sitting patiently while the Great Cortado sweated at his villainous work, waiting to take Miles's last breath from him and release it on the wind. A wave of sadness washed Miles's fear away. He felt sad that his life would end just as it seemed to be beginning, sad for Little who would be left alone again, sad that he would never get the chance to say good-bye to his friends, or to follow in his father's footsteps and perform with . . . perform with . . .

"Varippuli!" said Miles, although his tongue said something more like "Owahooie." The saw blade ripped through his clothing and scraped painfully against his skin. He sucked his stomach in even further, and scrabbled in his pocket for Tangerine. He grasped the saggy bear gently and closed his eyes.

"Forgot the tinfoil," giggled the Great Cortado as he sawed. "Forgot the gravy. Forgot the ketchup. Didn't even preheat the oven to four hundred degrees."

Miles tried to block out the crazed ringmaster's voice and the stinging pain in his side. He made himself picture Varippuli, waiting in his cage behind the star-strewn curtain at the back of the ring. He listened for the tiger's heartbeat, and tried to turn the smell of Cortado's cheap cologne into the musty odor of the tiger. He opened his ears and waited for the roar. "Now," he said to himself. "Make it now."

The tiger's roar thundered through the big top like tropical rain on a tin roof. The audience shrieked, and those nearest the curtain scrambled for safer seats. The sawing stopped. Miles opened his eyes and saw that even the nebulous figure of the Sleep Angel had twisted on his stool and was looking over his shoulder. The Great Cortado's eyes widened, but he did not turn around. He mopped his brow again, and grasped the saw handle. "Even ghost tigers can be caged," he said, "and you seem to have lost the knack of your disappearing act. Good-bye, Selim." He pulled the saw through the box again, but Miles scarcely felt the bite of the blade. He heard a crash from behind the curtain and the terrified whinny of Delia Zipplethorpe's piebald mare, heard Fabio shout for the beast men, and heard the screams of the audience as the panicked mare burst like a comet through the silver stars, followed seconds later by the tiger.

The horse began to gallop around the ring, which was what she knew best, but the tiger crossed the sawdust in a couple of mighty bounds, heading straight for the Great Cortado. He leaped straight through the Sleep Angel, who vanished like smoke, and Cortado dived under the box just as the tiger landed. The mighty cat's weight slammed against the box, almost knocking it over, and waking Miles from his stupor in an instant.

There was a ripple of applause from the audience, who were unsure whether the entire act had been rehearsed, but thought it would be safer to clap in any case. The piebald mare's hooves thundered around the ring. The tiger had recovered himself and was creeping around the box, his belly slung low to the sawdust, while on the other side the Great Cortado struggled to his feet. His mustacheless face was shiny with sweat. He scuttled like a crab around the far end of the box, where Miles momentarily lost sight of him, and appeared by Stranski's box of tricks. He grasped two of the long knives that Stranski liked to throw right across the width of the ring. The blades were polished to a dazzling shine, and Miles knew just how keen the edges were, because he had sharpened them himself. Some of the swagger had returned to Cortado's step. "Knives, Selim!" he said. "I wrote the book on 'em." He swished the two blades around his head in a flurry of glinting steel, and the audience cheered. "Who do you think taught Stranski, eh?" He began to circle the box again, as the tiger rounded the other end. "Heere, pussy pussy," he sang quietly. "No more pussycat, no more Barty's brat."

Miles could see Fabio crouched at the curtain, watching intently. Two of the beast men appeared beside him with a net, and Fabio motioned them to wait as the mare galloped by. Miles could not tell if Fabio had realized that Stranski was not Stranski, and whether the net was for the tiger or for the Great Cortado. Miles tried to call out to him, but his tongue was still not cooperating. He could feel warm blood trickling down his side. The Great Cortado was circling more slowly now, waiting for the tiger to get close enough. The audience held its breath, and the drummer in the circus band—who had drumming in his blood and couldn't help it—began a long roll on the snare drum.

Suddenly Cortado lunged forward and aimed a swipe at the tiger with his blade. The tiger pounced at the same moment, and the blade glanced off his foreleg as the tiger bowled Cortado over. A cymbal crashed, and the little man somersaulted backward, dropping both knives and fetching up against Stranski's box of tricks. He scrambled to his feet as the tiger turned and launched himself again. Miles watched in dismay as the the Great Cortado reached deep into the box for another knife. If he got it out in time there would be no way the tiger could avoid being skewered on the blade.

Cortado was already withdrawing his hand as the tiger soared through the air toward him, but it seemed that fate was not on his side this time. His hand gripped only a pair of long white ears, and he dropped the struggling rabbit in fright as the tiger's mighty paws met his chest and sent him crashing again to the floor. The tiger reared to strike and Miles closed his eyes tightly. "Don't kill him," he said silently. There was a roar from the tiger and a cry of pain from the Great Cortado. Miles opened his eyes despite himself. The audience was panicking now, and those nearest the exit were beating a hasty retreat while others scrambled backward and crowded onto the higher benches.

The tiger had backed off and the Great Cortado was crawling toward the banked seats, a trail of blood staining the sawdust behind him. Fabio and the beast men were advancing across the ring, holding the net wide, but it was still not clear who their intended target was. Suddenly Cortado stumbled to his feet. Fabio and his boys broke into a run, but the Great Cortado was too quick for them. He reached up and grasped the piebald mare's saddle as she thundered past, and swung himself up onto her back like . . . well, like a lifelong circus performer. Miles saw a streak of red and gold as Hector the monkey leaped from somewhere in the crowd and clung to the Great Cortado's shoulder, beating at his head with tiny fists. Cortado tore him free, and the monkey scrabbled at his jacket for a moment before losing his grip and somersaulting backward into the sawdust. The Great Cortado grabbed the reins with one hand, holding the other to his bleeding face, and before anyone could stop him he had galloped out through the fleeing spectators, who dived to either side to avoid the terrified horse and her wounded rider.

Fabio and the beast men ran after the mare, and the audience broke into a cheer, no longer concerned whether the act was elaborately staged or totally out of hand. It seemed as though only the villain had suffered any real damage, and it was certainly the most riveting show that any of them could remember seeing. Miles realized he was still holding his breath, and he let the air from his lungs in a long sigh, the blood pounding in his head.

"Miles," said Little's voice, "are you all right?" He could hear her snapping open the clips that held down the lid, but he couldn't twist his head to see her. She sounded out of breath. "Wiggle your toes, Miles," she said. Miles wiggled, and for a moment he had the strange sensation that the other half of the box was on the far side of the ring with his feet poking from the end of it. He wanted to say "I'm fine," but his tongue had now gone entirely to sleep, and he gave up trying. Little hauled the box lid open, and took Miles's arm as he climbed unsteadily out.

"You're hurt," said Little. "Sit down and I'll get Gila." She set Stranski's stool upright, but Miles shook his head. His legs felt they would buckle at any moment, but he was not ready to sit down yet. He walked shakily to where the tiger stood in the bloodied sawdust, a steady rumbling growl coming from his heaving ribs, and placed his hand on the magnificent beast's shoulder.

The tiger turned and gazed into Miles's pale face. "Your father would be proud," he said. The audience cheered wildly, and despite the dizziness in his head and the stinging pain in his side Miles felt a wave of pride and happiness sweep through him. He was where he belonged, in the center of a circus ring with a tiger by his side. He took a deep bow, and the audience stood in their seats as the applause grew into a deafening roar.

As he straightened up, beaming through the pain, Miles felt a tug at the end of his jacket. He looked down to see Hector's little white face looking up at him, chattering excitedly. The monkey reached into the pocket of his waistcoat and pulled out what looked like a slim wallet. Miles laughed. He reached down to take it, and realized that it was not a wallet at all. It was a leather-bound notebook, the third of Celeste's diaries, still smelling faintly of the Great Cortado's cheap cologne.

CHAPTER THIRTY-SIX
INTO THE LIGHT

Miles Wednesday, rubber-tongued and almost-halved, arrived back at Partridge Manor shortly after midnight, with Little by his bandaged side. He had never felt so tired, and wanted nothing more than to fall into his bed, but as they passed through the main hall of the manor the drawing room door opened and Lady Partridge appeared. "There you are, Miles dear," she boomed. "Are you all right? I was worried sick! Are you badly hurt?"

"I'm just a bit sore," said Miles. His tongue still felt like it was someone else's, but he could speak well enough.

"Well, I'm just delighted to see you alive. We've been hearing the other side of the story from . . . well, you'd better come in and hear it for yourself." She opened the door wide, and a murmur of voices flooded out with the warm lamplight. Miles and Little entered the room to find Sergeant Bramley and Constable Flap, who were becoming as familiar as the furniture, seated on the sofa by the fire, and in between them the dejected figure of Doctor Tau-Tau, his face scraped and bruised and his eyes staring fixedly at the carpet.

"Well, Master Miles," said Sergeant Bramley, "I hear you've been taking this sawing-in-half game a little too seriously. I trust you're still in one piece."

"I am," said Miles, "but it was a close thing."

Constable Flap pulled up another sofa, and Miles and Little flopped down on it while Lady Partridge settled herself in her armchair. As soon as she was seated she began to attract cats like a lollipop attracts fluff.

"Where did you find Doctor Tau-Tau?" asked Miles.

"Walked into the police station, bold as brass," said the sergeant. "Rambling like a drunk and hand-cuffed to a metal bar. I couldn't get any sense out of him, so I put him in the lockup to cool off."

"I was making perfect sense," muttered Doctor Tau-Tau. "Just a slight numbness of the tongue, that was all."

"Yes, well," said the sergeant, "I sent Constable Flap in to question him in detail, and it turned out that he had come in to alert us to the danger from that Cortado villain. It was the metal bar and the slurry speech that made me think he had a screw loose."

"I'd been handcuffed to a motorcycle sidecar since the previous morning," said Tau-Tau, looking up through bloodshot eyes. "It's only because I always carry a penknife that I managed to unscrew the bar I was attached to and make my escape."

"Who handcuffed you to a sidecar?" asked Little with interest.

"The Great Cortado," said Doctor Tau-Tau, "when he kidnapped me in the woods outside Iota. Of course, if I hadn't been arrested for trying—"

"Yes, yes. We've been through all that," said Sergeant Bramley testily. He stood up and looked at his watch. "We'll be subjecting the prisoner to a full interrogation first thing in the morning, and then we'll find out where the Great Cortado is holed up, you mark my words."

Lady Partridge removed a small cat that clung to

her shoulder with needle claws. "Surely you're not thinking of going off duty at a time like this, Sergeant Bramley? A would-be murderer has just slipped through your net and is getting farther away by the second. As long as he's on the loose Miles's life is in danger, not to mention anyone else who gets in his way."

"That's all very well," said Sergeant Bramley, meaning the complete opposite, "but it's after midnight, Lady P."

"You can leave him here with us," said Miles, "can't he, Lady Partridge? Deputy Little can question him. There are a couple of things I'd like her to ask him about a family heirloom of mine."

Sergeant Bramley looked doubtful. "It would be . . ."

"Highly irregular," finished Constable Flap. He had worked with the sergeant long enough to be able to finish his sentences with great accuracy, though he seldom dared to do so. He was beginning to regret ever having suggested swearing Little in as a deputy. She seemed to be inheriting a growing share of his duties, and she was still, he noticed, wearing his favorite badge.

The sergeant disliked having his sentences finished by anyone. It had just occurred to him that without the prisoner on his hands he might get a few hours of sleep before beginning his pursuit of the Great Cortado, and after all a clear head was needed to hunt down a master criminal. Especially one on a horse.

"However," he said, hitching up his trousers, "if you're satisfied that he won't pose any danger . . ."

"I'm sure Doctor Tau-Tau can be persuaded to behave himself," said Lady Partridge. "If he can give us information that might lead to the arrest of the Great Cortado I may be able to put in a good word with Justice Ffrench when I meet him for bridge on Tuesday."

"Very well," said Sergeant Bramley. "If you'll excuse us, Lady P., we have important police work to do." He tipped the peak of his cap, and he and his crestfallen constable showed themselves out.

Lady Partridge swept the cats from her lap and hoisted herself out of her armchair. "I'm sure you could all do with a cup of tea after your various ordeals," she said. "I'll go and put the kettle on and Miles can ask you about his family heirloom." She gave Doctor Tau-Tau a hard stare. "And I strongly recommend that you leave nothing out," she said. "Justice Ffrench is a great believer in the benefits of long prison sentences."

Doctor Tau-Tau shuddered as Lady Partridge swept from the room. "Well," he said, attempting a friendly smile. "All's well that ends well, eh? At least Cortado didn't manage to . . ." His words faltered.

"To saw me in half?" finished Miles. Doctor Tau-Tau nodded.

"What I'd like to know," said Miles, "is where he got the idea that the Tiger's Egg was inside me in the first place."

"Ah . . . ," said Tau-Tau. "That's what I told him, when he ambushed me in the woods outside Iota. It was for your own protection, of course."

"How would getting me sawn in half be for my own protection?" asked Miles.

Doctor Tau-Tau sighed. "I have always had your interests at heart, boy, though I admit it may not always appear that way. I had persuaded the Great Cortado that the Tiger's Egg was probably somewhere in Larde, and he had spent the summer searching for it. He began with those Punchbiscuit people, who had owned the orphanage where he believed Barty's infant son had died. He soon realized that they knew nothing about the Egg, but he found them greedy and unscrupulous, and took an instant liking to them. It was Cortado who devised the clock-and-rat scheme to sift through the valuables of Larde in search of the Egg, and he kept them supplied with exotic clocks from an importer in Fuera."

"So that's how they got into the clock business," said Miles. "I thought that plan was a bit clever for Fowler Pinchbucket. But if Cortado was searching in Larde, why did he turn up at the circus in Cnoc?"

Doctor Tau-Tau's eyes bulged in surprise. "How did you know about that?" he said.

"I saw him in the audience," said Miles.

"It's true," said Tau-Tau. "He found out—by putting rumor and report together—that Barty Fumble's son had not died of a fever at all, and what's more that he was one and the same boy who had brought down the Palace of Laughter. He traveled to the circus intending to kill you then and there, but I told him I had befriended you and was within a whisker of finding the Tiger's Egg. When I urged him to give me a few more days a nasty little smile came over his face, and he told me that he would head straight back to Larde and release The Null from its unguarded prison. He said that the beast had shown a perverse instinct to destroy you, its own flesh and blood, last time it had escaped, and that it was up to me to find the Tiger's Egg before the beast found the boy. The whole idea seemed to amuse him greatly."

"So that's why you tried to escape from the circus," said Miles.

Tau-Tau nodded. "I made one last attempt to see if you really knew where the Tiger's Egg was all along, but when that failed I took to the woods to hide. I was not keen to come face to face with The Null again after all these years. I had no idea if it would recognize me, and I didn't want to find out."

"But you found out anyway," said Little. "It must have been very frightening."

"You have no idea," said Doctor Tau-Tau, shuddering at the memory. "If it hadn't been for my quick thinking . . ."

"Actually I don't think it was interested in you," said Miles.

"What do you mean? The monster had me hung in a tree like a ham. It might have devoured me whole at any moment!"

"It's not a monster," said Miles, "and it was looking for a cure, not a ham. Once it had swallowed the sleepwater it dropped you like a sack of potatoes."

"No amount of sleepwater will ever cure that thing," snorted Doctor Tau-Tau.

"But maybe a Tiger's Egg could," said Miles.

"If I ever find it, perhaps," said Tau-Tau, but there he stopped. His eyes bulged and his jaw dropped, and he stared at Miles's chest. "By the smoke of ages—what a remarkable creature! Let me see it closer."

Miles's hand instinctively went to his pocket, and he found to his dismay that Tangerine had climbed half out of his portable home. "It's just a toy," he said quickly, shoving the small bear back down into his pocket next to his thumping heart. "It's clockwork," he added.

"Clockwork? Are you sure?" Doctor Tau-Tau stared at Miles's pocket with a puzzled frown, but at that moment the door opened and Lady Partridge swept in, wheeling a hostess trolley before her. The trolley was piled with cakes and biscuits. A pot of tea steamed on the top tray, and cups rattled in their saucers. Tau-Tau helped himself to a cake without a word and sat back on the sofa, chewing slowly and staring through Miles as if he were transparent.

"You haven't answered my question," said Miles, hoping to distract Doctor Tau-Tau from thinking about Tangerine.

Doctor Tau-Tau shook his head and focused on Miles. "What question was that?"

"Why did you tell the Great Cortado that the Egg was in my stomach?" He glanced at Lady Partridge, but she was busying herself with cups and saucers.

"I had to tell him something," said Tau-Tau. "He had been tracking The Null on a stolen motorbike, and he was watching from the trees when I put it to sleep with a superb shot from my blowpipe. He was not pleased. He ambushed us as we came back through the woods and knocked the constable out cold. He planned to dress up in my clothes so that he could get close enough to kill you himself."

"But we know the Egg isn't inside me," said Miles. "The Fir Bolg said so."

"I know that, but I had to think fast. I hoped this might stall him long enough to give me a chance to escape and alert the authorities. I told him he should disguise himself as Stranski, who was more his size, and who would have you locked in a box the following night with a saw in his hand."

"Where *is* Stranski?" asked Miles, sitting up suddenly on the sofa.

"Sleeping like a baby in his wagon," said Doctor Tau-Tau. "I gave Cortado my last bottle of sleepwater so he could knock him out and steal his outfit. There was enough in there to put a man out for two whole days. Without the sleepwater he would think nothing of killing Stranski to get him out of the way. He drove us to a spot near the circus and hid the motorbike in a bush, with me still handcuffed into the sidecar. He watched me the whole night long, and it wasn't until he left for Stranski's wagon that I had a chance to escape. He forced me to drink a little sleepwater before he left, but I managed to hide it in my cheek and spit it out afterward. Only my tongue was affected. A small dose of sleepwater will numb your tongue better than any dentist's needle."

Miles nodded. His own tongue still tingled.

"Then it's no wonder Sergeant Bramley couldn't understand you," said Lady Partridge. "It seems clear, however, that in this case you tried to do the right thing. You almost certainly saved Mr. Stranski's life, and you did your best to save Miles's too, although frankly it sounds as though you contributed to the danger in the first place." She handed out the teacups. "If you can just help us to pinpoint the Great Cortado I feel sure there's a good chance we can keep you out of prison."

"Lady Partridge," said Doctor Tau-Tau, straightening himself up and placing his fingertips to his temples, "you are speaking to the greatest clairvoyant in the Northern Hemisphere. Pinpointing is child's play to a man such as me. To me," he added, "pinpointing is mere child's play."

• • ● • •

Miles Wednesday, circus-scarred and just twelve, sat against the smooth trunk of the twin beech tree on a cool October morning, a newspaper and The Null's breakfast sitting on a root beside him. He rested his gaze on the long sun-striped grass of Lady Partridge's garden, letting his eyes unfocus. The wind sighed in the branches like the breath of a mighty animal, carrying the sour smell of tamarind pods from a nearby tree. He thought he heard a distant rumble, but he didn't strain his ears. He watched the grass, and he waited for the movement he knew would come. The tamarind smell had turned to tiger now, and he smiled to himself.

"I don't know what you have to smirk about," said the tiger.

Miles focused his eyes. The tiger sat a short leap away, his magnificent stripes blending with the grass, regarding Miles with a hint of amusement.

"I'm not smirking, I'm smiling," said Miles. "I'm still alive, for a start. I wasn't able to thank you properly the other night."

"I didn't hang around," said the tiger. "I had the distinct impression some of those kiddies wanted to paw me with their sticky fingers, and they might have ended up without them."

"How did you get away?"

"I'm a tiger, not a dodo. I am a master of stealth, camouflaged in stripes, and a circus tent is nothing if not stripy."

"Well, you saved me in the nick of time anyway," said Miles, scuffing his toe in the soil. "Thank you."

"Think nothing of it," said the tiger. "I'm only sorry I didn't get to finish the job on that little reptile, although I suppose eating a man in a magician suit might not be considered family entertainment."

A screeching cackle drifted across from the gazebo and the tiger was on his feet in an instant, his mighty teeth bared and his tail lashing to and fro in the long grass.

"It's all right," said Miles. "It's just The Null. I bring it breakfast every morning when I'm here, and today I'm a bit late."

"Keeping that creature here is not a good idea," said the tiger. "I have advised you before you should have nothing to do with it. There is nothing to be gained from foolish bravado."

"I can look after myself," said Miles indignantly, "and if it wasn't for my foolish bravado I might never have become friends with you."

The tiger growled, making the hair stand up on

Miles's neck. "It's a foolhardy mouse who calls the cat his friend," he rumbled. "And being plucked from the jaws of death by myself or your strange little sister can hardly be called looking after yourself."

Miles said nothing. The tiger stood, his tail switching in the autumn grass. His amber eyes were fixed on Miles, but his ears were turned toward the gazebo. It was Little's voice that broke the silence. "Miles saved me from the Circus Oscuro," she said, flopping down in the grass beside Miles and smiling at the tiger. "And I help him out when he needs me. We look after each other."

Miles looked away. He could feel his eyes stinging with tears. The tiger gave a low rumble. "Perhaps I was a little harsh," he said. "It's no bad thing to face danger with courage, if there is a good reason for it, and courage is something you don't seem to be short of. Keeping that hairy nightmare as a pet is another matter altogether."

"The Null is not a pet!" said Miles. "The Null is all I have left of my father."

The tiger stared at him, but Miles could not read the expression in his gaze. "Your taste for riddles is as strong as ever," said the tiger, "and my patience with them is no greater than before. Just remember that I may not always be around to help you stand your ground."

"Where are you going?" asked Miles.

"Nowhere out of the ordinary," said the tiger, turning away toward the sunrise.

"Then we'll see you again," said Miles.

"No doubt," said the tiger.

"Good-bye then, Varippuli," said Miles.

The tiger paused for a moment and looked back over his shoulder. "Good-bye, Miles," he said, "and remember to keep your eyes clear and your claws sharp."

The tiger disappeared among the bushes, and Miles stared after him with an uneasy feeling. "What do you think he meant by that, about not always being around?" he asked Little.

"The tiger lives alone and relies only on himself," said Little. "It's hard for him to understand that our friendships make us stronger. And that reminds me." She gave Miles a sudden hug. "Happy birthday!" she said.

"Is today my birthday?" said Miles in surprise. In Pinchbucket House there had been no birthdays. He had only learned of his from the Bolsillo brothers the year before, and he had not got used to keeping track of the date.

"Of course!" said Little. She sprang to her feet. "And I have to get back to help Lady Partridge with your birthday surprise. She's made a big cake, and the Bolsillo brothers are coming over with Tembo and Mamba, and . . ."

"Don't tell me!" said Miles, laughing. "I'm not supposed to know if it's a surprise."

"Then how can you look forward to it?" said Little.

"You can't, I suppose," said Miles. "A surprise is supposed to be more fun."

"People are funny!" laughed Little. "In that case I won't tell Lady Partridge that I told you. Then it will be more fun when she finds out."

Miles picked up the newspaper and The Null's breakfast and stood up. "Just don't tell her at all," he said. "Trust me."

"Whatever you say, Miles," said Little. She smiled and tucked her hair behind her ear, and the day seemed to grow warmer. "Say hello to The Null for me," she called as she turned and ran back toward the house.

The Null was crouching like an inky blot in the corner of the gazebo, away from the sunlight that slanted in through the barred window. Its red-rimmed eyes stared at Miles as he entered. He pushed the metal dish between the bars that separated the creature from its visitors, but The Null did not move. "Hello," said Miles. "Remember me?" He sat down in the worn armchair and shook open his copy of the *Larde Weekly Herald*. The headline filled most of the front page. "ESCAPED NUTCASE MAULED BY SAVAGE TIGER," read Miles. "Police are today searching for a dangerous tiger that disappeared after maiming an escaped lunatic. The Great Cortado, forty-five, was attacked by the beast while attempting to saw a local boy in half, and is also being sought by police after making his getaway on a stolen horse." Miles stopped and turned the page. "Let's try this instead," he said. "YOU WON'T SEE ME FOR DUST, SAYS FEZ-TOPPED SNITCH. Itinerant fortune-teller Doctor Tau-Tau, forty, faces deportation after telling police the likely whereabouts of fugitive lunatic the Great Cortado. In a deal reached between police and local magistrate Justice Emmanuel Ffrench, charges of Assault with a Blowpipe and Making Incoherent Statements were dropped on condition that the sideshow psychic agree to leave the country at once. 'I no longer feel safe here anyway,' Doctor Tau-Tau was quoted as saying. 'I will be going where my talents are better appreciated.'"

Miles stopped reading and sat for a while in silence with the beast that had once been his father. He knew that talking to The Null might be no more useful than shouting into an empty barrel, but having lived in one of those he also knew there could be more to an empty barrel than meets the eye. He was supposed to practice reading from the newspaper each day, but the things he wanted to say could not be found between the covers of the *Larde Weekly Herald*, and so he put the newspaper down and began to talk.

He talked about his travels with the circus and his adventures with the Fir Bolg, in search of the father he had lost to a fathomless darkness. He spoke of his mother, the beautiful Celeste, and how he wished that he could see her face, even in a picture. He spoke about her twin, whom he hoped one day to meet, and about Little, the girl who had given up her wings to be his little sister. He laughed as he told The Null how odd she had looked when she came, bearded and covered with hair, to rescue him. He spoke about the tiger who was always there when he needed him, and how, though he still didn't fully understand it, he somehow carried that magnificent animal's soul hidden in a small stuffed bear in the pocket of his jacket. And finally, as the patch of sunlight crept across the straw-carpeted floor, he told the brooding shadow in the corner about the small stone that contained the power of that tiger's soul, and how he would study his mother's diary until he learned how to master that power, so that someday he could use it to bring his lost father back from the darkness and into the light of day.

The Julie Andrews Collection
encompasses quality books for young readers of
all ages that nurture the imagination and celebrate
a sense of wonder.

For more information about
The Julie Andrews Collection, visit
www.julieandrewscollection.com.

Words. Wisdom. Wonder.

Did you like this book? Julie Andrews would love to read your review of THE TIGER'S EGG, or any of the books in the Julie Andrews Collection. Write to her at:

JULIE ANDREWS
THE JULIE ANDREWS COLLECTION
HARPERCOLLINS CHILDREN'S BOOKS
1350 AVENUE OF THE AMERICAS
NEW YORK, NY 10019
or
INFO@JULIEANDREWSCOLLECTION.COM

From time to time we will post reader reviews on the Julie Andrews Collection website. Please include permission to quote your review and include your name and location when you submit it.

Other books you might enjoy in the Julie Andrews Collection:

BLUE WOLF by Catherine Creedon

DRAGON: *Hound of Honor* by Julie Andrews Edwards and Emma Walton Hamilton

DUMPY AND THE FIREFIGHTERS by Julie Andrews
Edwards and Emma Walton Hamilton,
illustrated by Tony Walton

DUMPY'S APPLE SHOP by Julie Andrews Edwards and
Emma Walton Hamilton,
illustrated by Tony Walton

DUMPY'S EXTRA-BUSY DAY by Julie Andrews Edwards
and Emma Walton Hamilton,
illustrated by Tony Walton

DUMPY'S HAPPY HOLIDAY by Julie Andrews Edwards
and Emma Walton Hamilton,
illustrated by Tony Walton

DUMPY'S VALENTINE by Julie Andrews Edwards and
Emma Walton Hamilton,
illustrated by Tony Walton

DUMPY TO THE RESCUE! by Julie Andrews Edwards
and Emma Walton Hamilton,
illustrated by Tony Walton

GRATEFUL: *A Song of Giving Thanks* by John Bucchino,
illustrated by Anna-Liisa Hakkarainen

THE GREAT AMERICAN MOUSICAL by Julie Andrews
Edwards and Emma Walton Hamilton,
illustrated by Tony Walton

HOLLY CLAUS: THE CHRISTMAS PRINCESS
by Brittney Ryan, illustrated by Laurel Long
with Jeffrey K. Bedrick

THE LAST OF THE REALLY GREAT WHANGDOODLES
by Julie Andrews Edwards

THE LEGEND OF HOLLY CLAUS by Brittney Ryan

THE LITTLE GREY MEN by BB,
illustrated by Denys Watkins-Pitchford

LITTLE KISSES by Jolie Jones,
illustrated by Julie Downing

MANDY by Julie Andrews Edwards

THE PALACE OF LAUGHTER by Jon Berkeley

PEBBLE by Susan Milord

SIMEON'S GIFT by Julie Andrews Edwards and
Emma Walton Hamilton,
illustrated by Gennady Spirin

THANKS TO YOU by Julie Andrews Edwards and
Emma Walton Hamilton